Dicing with Danger

Acknowledgements

To produce a novel, self published or otherwise, takes a lot of effort, energy and determination. Thankfully I am blessed with a sufficient amount of determination but the energy and effort are largely the result of being surrounded by good friends and a fantastic family who have spurred me on when necessary.

There are many people who helped make this book possible and I would like to take this opportunity to sincerely thank them. They are:

Robert Banham: for always allowing me to be the person I am and for not getting grumpy when I go off into my fantasy world. As you know, I don't 'do' reality. You are always there for me, even when I felt so low I wondered what the point to it all was. Thank you and I love you.
Chloe Banham: for growing into a beautiful and respectful young woman who I am so proud of. I hope all your dreams come true.
Mum: for being my No. 1 fan (even though that's what Mum's are supposed to be), also for believing in me from day one.
Dad: You've enabled me to get yet another step closer to realising my dream. Thank you so much.
Bob French: for your assistance with research on medals.
Casey Clay: for allowing me the use of your first name – it and you are so cool!
Connor: for the inspiration in the first place to create Detective Casey Pitt. He became a 3D character for me because of you.
Karen Young and Sis Unsworth: (My 'Reading Circle'). Your upbeat comments, words of encouragement and constant enthusiasm for 'the next one' keep me going. You're the best!
Tux and Rosita: for being fab friends and for being at the other end of my neurotic emails when I announced on so many occasions that I was, yet again, giving up writing! Special thanks to Rosita Pounders for providing answers to incredibly random questions about our American brethren.
The Rayleigh Library Writers Group: for giving me the strength, inspiration and energy to continue my passion. I value our friendships and I wish each of you the best of literary luck.
My family and friends: without you life would be very dull.

For Chloe

Please email me at sarah@sjbanhamauthor.co.uk

ESSEX COUNTY
COUNCIL LIBRARY

Front Cover Photo: 'California' by SJ Banham. Designed by Robert Banham

Printed by Basildon Printing Company Ltd, Fleet House, Armstrong Road, Benfleet, Essex, SS7 4FH, England

Dicing with Danger © SJ Banham 2007. All rights reserved, no part of this publication may be reproduced or transmitted by any means, electronic, mechanical, photocopied, recorded on any information storage or retrieval system without prior permission in writing from the author.

Prologue

"Stand up and show them you're not afraid!"

Vice President William Dicing's words to his family came as if he were addressing a conference. Despite regular threats against him through the mail, he continued his professional and personal lives as normal. His family were told to behave perfectly normal but remain vigilant. These terrorists wanted to frighten but he refused to let them have the upper hand. It wasn't what he was about.

His wife, son and daughter looked bleakly at him. Judith, his wife of thirty years stroked a hand over his, a show of support in front of their family. Michael, an attractive twenty-four year old with dark hair like his fathers, sat listening intently at the mahogany kitchen table while his sister, who'd inherited the red hair from her mother's gene-pool, wouldn't hear any of it.

"Why ignore the threats?" Genevieve complained wrinkling her freckled nose. "If they mean business why not get the Army in and hunt them all down?"

"That's not necessary, honey," William said gently, calming her excitement. "We get a lot of threats each year, if we took every one of them to heart we'd never get anything done."

"You've had others?"

"Yes, of course. You don't get into power by having everybody like you. Life isn't like that."

"Oh great!" her tipped her head adopting an air of impertinence. "Didn't it occur to you Daddy, that *I* might have a problem with that?"

"Genevieve, I take everybody's thoughts into consideration when I make family decisions. You already know that."

"But what about the other threats?" she pressed. "What happened with those? I don't remember anyone informing me about them."

Judith took over. "Like your father says, Gen, honey, if you took them all to heart, well, we'd all end up in some hospital somewhere on anti-depressants!" She forced a laugh hoping to diffuse the obvious agitation.

"So, why's this threat any different?" Michael put in. "You're obviously taking this one more seriously, why?"

"We take them all seriously, son," William countered, "but we don't necessarily act on them all. This threat was - a little different, that's all."

"How?"

"It was..." Judith took over again watching her husband contemplate the best way to break the news, "different because...." She exhaled sharply. "Look you're not children anymore, you're adults and we feel you should be aware of the situation that's all. Keeping you in the dark is not the best way to handle it anymore."

Even as a child Genevieve was outspoken and now, at twenty-two, she was no different. It had got her into trouble in the past but she never learned from it until it was too late.

"So, why *is* this one different?" she asked again, expecting immediate answers. "What did they do? Threaten to kidnap *us*?"

Judith and William exchanged shocked expression at each other for a moment then on to their children. The look said everything.

"You mean, *it was*?"

"Are you serious?" Michael choked.

"What the hell did *we* do?" Genevieve shrieked dramatically, gesturing at her brother. "*He* hardly leaves the house and I hang around with Cassandra. We're not exactly a threat to national security, are we? This is crazy!" She threw her hands in the air and pushed them through her thick mane. "So what is it, we're going to die at the hands of some crazed gunman just because we happen to be the offspring to the all-important VP?"

It was exactly the kind of response they'd expected from her. A quiet and shy wallflower she was not. While it was not in her nature to be anything else, her feisty high-spirited nature was exactly the reason they decided to deal with the situation they way they had.

"That's quite enough, Genevieve, calm down! Your father and I take it very seriously keeping you both safe and secure. We always have. Nothings changed there."

"But -!"

"Please, " Judith eased her hand over her daughter's slender fingers, "and nothings going to happen to you or Michael anyway. We just have to be vigilant, that's all."

"You're telling us that someone's been threatening us and then says its okay? Well sorry but I don't think this is at all okay." She pushed her chair from the table and stood, three sets of eyes providing an instant audience for her outburst. "You know what, Daddy, this is because of *you!* *You* chose to do this job, *you* chose to be in this position and now *your* threats are extending to us? I didn't ask for any of this and now my life is in danger! How unfair is that?"

She stormed out of the room and thudded upstairs as if she were six years old again and protesting over eating macaroni and cheese. Judith rolled her eyes at Michael then William.

"Okay, okay," she said waving her hands in surrender. "I'll go talk to her. I don't know what I can do, but I'll talk to her."

Moments later she knocked on Gen's door.

"Go away, I don't want to see anyone."

"That much is obvious but this is important. Come on, we have to talk about this." She waited for a moment, heard no response from the other side and added. "Gen, this isn't going away. Open up, come on."

Gen opened the door, huffing. "Okay, I'm listening but that doesn't mean I have to like what I hear."

"Of course not but just hear me out, that's all I ask."

She sat down gracefully on her daughter's bed. Just out of her forties, Judith looked every bit the wife of the VP. Dressed, even on this Saturday afternoon, in a white chiffon blouse, pearls adorning her neck and a peach skirt covered her legs ending, conservatively, just below her knee. Respectable and decent was how the public perceived her. It made all the difference to her husband's position. She was liked and likable and, more importantly, an asset.

Now, if only she could talk some sense into her daughter.

Genevieve threw herself onto her bed front first landing on a large, pale pink cat with a white velvet collar. It had been a gift from her father after one of his international trips. As she turned slightly, the expression on its face was that of a sedate smile as if content at being squashed under her young breasts.

"Getting a little old for these things aren't you?" Judith smiled.

"No." She pulled herself over and lay on her back still holding the cat to her chest. "I don't know, I guess. It's not fair. He chose to do that job. It wasn't like we asked him to do it and now I have to keep looking over my shoulder every time I leave the house? It's going to be impossible! I can't go to the mall with Cassandra or hang around with the guys or anything." She sighed again. "Life's so unfair!"

"Honey, you'll have twenty four hour protection wherever you go, you won't have to worry about a thing."

"Oh sure, that's going to look fabulous isn't it? Me marching down to Cassandra's with some suit behind me, his finger constantly stuck in his ear! I can see it now." She furrowed her eyebrows and imitated the deep voice of a bodyguard. "Subject is heading south, subject is heading north, subject is eating French fries and being driven out of her mind!"

Judith couldn't help but laugh. "It won't be that bad."

"Come on, Mom, its not like nobody knows who the suits are. It's blatantly obvious," she whined. "Not to mention embarrassing. You know how many girls I know who have twenty four hour protection?"

"No, honey, I don't."

"You're looking at her."

"I'd bet a lot of your friends would like it though."

"Are you kidding me?"

"It is for your own good, Gen. You're very lucky to have that privilege. Those 'suits' as you put it, put their lives on the line for you, you know."

"Yeah, 'cause Daddy tells them to. He says jump and they jump."

"They're protecting you. Any other girl would be thrilled at that idea, Gen."

"Any other girl didn't have to grow up with it though, did she?"

"Your father and I just want the best for you and Michael and if that means tougher security then tougher security it is. We would simply die if anything happened to either of you. You are our lives."

Genevieve sulked again.

"Hmph! Some life, daughter of the VP. It's crazy enough having to constantly live down that honour without having it thrust upon your social life too. Do you have any idea how irritating it gets?"

Judith stroked her daughter's hair, taking a copper tendril and winding it gently around her finger. The colour was a stark contrast to her own pale flesh.

"Just relax, nothing's going to happen, but if anything did, well, we just need to remain alert. Would you prefer no security?" she asked but didn't expect a response. "Prevention is better than cure."

"It's manic!"

"It's life."

"It's unfair!"

"It's necessary," Judith emphasised her point. "You know your father loves you and Michael so very much. He's doing this job for you, for all of us. We're just trying to protect you, that's all." Genevieve suppressed an angry laugh. Judith nodded reinforcing the fact. "He is, honestly."

"Daddy's a lot like me, isn't he?"

"How so?"

"We never do anything unless we really want to."

Judith hugged her. She was right. There was no point in disputing the fact.

"That's what happens when strong minded people get a hold of strong minded dreams. Nothing much will change really. You can still do all the things you do already, just be aware of your surroundings, that's all."

"I can still go out?"

"Of course. I don't see a problem – just be sensible."

"Still go to Cassandra's and the mall?" Her tone teetered on whiney, manipulating, like a small child wanting its own way. And she was getting it.

"Would it do me any good to tell you otherwise?" Judith asked.

Genevieve smiled knowingly. She had won over her mother, that was something. Now all she had to do was get around her father. Her mother wasn't too bad at all. She seemed to know what her life was like even if her father had no idea.

"Now come down stairs and show your father you're okay with this. He's been going through hell wondering how you two would react."

"I guess he found out."

"You bet he did."

Five days later, protection was finally called off. No attempts had been made and no more warnings received. It was quiet. William liked quiet. Genevieve liked it even more. Quiet meant socialising possibilities!

Genevieve stepped outside the family house breathing in the midday air. Knowing nobody was watching her, suit or otherwise, was liberating. She looked up to see Michael watching her from his bedroom. If he wanted to stay inside, that was his problem. She grinned spitefully, *she* wasn't going to be afraid. She wasn't going to stay in the house another day like him and she most definitely wasn't going to stop having a social life.

She exhaled walking away from the house. Today was going to be perfect. She and Cassandra would hang together, maybe take in a movie and chill out.

She had gotten her way and life was damned near perfect. She put in her ear-plugs and switched on her IPod to its loudest setting, grinning at the world as she walked down the street. This was what it was all about. Living. It didn't matter what anybody else thought, this was her time, her life. And she was going to make damned sure she enjoyed it her way. The music played loud, encouraging her to sing which she did happily.

She didn't hear the van pulling in rapidly next to her. She didn't hear the man fling open the sliding door. Nor did she hear his rapid footsteps approach her from behind. The first thing she became aware of was the hand covering her mouth and another forcing her arms behind her.

After that everything was dark.

Chapter One

"Casey! Down here, I can hear something!" Detective Dan Chandler called excitedly. "I can hear something, listen."

He moved down on all fours pushing his ear to the drain on the hot broken concrete road. His partner, Detective Casey Pitt, joined him.

The noise was muffled but there definitely was a sound. Casey listened hard, both men leaning into the concrete with their butts in the air. Dull clanking - metal against metal – or so it seemed to Casey, emanated from the curb side.

"What do you think?" Dan looked up, squinting at the silhouette that was his partner's face. Despite the midday sunshine, an offering of clouds were moving in quickly promising rain soon if the forecaster on Radio DC this morning had predicted correctly.

"Could be, but we won't know for sure 'less we get our asses down there and take a proper look, will we?" he grinned, eager at their potential find. The two stood as Casey pressed the button on his radio attached to his bullet proof vest. "Chief, I think we've found something."

"What is it?" By the tone of Chief Mackenzie's voice, it was clear he was agitated.

"We're off Hillside Road. There's a section of unmade road here, it's under construction. We can hear noises from the drain. I think we should take a closer look."

"Get right on it, boys. We're on our way."

The two ran to the end of the unmade area locating the pipe work easily down the edge of the slope. Large round concrete tubes jutted from the road while heavy wires and grids poked out. It looked like the aftermath of an earthquake rather than the slow construction of a road.

In the distance cars and trucks whizzed by at considerable speed, none of them aware that the police were conducting a missing person search just yards from them or that the missing person was the Vice President's daughter, Genevieve Dicing

By the look of the photograph the officers had been given, the girl was beautiful to say the least. Long red curly hair hung past her shoulders and green eyes looked powerfully into the camera lens. Her mother, a keen photographer, had taken the picture not six months ago, hardly expecting that it would end up in the dust covered hands of the police.

The detectives walked into the largest pipe without the need to duck. It took a moment for their eyes to adjust to the darkness inside.

"Can't see a damn thing, down here," Dan said, reaching for his flashlight, "smells better than I though it would, though."

"It's a storm drain, not a sewer. Shh! Listen," Casey stopped, "did you hear that?"

The two stood perfectly still waiting for whatever it was Casey thought he heard.

"Don't hear anything but the traffic up there, what was it?"

"Maybe nothing." Casey aimed his flashlight up ahead just as a rat rustled past the metal bar to his left. "Come on."

At the end of the pipe, a large round barrier ceased further progress.

"Looks like we're going to have to break in," he said. He took out his pocket-sized tools and grinned. "I've got just the thing for this."

Thirty seconds later the door opened. The tunnel darkened the further in they went.

Clank, clank, clank.

Automatically, both officers took out their weapons holding them on top of the flashlights, unsure what they expected to see. The sound was near, that much was certain. Every fifty feet or so a drain cover from the road above cast light downwards in strips. Eerie shadows were cast on the concave walls. The slope of the tunnel forced shallow water to lick at their boots while the water veered off into three tubes and three possible directions. Casey looked down aiming the light ahead of them.

"Looks like we're getting somewhere now."

"If it was her, why doesn't she make more noise?" Dan complained. "We don't know which way to go, two of us, three tubes."

"Maybe she can't." Casey whispered back looking at each of the tunnels in turn. "We'll take the ones each side."

"What if they're both wrong? It could be the middle one?"

"Then I guess you're right and she's going to have to make more noise," he shrugged. Taking a quarter from his shoulder pocket, he held the light over it and flipped it hoping it didn't land in the water. "Heads you take the left tunnel, tails the right one."

"Heads."

As the coin came down Casey grabbed it and held it flat on the back of his hand.

"Heads it is, Danny. Keep in touch."

He could hear Dan wading through the now knee-high water in the furthest tube and walked away from the sound hoping all the time their radios would still have reasonable reception down there.

But now, as Casey waded knee-deep through the water, he heard the same metal against metal sound again.

Clank, clank, clank.

He was wrong, it did smell down here. It smelled of fear. The temperature had fallen too and he shivered stopping to allow the water which swirled around his legs to settle. He tried not to think about how full his boots were and how wet his toes had become. He waited for silence to engulf his position, closed his eyes and listened.
Clank, clank, clank.
That wasn't far away, and he could even put a direction to it. He paddled through the pipe thanking God that the rain forecast for today had not begun. It would be an awful job trying to manoeuvre in here with constant rain from the drains above. His radio suddenly crackled into life shattering the silence.
"Anything?" Dan's voice asked.
"Could be. Give me a minute, standby." He waited for another clanking sound before he did anything else. Standing silently in the water with just the sound of his own breathing for comfort, he waited for it. He was cautious not to call out in case the noise was the kidnapper setting a trap. If he ran he'd had no chance of catching him in this maze of tunnels. The softly-softly approach was far better and Casey liked nothing more than to bring on the element of surprise by clicking his weapon at the back of the perpetrators head. Total control, that's what it was all about.
Clank, clank, clank.
There it was again. It was slower but it was definitely there. He would have to call out, take a chance that it was her.
"Hello?" he called, "Miss Dicing?"
His radio cut back in again.
"I can't ….that far from you. … nothing here at all. I'm……back…" Dan's radio crackled.
"Missed that, Dan, say again?" *Darned radios cutting out underground*, Casey thought. "Dan?" *Must've hit a dead zone.* He continued with his primary objective, calling as he went. "Miss Dicing, can you hear me? This is the police, Miss Dicing. If you can hear me, please respond."
He walked further, turned a corner and came to two tubes forking in opposite directions. He guessed Dan would come out from the left so chose the right.
"Miss Dicing?"
He stopped again, letting the echo of the water slow to a stand still, waiting for the all important answer.
Clank, clank, clank..
"Genevieve, we're here to help. This is the police. Can you call out, let me hear your voice?"

"I'm here!" a weak voice, almost a whisper, called back.

"Where are you, I can't see you." He shone the light all the way down the tube wading quickly the rest of the way until he came upon another circular grid barring his way.

"I'm here!"

Her trembling body, submerged up to her neck, sat slumped over against the bars. She needed medical attention. Her pale eyes squinted at the brightness of the light and she turned away.

"I'm Detective Casey Pitt. I'm here to get your out. You're going to be fine. Are you injured?"

"No, I'm freezing!"

"I'm here now, it's going to be okay. I'm going to get you out of there."

"How?" she looked at the bars between them. "How are you going to get in?" she trembled. "It's locked. I'm trapped in here."

"Who locked it?"

"I don't know, his face was covered, but he had a gun and he's coming back. Hurry, please!"

Casey pushed the flashlight under the strap on his shoulder, put away his weapon and picked at the lock.

"I'm cuffed under here. I've tried to get out but I can't. I'm trapped!" she cried. "My ankles are tied and I can't move, you've got to get me out of here!"

"It's going to be okay now, try to stay calm." He pulled open the barrier and went through

"He said when it rains, the drain will fill and I'll drown."

Casey pulled his radio nearer to his lips.

"Dan, where are you?" *Still nothing.* "Dan? Chief? Can anyone read me?"

"...Casey... break-...Did you..."

"Damn it!" he told her, "radio's down. Chief, if you can hear me, I'm in the storm drain. I have her – repeat. I have her. She's alive but I need back up immediately. I've lost contact with Dan."

"Casey...in, come in? Did...?"

"I'm in the storm drain." He said deliberately. "Back up needed *immediately!*"

"What if they can't find us?" she wept.

"They'll find us." He took out the key and fumbled underneath the water for her hands. Long slender fingers shook from within the cuffs.

"Can you open them? What if he comes back, he has a gun."

Casey smiled casually, "Yeah, well, so do I." Her bloodied and beaten face was a far cry from the photograph he had seen. "Pretty name, Genevieve."

"What? I - I guess."

His hands struggled underneath the water as he tried to locate the key hole for the cuffs but it was difficult, something was blocking the hole. Above her hands another bar stopped her moving above the water.

"My partner will be here in a minute, you can meet him."

"I don't care about meeting anyone, I just want to get out. Is it raining yet?"

"No, it's a beautiful sunny day out there."

"If it rains, I'll drown."

"It's not gonna rain."

"He said it would." She sobbed.

Casey shook his head. "Well, I'm saying it won't."

Just as he said that, a flash of lightening soared through the drain.

"What was that? Is that a storm?" she blinked. Fear rose in her eyes. "Oh my God, it's going to rain, I'm going to die!"

"Genevieve, listen to me. I won't let that happen." He looked down at her shuffling his shoulder to get the light to shine onto his subject. It was harder than he thought. Where the hell was Dan? "Did you see what he put on the cuffs?"

"No. You can't do it can you?" She laughed, resigning herself to her fate.

"I'll do it. I'm taking you back up there with me in a minute. I've just got to…"

Her chin puckered and her lips trembled in the cold.

"But I might not have a minute."

The light coming through the drains was much less now. If it wasn't for his flash light they'd be there in complete darkness.

"Why? You going somewhere?" Casey fumbled with the cuffs.

Shocked at the question, she stared at him and swallowed. She hoped she wasn't going anywhere but up to the surface but she didn't know what fate had lined up for her.

"You got a boyfriend, Genevieve?"

"What?" her confused expression told him clearly she could barely remember her own name let alone recall if she had a boyfriend.

He shot her a half smile, "Well, do you?"

"Maybe, does it make a difference? I know what you're trying to do. You're trying to calm me down, aren't you? I've seen it on TV, the cops do it all the time."

"So," he asked, unconcerned with being found out. "Is it working?"

She tried to imagine how he was doing with the cuffs hoping he could see more than her. She could feel his warm hands against hers. Any connection to a human being was good, but so much better with one who was on her side.

"A little I guess."

"So, do you?" His voice was deep, rough and manly. "Have a boyfriend?"

Through glimpses from the torch light, it was the first time she could see his face clearly. He had short hair, spiked a little on top and had an angular shaped face with an unshaven chin. Dark shadows and over exposed light patches made it seem distorted but she could still see he was an attractive man.

"No. How about you?"

"No, I don't date guys." He came back quickly, softening the moment. "Date girls though. Does that count?"

She smiled. It was the first moment in a long time she felt able. "I – I guess."

She'd been through a traumatic experience and finding her was one thing but getting her out was proving to be quite another. Suddenly another sharp spark of lightening flashed through the drains causing a bright blue fleeting effect over their faces, this time is was joined by a loud roar. She looked up at him just as he looked down, both startled.

"I've almost got this, Gen, hang on."

He forced a smile, keeping her calm and staying in control of the situation. Another flash and more thunder, the noise echoed inside the drain making it seem ten times as deafening. A chill ran through him.

"Stop it, stop the noise!" she screamed trying to find some way to cover her ears. She tried to raise her shoulders but that was no good. Eyes closed tightly she huddled into herself.

Casey hugged her. "It's okay, I'm going to have you out of those in a moment. If I can just…"

"What's stopping them? Why won't they open?"

"Their stuck tight. It's as if…"

In all the years he'd rescued people from horrific situations never had he come across a set of cuffs more difficult to open. The kidnapper had somehow melted the lock from what it felt like. Rain slowly began to fall through the drains and down the sides of the walls. At first it trickled, then it came harder filling the already deep water. If it came up much higher it would cover her mouth then her nose.

"You've got to do something!" she shrieked, panic filling her voice, "I'll drown!"

"It's going to be fine."

"But the water! Oh my God, I'm trapped!"

"Genevieve, look at me," he said forcing her head level with his." Look at me, I won't let you die. Do you hear me, I *won't* let you die!"

He reached down to her cuffs once more and pulled out his weapon.

"I'm going to have to shoot it off okay?"

"What if you miss?"

"No, I'm a great shot," he grinned. "I'm going to have to go underneath the water for a moment and you'll have to hold the flashlight for me in your hands okay? I need to see where I am going to shoot."

"You're crazy! If I don't drown I'm going to get shot, I'm going to die! I knew it!"

"Gen, *listen to me!*" he shouted silencing her panic. "It'll take two seconds but you've got to stay calm, okay? This isn't going to work if you freak out on me. Now hold the flashlight."

He fumbled with the strap holding the light on his shoulder and took a deep breath to go under the surface. He thrust it into her hands, long soft fingers grabbed it and held it in the position he commanded even though she could barely feel it through the cold. He pulled her arms away from her back, holding them there in his fists. With her constant immobilisation and the freezing water surrounding her, she screamed with pain as if her arms were about to be broken. Then, he re-surfaced.

"Okay, you are going to have to take a breath and go underwater a little."

"What? Why?"

"I need your hands to be up as far to the surface as you can get them. The gun won't shoot under water, so I need to get a clear look. Okay? You understand?"

"This is crazy!" she cried. "You should just let me die here. Tell Mom and Dad I love them."

"Tell them yourself, Genevieve. I just need you to tell me you understand what I said. About the gun? I need you to ..."

"Yes! Of course I understand."

She filled her lungs with a long deep breath and went head first into the water bringing her hands upwards as far as she could lift them. Casey assisted as much as he could before her bones broke, aimed the gun and pulled back the trigger. Even under the water she could tell the difference between a gun firing and the thunder. Her hands flew apart above the water while Casey took the restraints from her ankles. She took in a large gulp of air too quickly and choked. Her arms ached like hell.

He surfaced and took the flashlight. "You okay?"

She was about to answer when something else caught her attention instead. Another flash light was aimed at them. Casey turned around, shone the light in front of him and swallowed hard. Her abductor had returned and he wasn't alone. He had Dan.

He was cuffed, wading through the water in front of the kidnapper. Casey automatically stood in front of Genevieve protecting her from further harm, immediately went for his weapon.

"I wouldn't try that if I were you," the gunman told him. "I've got one pointed at your partner's spine and I'm betting it'll make a mess!"

"Why don't you let him go? In fact, why don't you let us all go?"

"Because that wouldn't be very sporting, would it?"

"This is a sport to you? Jeez, you've got to get out more, man."

"He's going to kill us!" Genevieve whispered. He searched for her hand offering comfort behind him. She took it gratefully, holding it tight, savouring their bond.

"I'm not going through all of this for no reward," the abductor said without flinching.

"What did you have in mind?"

"At least one death, hers preferably, but all three of your would be better."

"Really? That's original. Scum like you usually want money or diamonds."

"Shut up! Maybe I'll start with him, then her next."

"Leave him alone!" Genevieve shrieked imagining someone else's death on her hands since she was the one who was kidnapped. "Why didn't you just try to kill my father? Surely the Vice President would be worth more to you than me or a cop."

"Vice President?" he looked genuinely puzzled, then laughed. "Your Daddy's the Vice President? You're kidding me?"

She was stunned and confused.

"You didn't know?" Casey interrupted. "You didn't do your homework very well, did you?"

"Maybe I did and maybe I didn't." Then he grinned, "I guess I'll have to put my price up now."

"Who's paying you?"

"Why do you care? You going to up my money?"

Dan and Casey shared eye contact, each hoping the other would be thinking the same thing. Dan bent down stabbing his foot hard against the man's shin while Casey took a shot, hitting the assailant's shoulder sending him against the wall.

But it was all too quick, the gun went off behind Dan's back and he fell rapidly to the ground. Another blast came along with a crash of thunder as blood poured from Casey's chest, seeping down his shirt mixing with the water. Then Casey shot twice – a reflex action – falling backwards into the girl.

Genevieve's piercing scream rang through the whole drain. She covered her ears and shut her eyes, shielding them from the horrible scene happening in front of her.

The flashing and thundering continued outside as Casey's last memory, before he passed out, was of his partner slipping gently beneath the surface.

Chapter Two

Casey Pitt stood inside his shower enjoying the water at it beat down onto his head. Moments ago, his light brown spiked hair stood up like soldiers to attention but now it lay flat, plastered against his skull.

The Californian sun shone irritatingly hard through the bathroom window onto his face but he turned away washing his underarms at the same time. Once showered, wrapping a towel around his hips, he wiped the mist from the mirror and stared into it. Not the best image to portray to his new boss, he thought staring at the scars on his face and body, but having little choice over his features he slapped cologne onto his chin and cheeks and went into his room to get dressed.

It had been a little over two years since the day in the drain, the day it had all gone wrong. He'd lost his best friend and partner in a single moment and had never quite got over that fact. Dan's death was the result of a coin Casey flipped. Dan was gone, he'd reminded himself over and over in the shrink's office, but not forgotten.

Never forgotten.

Even at the funeral, standing next to his colleagues and Dan's family, Casey knew his partner was going to be a hard one to forget. He couldn't even if he wanted to.

He pulled on the white shirt he'd prepared and fastened it. Over his boxer shorts went a beige pair of trousers and the suit jacket over the shirt. Lastly he knotted his tie, buttoning down the collar before raking back his hair. The picture of eagerness, he was the epitome of hard work and ready to sink his teeth into his new job.

He needed this. Needed something else to focus on. Something other than Dan.

Casey grabbed hold of his car keys from the dresser, climbed into his car and left.

Palm trees danced gently to a song known only to them. People went about their business hardly noticing anybody else around them. In the parking lot of the Beverley Centre, the plush shopping mall in the heart of Beverley Hills and the arranged meeting point, Manny Weston's overweight body stood in his light grey suit in the blazing Los Angeles sunshine. He wiped his forehead before tucking the handkerchief back into his breast pocket.

Since retiring from the force, Casey hadn't found work - unless becoming a night watchman was fascinating to him. It wasn't. Nothing stirred his interest for some time, depression taking over. Then, a chance meeting in a bar brought forth a position that *had* interested him. He needed a little action not some job that forced you to fall asleep or long to drop dead with boredom.

Becoming a body-guard sounded interesting. Almost like the real thing but without most of the paperwork. That part of police work he didn't miss and never would. The best part was, you were still considered to have all your marbles.

Manny was very eager to take him on. Someone with Casey's experience was rare and always a good choice in this game, despite his reasons for retiring.

"Listen, kid, this is the plan," his new boss told him in a step by step kind of way, handing over an envelope he promised contained a picture of a woman and a door key. "The girl doesn't know a thing, you got it?" his New York accent warned. "She's going to come out of the south entrance with a couple of friends and call a cab. They won't have a clue who's driving it, they won't even care."

"Got it, Sir." Casey nodded glancing at the picture. "And that's where I come in?"

The woman in the photograph was clothed in a peach suit and wore a large rimmed cream hat that wouldn't have looked out of place during a state visit. Her face was a little blurred but he was pretty sure he could pick her out from a crowd, especially given her attire.

"Okay, then you drive her to this address and await further instructions, you got that?" Casey nodded. He turned over the picture and read an address on the reverse. "It's a safe house," Manny assured him. "It ain't pretty but they never are. If she complains, tell her you know a different way to the address she gives you. Make up something. You know the kind of thing. From the little I know about her, her head's filled with fluff anyhow, she won't have a clue. It's a simple babysitting job this one, okay? I'm working you in gently." He glanced at the picture once more before handing it back, waving his cigar in the air. "Women like her are usually so far up their own butt, they hardly know where the drivers' taking them anyway."

Casey looked down at his suit. "Won't I look a little over dressed for a cab-driver?"

Manny frowned. "You think this woman's gonna give a stuff about what you're wearing?" He didn't wait for a response, instead he placed his puffy arm around Casey's shoulder. Stuffing the cigar into his mouth again, he continued. "You could be wearing a tutu and red Indian feathers for all she'll notice! She probably couldn't even place you in a line up and she's gonna spend at least ten minutes in your cab!" The burly man's accent was broad as his humour was dry and cynical.

"Who is she anyway?"

"Didn't ask, never do. Sometimes its better that way, it's all on a need-to-know basis. Soon as I know you will," he smiled. Casey nodded. "You okay with this, kid? 'Cause I hear you're a good guy and I got all kinds of contacts in DC and they tell me good stuff, you know? Now don't take offence but I pulled your records. I read your history. I read what happened to your partner."

Casey raised his chin up taking any comments on the chin like the man he was.

"Yes, Sir."

"You had it pretty tough for a while from what I read. Lost it back there."

"I'm fine now, that's what matters."

"Yeah, kid, so long as you ain't gonna freak out on me or the girl, I got no problem. Listen, I know all I need to know just by looking at you. This is a good one to begin with for you, she's a pretty easy start, I reckon. Work you in gently, learn the ropes and then try something a little tougher later on. You get paid at the end, got that? Couple of hours work and you can have an early lunch. Relax a little, okay? This ain't the force anymore, kid. I run a business, I'm a business man. Got it?"

"Yes, Sir."

"Good," he held his ear listening for new information coming through the earpiece. "'Cause we don't go filling out no reports here. We do our job and we go home, okay? That's the best part of this job, no strings. ETA's four minutes. You sure you're ready for this?"

"Absolutely."

"Yeah, I thought you would be. Oh, and kid?"

"Yes, Sir?"

"You're not a cop anymore, okay, but let me give you some advice. You've got your piece, right?" he asked. Casey nodded. "Never put it down, ever. Even on easy ones like this, you're there to protect the client, *whatever* it takes, okay. If you have to use it, then use it. You understand, even if she's a total pain in the ass, you're there to protect her. Right?"

"Yes, Sir."

"Good. Good luck, kid. Like I said, get to the address and we'll catch up with you there."

Casey was pushing thirty, but to a guy Manny's age, thirty probably was just a kid. But Casey was confident enough. He knew his job. He walked to the cab, put on his sunglasses, sat inside and waited for the call.

As planned, an elegant young woman left the shopping mall with two friends; another young woman dressed equally as stylish and a man in a black polo shirt and trousers. The three of them leaned into each other exchanging air kisses. She put out her arm for a cab and Casey pulled up in front of her. The man opened the back door loading up the back seat with bags as Casey watched him from the rear view mirror.

"Here," he said handing over a hundred dollar bill to the driver. "Take her home, okay? 2255 Santa Monica Boulevard."

"Yes, Sir," he said looking to the road ahead keeping a mental note of the address he was heading to and the security around him. The woman removed her oversized hat revealing red hair pulled back into a bun and leaned inside the rear, still exchanging air kisses with the two.

"We must do lunch, darling. Don't forget, will you?" her friend called hanging on the arm of the man. "I'll take care of Glen for you," she giggled as if the three were continuing some private joke.

"I'll see you tonight, Glen?" she confirmed. "Call me for drinks, okay?"

"Of course, I can't wait."

Casey waited patiently until the tedium of fake hugs and false kisses were over before pulling out of the space.

She sat checking her nails. "Darn it! I chipped one. That blasted door back there, I knew I'd chipped one. Now I'll have to re-schedule my appointment. Driver, make it quick please, will you, I haven't got all day." She fumbled in her purse for a moment and took out her cell phone immediately dialling a number. "Charlotte darling, I just chipped one. Can you believe it, I know, it's impossible isn't it? Can you come over this afternoon? Well, darling I would but Glen's taking me out for drinks tonight so I need them looking perfect. I have a feeling he's going to be a pretty special night too if you catch my drift," she giggled. "Yes, and the one I have in mind wouldn't look half as good on a hand with a chipped nail now, would it?" She held up her left hand and stared at her bare ring finger admiring the vision her mind had conjured. "Four-thirty? Yes that's fine. Don't be late, will you. I have a very busy schedule."

As quickly as she had picked up the phone she snapped it shut and threw it back into her bag, still staring at the chipped nail, painted in 'Peach Frost' to match her suit. She looked out of the window before glancing back to her purse once more and took out a small black book. Casey glanced up to see her back on the phone again.

"Antonio, darling," she grinned widely holding her phone between her ear and shoulder. "Yes, I'm fine. Listen, I know you're coming at three this afternoon but really, do you think that's enough time?" She pulled a

small pocket mirror from her bag and flipped it open rousing her hair. "It's just that I have a feeling that Glen might be popping the question tonight and I want everything to be just perfect. You know how it is. You can't? But Antonio, whatever shall I do, it looks absolutely hideous!" her free hand flung in the air adding to the dramatics she was causing. "Two-forty-five, yes I suppose that will have to do, ciao darling."
Casey glazed over listening to her calls. Manny was right, this girl was completely self-absorbed.

"Oh, driver." Casey looked into his rear view mirror. "Yes you, excuse me, but I think you've taken a wrong turn somewhere. It's Santa Monica Boulevard."

"Yes, Ma'am that's right."

"No, no, this isn't right at all. I've never been this way home before. Are you new or something?"

"It's definitely this way." He watched her looking outside with a frown.

"No, this is all wrong. Give me your badge number, please. I'm going to report you."

"Ma'am?"

She snapped open her phone again and tapped in another number.

"Yes, Glen, this driver's all over the place! Looks like we're heading for Pasadena of all places. It's entirely the opposite direction, can you believe it? I know! Well, people just don't give you the respect these days, do they? Can you come and get me?" she said loud enough to reach Casey ears. "Driver stop the car, I want to get out."

"Sorry, Ma'am, I can't do that."

Her face was motionless with confusion. "Glen, did you hear that? He says he won't stop the car. What shall I do? What? Oh, alright then. Driver, I *demand* you stop the car right now."

"No, Ma'am I can't," he smirked as if the word 'demand' would make a difference to him.

"You most certainly can and you will. Stop it this instant or I'll call the police! I have a phone here and don't think I won't call them. This is tantamount to kidnapping!"

Casey let out a small laugh. "I'm not kidnapping you."

"Glen, hurry!" she whispered before shutting the casing and moving forward in her seat. "Listen, I've been kidnapped before. I know what its like and if you don't stop the car right now, I will consider this abduction!"

He pulled the car over and stopped abruptly turning around to face her as the cars spun past on the road beside them, beeping their horns from his sudden stop. He turned around to face her.

"Miss, I'm not kidnapping you. Calm down. I'm protecting you. I'm a bodyguard and I was sent to get you."

Her face was a picture. "What are you talking about? I called a cab not a bodyguard service! Where the hell are you taking me?"

"I have an address, just keep calm, everything's going to be fine. My orders are to get you there and await further instructions."

"Your orders? What's going on? This is preposterous! It's all some kind of joke. Did Cassandra hire you?" She forced a smile. "That's it isn't it? She put you up to this because of the drinks tonight, didn't she? I knew she was up to something, she and Glen seemed too chummy earlier." She said trying not to become too bewildered at the practical joke.

"No, it's no joke. It's for real."

"Listen, I'm a very busy person and while I'd love to play silly games and practical jokes with you I really don't have the time right now. I have a whole day of appointments and if I don't get back home to rest pretty soon, my face will look awful and I have a busy night ahead, do you understand?"

"Perfectly."

She sat back a little more relaxed in her seat after the outburst.

"Oh, thank goodness for that, I was beginning to get a little worried we were going to have a problem."

"No Ma'am, no problem at all."

"Good then can we just go back home please."

"Sorry no, I told you, I have orders."

She sat forwards again and squealed at him.

"What? Oh this is ridiculous! You're not going to take me home?"

He shook his head. "No, Ma'am I'm not."

She inhaled deeply, closed her eyes and remained silent for a moment.

"Of all days," she whispered to nobody in particular. "Okay, let me out!"

"No."

"*Now!*"

"No!"

She leaned forwards and pulled the lever to open the door. Casey had no choice but to get out too or he may lose his first client under the wheels of the car and that wouldn't look good on his résumé!

She grabbed her bags, kicked open the door and slammed it shut rather clumsily with her stiletto-clad foot. Casey stopped her.

"You've got to get back in that car, Miss, do you understand? This is dangerous. You could be killed out here."

"You can't treat me like this, do you know who I am?" she spat. Wisps of curly hair, though tied back, blew with the traffic breeze. Green eyes glared while her soft peach coloured lips pouted.

Casey stared motionless for a moment. "Yeah I think I do." A chill shot through him taking him back to the day in the drain. He nodded, trying to smile. "We've met before."

"Well, you've probably seen my face on TV or something. I'm *very* famous. But I'm not getting back into that cab. My boyfriend will be here in a moment to take me home. Now I suggest you leave me alone or I *will* call the police."

"Genevieve Dicing."

His voice brought with it a strange ring which caused her heart to skip a beat. It wasn't the kind of feeling she usually got from an admirer, of which there were plenty. With her looks it was hard not to be admired but she enjoyed it, and used it to get what she wanted. This didn't feel like that though, this felt more like a scene from a long lost dream or worse still, a nightmare.

"Yes, that's right. So, big deal, you know my name."

"You don't remember me though, do you?" he asked, cars flying past making it difficult to be heard. He watched her trying to recall him. All at once the dark, surreal scene flew into his mind and he wondered if she would remember it the same way. The cold of the water, the echo of shots firing in the semi darkness, the moment Dan Chandler lost his life.

"Look, I'm not interested in your practical jokes. I'm a very busy person and I have contacts in very high places. If you don't leave me alone you'll find yourself without a job. I fire people all the time, don't think just because you think you know me I won't do it. I have hair and nail appointments in a couple of hours and if I don't get some rest, my face will virtually fall off before tonight and I'll look…"

"Just ask yourself, Gen, how many cab drivers' dress like this." Then he tapped the breast pocket, "or carry one of these."

She dismissed his comment in an instant.

"A gun?" she held back her words for an instant, trying not to let the idea of this man or his gun frighten her. "This is LA. Lots of people carry guns. Sorry, I just haven't the time for this." She looked around hoping Glen would be here very soon. Was he threatening her? She watched him lessen the gap between them. The last time she was this near a gun, events had taken a horrible turn.

A white BMW screeched to a stop along the shoulder a short distance from them. Casey immediately placed a light hand over the weapon should it be required.

"Thank God, Glen!" she called over the noise of the traffic. "Glen, darling, Glen?" she held her hat, over-dramatising the breeze against it. "Glen, you wouldn't believe what…"

It was obvious to Casey Glen was holding something dark and shiny in his hand. It was a gun. He aimed it straight ahead taking his position above the car door.

"Put down the weapon!" Casey shouted past her, "Put down the weapon and step back! Miss Dicing – get down!"

"Weapon, what wea-" she said softly taking in the scene with disbelief. Glen held it higher aiming past her. Casey watched, thankful, as Glen saw sense and put the weapon on the ground.

"Get back inside the cab, Miss."

"What? No, this is Glen, It's alright, it's just…"

"Get *back* in the car."

"But…"

"Now!"

Finally, but reluctantly, she complied. Casey edged back grabbing hold of the car door before speeding off down the freeway. In his rear view mirror he could see Glen fading off into the distance with a cell phone up to his ear.

Chapter Three

The silence from inside was deafening. Casey looked in his mirror over and over, first to ascertain Glen's whereabouts and secondly to see Genevieve's expression. She looked startled, bewildered and angry.

"What the hell just happened back there?"

"I was doing my job, Miss Dicing." Casey replied calmly. "Are you okay?"

She looked at his eyes in the mirror.

"Okay? Am I okay? I-I don't really know. First I'm being kidnapped by God-knows-who and then, when Glen tries to rescue me, you pull a gun on him. No, Mister, I don't think I'm okay actually. I think I'm little mad right now!" She turned in her seat to look out the back window. "What's going on?"

"I have orders to…"

"Yes, yes you have orders, you keep telling me. But screw your orders, I want to go home! This isn't at all convenient, I have appointments!"

Manny was right, she was unbelievable. She didn't have a clue about anything.

"I'm afraid it's not possible to get you home right now," he stated as calmly as he could muster, despite his rising temper. Stay focussed on the job, he reminded himself, control is everything.

"Not possible? This is crazy. I demand you stop this vehicle now! This very instant."

He suppressed a grin knowing she had already tried that routine, but this was far from an easy assignment. He grabbed the radio on the front seat and called in.

"Mr Weston?" The radio cracked into life.

"What is it, kid?"

"Um, Sir, things went a little belly-up. I'm heading for the address right now but I may need back-up."

Silence. That was the kind of silence that meant nothing good could come out of the situation.

"Sir?"

"Yeah, kid, I read you." Weston didn't sound happy. "Keep to the original plan, I'll be in touch."

"What?" Genevieve asked. "Does that mean you're still not taking me home?"

"It does."

"I don't believe this. This is quite possibly the craziest day I've ever had." She sat back in her chair pouting like the spoiled brat she was. "I could call the police, you know."

"You could but I don't think that would help you."

"You don't, huh?"

"No, I don't."

"You know I have two rules in life," she told him. "The first is that I never do anything I don't want to and the second is never to forget the first."

"Really, that's interesting 'cause I have two rules as well."

"You do?"

"Yeah."

Her attention was drawn back to her finger nails again, checking each one in turn before polishing it with the other fingertip.

"Let's just pretend for a moment that I am actually interested in your rules. What might they be?"

"The first one is that I always follow orders."

"Really?" she said sarcastically. "How noble of you. Cover puddles with your jacket too, do you?"

Casey arched an eyebrow

"And what is the other"

"To protect the client's life with my own."

"Is that right?"

"Yes, Miss Dicing, that is right."

"Well, aren't you the regular hero? And what do they pay you for the privilege of guarding my life, six-seventy-five an hour?"

"The money isn't important. Lives are."

"Great!" she huffed. "Not only am I being kidnapped by Mister Employee-of-the-Month but he turns out to be a saint too! So you go to bed at night with a clear conscience, do you?"

He shrugged, "I sleep okay."

"Of course you do. You probably don't have a life though, do you? I, on the other hand, *do* have a life and why don't I let you into a little part of it? If I don't get back to it real fast I'm probably going to lose the chance of becoming Mrs De Salle," she snorted, tapping one nail after another on her exposed knee.

"So far that's been a pretty important part of my life, but you probably don't give a damn about that do you, since your precious orders come first!"

"I guess that would be a fair assessment. If it helps your cause at all," he added with a lop-sided smile, "it is *your* life I'm protecting."

"Oh it helps considerably!" she lied. "You don't know how much better that makes me feel. And have you any idea *what* type of danger I'm supposed to be in?"

"I don't have that information."

"You don't?"

"No, ma'am."

"No, of course you don't. Your orders probably force you to keep that titbit of information from me don't they, and you being Mr Perfect Bodyguard couldn't possibly go against that," she chided. "So, what *do* you know?"

"That I'm supposed to carry out…"

"Your orders, yes I got that part." She sighed ungratefully making him even more than aware his protection was causing her untold inconvenience.

"There's one thing you might want to consider," Casey suggested. "You might want to think about why your boyfriend just aimed his gun at you."

"At me?" she laughed, holding her hand to her chest. "Don't be ridiculous! Why would Glen point a weapon at me? It was quite obvious he was aiming it at you. And quite justifiably too. He was coming to my rescue, remember? From being kidnapped by you."

"Like I said before, Ma'am, I'm not kidnapping you."

"No, no, of course, not. You're just following your precious orders and making my life unbearable!" She glanced out of the window watching the speeding cars fly past her shaking her head softly. "Such a mess! Such a mess!" she grumbled glancing down at her diamond encrusted watch. "As if Glen would shoot at me. How ridiculous an idea is that? Absurd. So, Mr Bodyguard, any idea how long it's going to take to get to wherever we are going?"

"Another minute or two."

"Good," she threw her body back against the seat and folded her arms over her well-curved chest, "Because I'm famished! Oh and by the way, you might like to remind yourself *I* am not your client since *I* didn't employ you. God knows who put you up to this but since it wasn't me, I still consider this abduction. When this big practical joke is all over, I'll have your cab badge for this and don't think for a moment you'll be able to get another job as easy as that because I will make it damn difficult for …"

He'd stopped listening a while back. It didn't make a lot of difference whether she thought he was a cab driver earning a little on the side with the joke or if he was the President of the United States of America himself. He was not paid to listen to her opinions, his job was to guard her life and so far he'd done exactly that.

Once they pulled off the main road and into the seedier part of Hollywood, the road lead to the safe house. Casey kept a firm eye on the road behind as well as in front. They travelled further but it seemed nobody was on their immediate trail. He pulled up outside a small white-washed building quickly checking the back of the photograph once again.

"You're stopping here?" she asked with horror. "But it's a dump! I can't walk into a place like that."

"It looks in pretty good shape to me."

"Yes," she sneered, "it probably does."

Casey got out looking around all the time, opened the door for her and taking her bags from the back. He ushered her to the front door and the two went inside.

"God, this is horrible!" she said as he shut the door behind them. "It smells awful, don't these people have a maid?" She was terrified to touch anything in case she received some deadly disease.

"I guess not."

"Who lives here?"

"We do."

She glared at him. "Surely not."

He shrugged. "For now at least."

The scent of what someone had eaten the night before filled the air. It clearly was a safe-house, he had seen many in his previous line of work, but how it was used was not his business. It was just unfortunate that they hadn't cleaned up after themselves.

Candy wrappers littered the small sixties style coffee table between the brown couch and wooden chairs and empty Coke cans joined them. An overfilled flat metal ash-tray precariously perched on the arm of the couch as if whoever had occupied it last had left in a hurry. The odour of cigarettes filled the room.

"Open a window or something, can't you?" she ordered. She spotted a clean towel in the kitchenette and lay it down on the couch before sitting on top of it. Casey watched her actions. "What? Well, I'm not in the habit of having anything like this touch my clothing ordinarily so I'm hardly going to start now." She fanned her face and neck with the floppy rim of her Chiffon covered hat. "Didn't you hear me? I said open a window."

"Oh, I heard you loud and clear."

"Good. Then hurry up will you, I'm suffocating over here."

"No."

"No, you won't hurry or no, you won't open it?"

"Just no," he shrugged.

She could see his impertinence as clear as day. "Fine," she huffed, "then I'll open them."

He grabbed her hand stopping her instantly.

"The windows stay closed."

"But it's so stuffy and they don't even have air conditioning. Can't you smell it in here, it's awful."

"I said they stay closed."

"I'm going to die of suffocation here if I don't get some air!" she insisted, snatching back her hand. "Open the damn window!"

"If you want to die from something a little more painful than hot air and ash then by all means be my guest." He raised his weapon as though to threaten her with it. "But I'm warning you, it's not going to be pretty."

She looked at the barrel of the gun, her anger and fear rising in equal measure.

"What? So you're going to shoot me now after supposedly being my bodyguard?"

"I'll do whatever it takes."

"You'll be sacked before the days out."

"What do you care?"

"Fine! Keep them closed!" She threw herself down on the chairs. "I really don't care. I have some calls to make anyway."

"Switch that thing off! You can be traced."

"I said I have calls to make and I'm going to make them whether you like it or not, Mr Perfect Employee."

"And I said switch it off. *Now!*"

"I can't open a window and I can't make a call? What kind of man are you?"

"The type that's trying to stop you from getting killed."

He grabbed the phone from her hands and threw it onto the settee before going off to check the window, standing back from the curtain just enough not to be seen from outside. If Weston was on his way, he'd better make it soon. Casey didn't know how long he'd be able to cope with this female's self-centred attitude

She had certainly changed from the first time he set eyes on her. Sweet and vulnerable she was no longer. He looked around, glimpsing her position on the sofa, the epitome of sophistication with long legs crossed at the knee and studying her nails again.

Casey looked back outside.

In the storm drain she was defenceless and vulnerable. Death could have been minutes away or even seconds. It was obvious to all that if he hadn't released her restraints she would have been killed. In truth she had a lot to thank him for- not that he either wanted or waited for thanks. It was his job, end of story. But a little common courtesy would be nice.

To put himself through that day again wasn't only dwelling on the past but the bad memories were made worse by the fact he could do nothing to change it. The psychiatrist had told him time and time again to let it go, to stop the self-torment. No good could come of it. Dan was dead. It was over. Life goes on.

The only good thing to come out of that day was that Genevieve Dicing had lived. In fact, she was very much alive, healthy, self-absorbed and free to insult him today.

"You said out there that we've met before. Was it at some gala? You know I have to attend a lot of those things in my position, I can't be expected to remember everyone I shake hands with."

"We've never shaken hands."

"Well, said hello then. Whatever."

He turned to face her. "You really don't remember me, do you?"

Genevieve sighed in her own spoiled way.

"If I did, I wouldn't have asked now, would I? Where was it then, some restaurant? You're not that awful little man who keeps sending me love letters are you? You know you people really are the worst."

"Love letters?" he tipped his head as his blue eyes filled with an emotion she couldn't quite place. He looked almost lost or in deep thought. At last he spoke. "You have a stalker? Is this why I've been hired?"

"Goodness, he isn't a stalker by any stretch of the imagination. He's just a pathetic little man who idolises me. He sends me letters and cards and flowers. You know the kind of thing. It happens all the time. If it's not one man it's another. Glen says he's innocent enough and I'm sure he is. I'm certainly not worried in the least and I definitely don't need protection from him. He's just a nobody." She shook her head softly to change topics and watched Casey return his attention outside. "Anyway, that clearly isn't you. Where was it you said we met?"

"I didn't and I didn't think I would need to remind you anyway."

"For goodness sake! I said it before and I'll say it again, I really cannot be expected to remember every time I meet a member of the…"

"You don't remember being left to die in a storm drain?" His words came out colder than he realised, rendering her silent.

She stopped looking at her nails as her mouth fell open at the thought of it.

"Of course I do. I could never forget that. It was the worst day of my life." She stared into space, her face falling paler. "I was in therapy for ages afterwards."

Casey nodded, he knew what that felt like.

She looked up, blew away the thoughts and replaced them with more familiar shallow ones. "And you wouldn't believe how much that filthy water played havoc with my hair! The whole episode was unbelievable but don't get me started on that."

"I wouldn't dream of it."

"It took me ages to get it back into condition. That was when I met Antonio. He's so considerate about that sort of thing. You know I had to have intensive work carried out on it and…" she stopped talking realising he wasn't listening anyway. "So what are you telling me, you were there too?"

"I was the Detective who found you. I'm Casey Pitt."

She looked him up and down. He had lost a little weight since then, received a couple of facial scars and aged inwardly.

"You?"

"Yep."

"You're saying *you* saved my life? You? You're *him*? You're Casey?"

He sighed keeping a vigilant look outside for a sign from somebody – anybody friendly.

"Yeah, that was me. Casey Pitt, at your service Ma'am," he said cynically as silence filled the room once more.

"I thought he was an older man. You're so much…" she didn't finish. "It couldn't have been you. Are you sure?"

He suppressed a smile at the most foolish question he had ever been asked.

"Believe me, it was."

"Well, in that case then," she stared back at her nails arrogantly, "I suppose I have to thank you, do I?"

"Not if you don't want to. I know how you are with your rules."

"Well, you see, the thing is, Mr 'whatever you said your surname was', I would thank you except you cost me a fortune in therapy sessions and hair appointments, not to mention the fact that I almost drowned that night too."

"Yeah, sorry about that but it's kind of an occupational hazard sometimes. When you're saving someone's life, you have to think on your feet, but, hey you lived and that was our main priority. I guess I could reimburse you for the sessions though it might take a while on six-seventy-five an hour."

"There's no need for sarcasm," she said softly.

"No, of course not, Miss Dicing, of course not."

The atmosphere was heavy around them.

"You know afterwards, when they found me, I thought you'd died in there like the others. What happened?" she asked.

Was she showing the first signs of concern or was it simply idle curiosity?

"I don't remember much about it, well, nothing except that my partner was killed. That part I remember only too... " he stopped. Thinking about it only led to re-living the nightmare all over again. Right now wasn't the time or the place for that

"I thought you'd been shot," she told him. "You went down so quickly."

"I was shot, but I lived. Sorry to disappoint you."

Genevieve looked down into her lap, she seemed genuinely troubled. "Any sign of anyone out there?"

"Nothing." Just as the word left his lips, he added, "hold on. Someone's here."

"Glen?" she sat up primly, hopeful.

"Wait here."

"Is it Glen? I knew he would come back for me. He'll explain this whole thing I'm sure."

"I said wait here." He left the room and slowly checked the front door, weapon ready. Casey opened the door a crack. It was Weston.

"It's okay, kid, let me in." His stocky body moved onto the step of the doorway as Genevieve peered from around the lounge door.

"Okay, it looks like things are a little more complicated than we realised." He confessed keeping his voice low. "It seems the danger is in the form of one Glen De Salle."

"Her boyfriend, yeah, I met him earlier."

"Right. He's a small fish but it looks like he's got big connections."

"You sure it's nothing to do with some admirer of hers, some stalker who sends her cards and flowers?"

Weston looked blank. "No idea what that's about. No, we're pretty certain it's De Salle. Now I've got another guy in the car, Baker. He's ready and willing to take over the assignment. He's a little more experienced with this kind of thing. He's been with me a couple of years, but it's up to you, kid. It's your call."

Casey looked over Weston's shoulder to the man in the car. Baker was slightly older, but Casey didn't want to give up that easily, especially on his first day.

"I'm fine. I'd like to stay."

"Great, that's the kind of answer I was looking for. Listen, my advice is to keep her here until you hear otherwise. These safe houses are all the same, they're not exactly five star but there's food in the cupboards. When you get word to move on out, just up and leave. Just keep the girl out of the picture until the cop's have dealt with De Salle."

"Glen?" Genevieve interrupted moving her slender body between Casey and the doorway. "My Glen? You're saying he's a danger to me?"

"Miss, it's best you keep inside," Weston told her glancing over his shoulder and attempting to push her back out of sight in one go.

"No, you've got it all wrong. We're going out tonight for drinks," she said as if it were relevant.

"I'm sorry, Miss. We have to react to the information we're given. It is for your own safety and I do have to ask you to go back inside."

"This is completely ludicrous! You send this guy to bring me here while I'm supposed to be home. I'm going to miss appointments. I supposed to be getting engaged tonight! I've got to get my hair and nails done and..."

Weston gazed at Casey, his expression was simple: was she for real? Casey arched his eyebrows and shook his head in disbelief.

"Fluff!" he mouthed. "I'm sorry we are inconveniencing you, Miss, but really there is nothing else to be done. The kid, here, is the bodyguard assigned to you and until we receive notice that everything is safe and you can go back home, he's gonna to have to stick to you like glue."

She stood with hands on her hips.

"And how long is that likely to be? I've got a two-forty-five with Antonio Stefan. I'm sure this will be news to you both but it's difficult enough to get an appointment with him let alone have it changed." Her voice gained strength. She grabbed the clasp holding her hair in the bun and let it spill around her shoulders. Deep red thick curls framed her face and the warm glow her hair brought made her complexion appear paler and her eyes a brighter green. "Look at it. It's not exactly going to look fabulous tonight is it?"

"I'm sorry, Miss, but you gotta calm down. This is all for your own safety."

"Calm down? I'm so mad here, you wouldn't believe it! Antonio *won't* re-schedule!"

Screeching tyres sounded out her squealing voice. Glen, at the wheel, slowed the car while his passenger, another man wearing black gloves, aimed a pistol out of the window at the doorway and shot repeatedly. Weston was hit immediately and fell into the gap between the door and wall wedging it open further. Casey pushed the girl behind him using the door as cover. Baker fired back from Weston's car but within seconds Glen had vanished. In this neighbourhood, gun shots wouldn't be out of place. Baker was on the radio just as Casey came into view. He leaned over his boss and felt for a pulse. Thankfully, he was still alive.

"You've got to get him to hospital," he shouted to Baker.

"You have orders?" Baker asked.

"Yeah. We're out of here. You get the license number?"

Baker shook his head. "Part of it but it was too quick. Here, take this car. They'll be expecting the cab."

Baker radioed for an ambulance as Casey ushered Genevieve hurriedly into the front of the Bakers car.

"You got money?" Baker asked.

"Some." Casey replied. Baker handed him a pile of notes.

"Take this. Stick to motels and get as far away as you can."

"For how long?"

Baker shrugged. "Until you get word it's clear. Call in from pay phones at least once a day. Ask for me. I'll wait for the ambulance. You've got to get moving. Good luck."

A moment later they were gone, a cloud of dust in their wake.

Chapter Four

Genevieve Dicing sat up front this time as the two of them sped along the expressway in the silver Ford without a single voice breaking the silence. She pulled down the visor, raking her hands through her long curls before resting against the door. The afternoon sunshine gleamed against her hair making each strand appear as embers.

She took a fleeting look at her driver. His beige suit matched his colouring, though he looked as though he were melting inside with the tie still knotted tightly under his collar. A scar travelled from the side of his lip to his lower cheek and another on his jaw line under his stubble. Both wounds must have been pretty deep, she thought, since they were obviously lighter in colour to the rest of his complexion.

Genevieve watched his profile as he drove. Other cars sped by into the beyond. She vaguely remembered him that day in the storm drain, though he seemed different back then, friendlier. Other events were safely tucked out of reach within her mind despite her therapists numerous attempts to help her retrieve it.

It wasn't something she wanted to remember, now or ever.

Casey remained silent. This assignment hadn't started easy in the least. He suspected Weston would have given it to Baker to begin with if it showed any sign of complications but he was glad he got it.

After leaving the force, unable to hold down a job for one reason or another had driven him nuts. Coming from an all-action position to more casual roles wasn't how he planned his career. He had thought the force was for life but after the incident it was clear keeping his mind on the job was too tough. What if another partner got killed? What if he lost it, if he found himself in a similar situation?

Consumed with guilt, he'd resigned his position but kept a lot of his psychological feelings out of the report since that was unlikely ever to gain him another position in this line of work. Weston understood, thank the Lord. Maybe this time things would be better.

Weston seemed as in the dark as Casey over this assignment and watching him get shot was no walk in the park. Casey felt nauseas. That kind of thing never got easier with time. It wasn't that he wanted to become desensitised, heck he had seen numerous people get injured or killed in the past – some even from his own weapon – but after Dan, it all seemed too real, too unnecessary.

Witnessing Dan's murder questioned his faith. Life was far too fragile. It was over in an instant and it made him want to protect life even more. Another reason to take this job, even if the client was a self-indulgent air-head.

"I thought that man said we had to get away from the city," Genevieve broke the silence at last. "You're heading straight for it."

"Yeah, that's right."

"What's going on?" she turned to him with a look of hope in her eyes. "Are you taking me home?"

"No."

Deflated, she said, "Well, then where the hell are you taking me?"

"We're going to my apartment."

"Why?"

"I've got to get some things."

"Like?"

"Supplies."

"Supplies? What does that mean?"

"In order to keep the both of us alive, I have to be prepared."

"Prepared for what? What's going on?"

"I just need to get some things from my place, spare ammo, change of clothing. It's nothing for you to worry about."

"You're kidding, right? Some guy just took a shot at me and you want to freshen up?"

Casey ignored her comments. At least now she understood it was for real and not some joke just to inconvenience her. He pulled off at the exit and continued towards Newport Beach.

"And what am I supposed to do while you're getting all this stuff, just sit in the car and wait?"

"You won't be in the car. You'll be with me the whole time." His vision was shared between the wind shield and the rear view mirror. "You won't be out of my sight for a second."

"What if that guy comes back, the one with the gun?"

"They won't know to come to my place, they don't know me," he shrugged. "We've got a little time to play with here. They won't be expecting us to go back to the city."

"And who exactly are 'they'?" she asked.

"I don't know."

"Well, that sounds as if you've got it all planned out. If they're not expecting you to come back to the city, why not take me back home too. Surely they won't be expecting us to go there either."

"That would be a bad idea."

Genevieve was exasperated. She wasn't usually in the company of people who didn't do exactly what she told them and it was irritating the hell out of her.

"Why? Why's it okay to go to yours but not mine? This really isn't fair!" she crossed her arms and sulked. She was spoiled brat material, the kind of overpaid movie star he expected to read about in the tabloids rather than the late Vice Presidents daughter.

"Are we sulking again?" He asked but expected no response. "Whatever you think of me, Gen, please try to remember I am here to protect you. If somebody's trying to kill you, I *will* take a bullet for you."

"Whatever!" she exhaled casually. "Do what you've got to do, but please reconsider. If I don't get a message to Antonio, I'll lose out big-time. I know it's not important to you how you look," she told him unaware how rude, insulting and patronizing she sounded, "but to me its *the* most important thing. Antonio isn't the kind of stylist who likes to be kept waiting."

"Your life is in danger. I'm sure he'll understand."

"You don't get it, do you?" she faced him. "Antonio is *the* best stylist around. Everybody wants him and he's coming to *my* house in a couple of hours. Antonio doesn't go to clients houses, they go to him. And if I don't get a facial and massage first there'll be no point in him coming at all anyway and no point to tonight."

Casey tried to stay cool despite everything.

"You won't let me use my phone, I can't go back to my house, and how the hell you expect me to go all day without a facial I really don't know! I'm supposed to be getting engaged tonight, Goddammit!"

"Do you have any idea what you sound like? Are you even listening to yourself?" he blurted, ignoring his brain's message to his mouth.

"You said it yourself, you've got someone trying to kill you and all you care about is getting a message to your stylist."

"It's important!"

"As important as staying alive?"

"This is my life, Mr Pitt! I don't expect you to understand but if I don't look good tonight, who's to say Glen won't propose? My whole life has been geared towards this moment, you don't know how hard this past year has been for me. Getting Glen to propose has been like extracting blood from a stone. He's not the easiest guy in the world to manipulate!"

"There's not going to be a tonight because Glen is trying to kill you. Why won't you listen to me and why would you want to marry a guy who wants you dead?"

"I keep telling you, he wasn't aiming for me he was aiming for you. He thinks you're abducting me. He was trying to rescue me, why don't you see that?" she huffed. "It's not rocket science."

"Lady, I have my orders and I'm sticking to them."

"This is pointless." She threw her arms dramatically in the air, "my life is over!"

"Not if I have anything to do with it, it isn't."

He pulled the car into a space outside his apartment. Sauntering behind him, she held her purse in one hand and the hat in the other. To any prying eyes they appeared to be a couple returning home from a shopping spree.

As he opened the main front door, she followed him up a flight of stairs until they were outside his apartment. Inside, they took in the cool temperature, white washed walls and a beige sofa upon a wooden floor. A dark brown rug stood between the TV and the sofa. A patio door lead out to a well stocked roof garden. She wandered by the window admiring the view.

"When does someone like you have the time and money to get a place like this?"

He had come to expect such a judgmental comment from her in the short time they'd spent together.

"Does that mean it meets with your approval?"

"It's not bad. It's not what I expected, but it isn't bad at all."

"I'll take that as a compliment. What did you expect?"

"I don't know. Take-out cartons on the floor? Beer cans everywhere else, pretty much what we saw earlier."

"Sorry to disappoint you again. Apparently I know how to tidy up." He walked through to his room and put her bags down on the bed. "Sort your stuff into one bag. We may not have time to keep taking a bunch of them with us."

She peeked through a smaller window overlooking a small outside garden.

"I never figured you for a gardener." She followed him into the bedroom where a simple bed was covered with a dark blue throw. A basic full length mirror and a set of drawers were the only other furniture within the room. The pale hues inside the room played beautifully against the colours from outside. "You haven't lived here long?" she added inquisitively.

"Long enough."

"You don't entertain much?"

"I don't have anybody to entertain."

"Why's that?"

"Listen, we're not here to chat and I don't do small-talk so let's just hurry the hell up and go, okay?"

"You don't entertain but you have a cool garden. How come?"

"What?" He stared at her; she wasn't going to accept the monosyllables he'd been giving. She wanted more. "I had a little trouble a while ago and spent some time at home. I guess I just got lucky with the garden, I needed to focus on something."

"What kind of trouble?" She took the bag he threw to her side of the bed and began filling it with her shopping.

"Nothing you'd be interested in."

"Try me, I might surprise you."

He looked up in astonishment. "I don't think so. And I don't usually talk about my personal life on the job."

"That's a shame, I've told you pretty much everything about mine." She said. It was true. The fact he wasn't interested in it or asked for any was irrelevant. "You live alone?" she looked around the room idly noting the lack of evidence of feminine items anywhere.

"Like I said, I don't talk about my personal life."

Genevieve laughed aloud, hands flying back onto her hips.

"Oh my God, you're not gay are you? That really would be a news flash, wouldn't it? Everyone's gay lately. Antonio came out recently, like we didn't already know it of course. You should see the colours he uses in his own hair. Honestly, there's blonde and there's blonde but I suppose he knows what he's doing."

"I'll bet."

"So, that's it then. You're gay?"

"No, Miss Dicing, I'm *not* gay!" It crossed his mind that if he were to show her exactly how un-gay he was, it might shut her up for five minutes.

"Shame! Antonio would love you. We could've double-dated. You, him, Glen and me. Sounds like a great night out."

"Wonderful."

"You say you're not gay but you don't have a girlfriend." She looked around the room again, "and the flowers outside are a dead giveaway. Come on, you can tell me."

"Miss Dicing -."

"Well, I can't see any panties around the place. No frilly pillows on the bed, no elegant furnishings in this room. There's no ring on your finger so you're not married and no white mark so I guess you're not divorced either."

"Just fill your bag so we can get out of here," he said flatly, paying no attention to her comments. He took a handful of T-shirts, a pair of jeans from a drawer and grabbed a couple of shirts from the wardrobe tossing them all into the bag as he went, opening a separate zipped compartment and filling it with spare clips for his gun.

"So, what then? You're not interested in anybody? Oh, come on, everybody is interested in someone."

"Just get ready."

"Maybe I could fix you up with someone. Cassandra's not dating at the moment. She'd love you. What's you're type?" She asked ignoring his comments. "I'll bet it's blonde's isn't it? It doesn't surprise me, most guys do. How about brunettes? Redheads?"

He removed his tie throwing it on the bed and unbuttoned his shirt suddenly catching her attention.

"You're undressing?" she flustered. "Shouldn't you, um, go to another room?"

"It's my place remember? If you don't want to look *you* go to another room but I strongly suggest you stay within my sight."

His shirt landed on the bed revealing his bare chest filled with muscles and a sprinkling of fair hair. She took it all in noticing the small round scar above his left nipple. He stared at her as he unzipped his trousers and watched her face filled with embarrassment as if he were a stripper about to entertain her. She turned quickly and sat on the bed with her back to him.

"What is it, you've never seen a naked guy before?"

"Glen and I have never, I mean I've never...not that it's any of your business!"

"Really? I thought you two were about to win the 'Couple of the Year' award! Just get yourself changed and into something a little less conspicuous. We need to get moving. We don't have much time, you must have something in that bag you can use, something a little more practical."

Genevieve fumbled with her purse while he looked directly at her back pulling on his jeans and zipping them up. As she turned back, the shirt covered up his broad shoulders.

"I don't think I've got anything. I went shopping for cosmetics not clothes."

He leaned forward pulling a piece of white denim from the bag.

"What's this?"

"Shorts, Versace. These things don't come cheap but I was lucky enough to..."

"Change into them." He cut her short unwilling to hear yet another designer shopping story.

"I don't have a top and before you say anything I'm not leaving here wearing a peach suit jacket and white denim shorts. It'll look top heavy. The textures are all wrong together and if I've learned anything over the years it's..."

Casey puffed out his cheeks. This was getting ridiculous, he half wished she *had* drowned that day! He pulled open a drawer too quickly, grabbing her attention, then hurled a white vest at her.

"Wear that. Look," he grinned mocking her, "it even matches!"

She clutched the two items to her chest and smirked. "Thank you. Most kind," she said plainly. "Where shall I change?"

"Right there."

"Here?" she nodded at the bed. "Right here, in front of you?"

"Yeah, that's right, in front of me." He cross his arms over his chest and rested on his left hip. He tried not to let his inner satisfaction show, but it was almost too hard.

"But...But..."

Finally, he held up his hands in surrender, turned around and placed them back on his hips. His muscles were tense and Genevieve found she was staring at them a little more than she realised.

"We don't have time for this, we have to get out of here, now." He glanced down at his watch. Maybe it was a bad idea coming here at all but he really wasn't prepared for a journey without supplies. This was not what he had in mind for his first day on the job.

He could hear her removing her clothes, the light fabric falling gently around her body and onto the floor. He imagined what was underneath and closed his eyes. White, he thought, white lace panties and a matching bra. She had a model's figure and that red hair spilling around her shoulders...*Stop it and focus!* Chastising himself, Casey swallowed turning back without waiting for her to finish.

He zipped up his bag but refrained from looking at her.

"What about my clothes, shouldn't we take them? What about my shopping and my hat?"

"Leave them on the bed. We don't need to get weighed down with anything we don't need. Travel light."

He was halfway out the bedroom door when he turned back to look at her. The white vest looked good against her tanned skin. She'd tucked it into the tiny white shorts and pulled her hair back into a pony tail. Despite looking like a million dollars, she was still going to be some distraction with those amazing long tanned legs.

She raced quickly to the other side of the bed and looked in the mirror.

"Do I look alright?"

He turned and left the room, a bag in each hand and still finding space to hold the keys.

"You look fine," he said, surprising himself with a sudden sexual urge. Boy, did she look fine! Forcing himself to keep his mind on the job, he issued her with an order. "Come on," he said. "Let's move"

Chapter Five

Back on the road, the heat was stifling proving that living on the west coast in July was unbearable. Even with air conditioning, the heat pounded against their bodies and was magnified through the windows. He longed to move back to Washington but life there just wasn't going to be the same again.

"We're going to be on the road for a while. You might as well make yourself comfortable."

Genevieve shuffled in her seat. She leaned forwards, fiddled with the lever beneath her and pushed her feet against the floor making the seat move backwards. Leaning back into the chair, she lifted her legs, bent her knees and let her toes touch the windscreen. She rested her sunglasses over hear hair.

Casey grinned.

"I told you to make yourself comfortable; I didn't say imagine you were on the beach."

She gave her first genuine giggle. It was music to his ears.

"I was just thinking, if I didn't have all those appointments this afternoon, I'd have ended up around the pool with a drink in my hand."

"Sounds pretty fantastic."

"Yeah. No point in stressing out is there? Instead though, I'm running from bad guys with guns. Never saw that one coming. What about you, Casey, what would you be doing if you weren't here to protect me from the baddies? Propping up a bar someplace or lying on the beach ogling the view?"

Wasn't this verging on 'personal-life' chatter? Ogling was hardly his strong point, it had been Dan's, but with the current sight on hand he'd certainly give it a go.

"I don't know."

"Oh, come on. You must have an idea. What do you normally do on a steamy afternoon like this? Have friends over? Watch a game?"

"Nothing."

"Nothing? You must do something. What about your friends, I take it you do have some."

He bit his lower lip at the thought. He did have one once, but now things were different.

"Not really."

"That's right, you said you never entertain but it's a little hard to imagine from a guy like you. You seem like a people person. What do you do for fun, hang out with your family?"

They were gone too. This conversation was futile, all it was doing was depressing him.

"I don't talk about my personal life, remember?"

She moved the large dial beside her seat rolling her chair back a little more. Her shapely breasts inside his vest were a major distraction but now her legs stretching out by the side of him were caught in view too.

"You said we're going to be on the road for a while, seems to me we have to talk about something." She was right, of course. He nodded, taking in her legs and unconsciously licking his lips. "So?"

He tried to centre his eyes on her face and nothing else, despite how appealing the rest of her seemed.

"So what?"

"So what do you want to talk about? You have no friends and you won't talk about your family."

"That's because I don't have any left."

"Family or friends?"

"Either."

"None at all?"

"One or two."

"There, see, you do talk about personal things." She smiled lowering her glasses over her eyes and leaning back. "Tell me about them. What was your mother like?"

"What? My mother, why?"

"Why not," she swallowed. "Come on, tell me about her."

"She was nice."

"What else? Did she bake cookies or was she a career woman?"

"Cookies."

"And your Dad?"

"Don't think he ever baked a cookie in his life," he laughed, "tried a couple of times but they were awful!"

"You know what I mean." She laughed. "Anyway, its good to see a smile on your face. You're like a robot, you're so serious all the time."

His face lit up when he smiled, made sexier by an unshaven jaw.

"He was in the force too."

"So that's why you joined?"

"Kind of."

"Is that how he died?" she asked outright, surprising him with her seemingly lack of emotion talking about a deceased relative. He started to goose all over despite the heat and the feelings of discomfort began.

"Yeah."

"How?" That uncomfortable silence struck again. She waited for an answer but impatiently filled the space with another question instead. "Why did you leave the force?"

"Listen, I can't do this, okay. If you want to talk, then go ahead." He shifted uncomfortably. "Tell me about your family instead."

"Okay," she smiled lapping up the opportunity to monopolise the chat again. "You know my father was Vice President Dicing and you probably know he passed away last year not long after…" she swallowed dryly, "well you know. I guess it was all too much for him. Afterwards my mother and I decided to move away from the political side of things and we came to LA last fall. My brother, Michael, stayed in Virginia. He visits sometimes, stays with Mom. She lives in a gorgeous house in Laurel Hills. Originally I was going to live with her but I wanted to be near the beach. Social lives are so much better near the beach, don't you think…" she went on.

"Then I met Glen at a party one night. He quite literally swept me off my feet." She didn't wait for him to put in the usual 'yes's' and 'no's' in the right places, she simply continued presuming he was listening. "I was wearing these really stupid heels and I would have fallen over, but he caught me. Funny isn't it how people meet. One month I'm in the paper as the Vice President's daughter and the next it's because I'm seeing one of the richest men in Hollywood!" she admitted freely. "I had it all mapped out. Glen and I would get together and with my background and his money, we'd be on the front cover of every magazine from now until the end of time."

"Is that really how you want to be remembered, by being a rich man's wife?"

Genevieve hardly heard him, she was still wrapped up in the fairytale she had imagined for herself.

"He's infatuated with me. Honestly, it's so unreal," she grinned. "All my friends were so jealous when we started dating. He phones me all the time and not a day goes by without him sending me flowers. He's besotted, poor lamb."

"Sounds like it," he said, stifling a yawn

"You can't avoid the paparazzi sometimes. I've only got to walk out of the gym and there all over me. It's impossible. That's why I have to keep in shape. Can you imagine the press if I put on a pound? Oh it would be impossible!" She continued. "Glen's lucky like that. He doesn't have to try to look good he just does it naturally." She looked at Casey. "All guys are, they just look better as the years go on. Of course if you keep in with the right people, the press just love you."

"Is that what you want, for the press to love you?"

"Of course it is, I'd be stupid not to. If you're in the public eye all the time, you have to have them on your side or they can break you. It happens all the time in Hollywood. You've only to look at some of the people out there. Put on a pound or two or have a bad-hair day and the tabloids will eat you alive." She put her head back down on the headrest showing off her slender neck and curved jaw line.

"After the kidnapping saga I realised how often I was in the public eye. It was then that I decided if I was going to be on every cover I wanted to look the part. And now with Glen on my arm I can't possibly lose, can I?"

She'd reverted back to her original me-me-me style while Casey drove them away from the city and towards the hills. At his place she'd appeared to soften slightly, another side of her had come through, a side he found he actually liked. At least, he told himself, if she kept up the self-chat he would be less distracted.

"No, not at all," he answered. "Unless of course, he kills you. That would probably put a major downer on your future plans!"

"How dare you say that, you don't know him! He's very sweet. It was all some kind of misunderstanding earlier. Do you honestly think Glen would try to kill me? He loves me."

"Of course he does," his sarcasm was slight enough for her not to notice. "So he gets someone else to do it, maybe."

"It's all a mistake, you'll see. Tonight I'll be sitting over drinks with him and we'll be laughing about this whole day," she told him. She lifted up her hand and studied her fingernail, "course I won't look nearly as good as I could since I won't be seeing Antonio or Charlotte today, but I'll work something out. I'm starving. Can we stop and get something?"

"No, not yet."

"When?"

"When I'm confident we're alone."

Genevieve grinned cheekily like a school girl. "You want to get me alone, do you?" She pulled down the visor and checked her face. "That would really surprise the press wouldn't it? Me showing up dressed like this with some nobody."

Casey kept his eyes firmly on the road. He wouldn't let this girl get to him, whether it was her cold selfish attitude attempting to intimidate him every chance she got or her unbelievable beauty surprising him every other turn. It would take him a lifetime to work this girl out.

"Of course, I don't mean that in a bad way," she added. "It's probably nice to be unknown sometimes it's just not for me."

"No offence taken. I wouldn't want the press on my tail every minute anyway."

"You'd be surprised," she told him honestly, "it's like a drug having them pawing over you for a picture or an interview. You can get seriously high on it."

"I'm happy with my life the way it is." He told her, "I'd change a few things but on the whole, if I had a choice I'd like a future with little or no interference from anybody. Quiet is good. Quiet is very good."

"Good," she quipped, "but dull! See, you do talk about your private life. Glen and I are perfect together. I can see our whole future together and its wonderfully exciting."

Genevieve was back in her own little fantasy land with visions of her version of the perfect life.

"We'd get a big place by the beach and have lots of staff plus a Nanny to take care of the children when their home from boarding school."

"You want' kids, huh?"

"Sure, why not?"

"Didn't figure you for a mother, wouldn't pregnancy ruin your figure, put a few pounds on you?"

She sat quietly for a moment thinking about the idea.

"Well, maybe we wouldn't have any children. Maybe we'll adopt a dog instead."

Casey laughed inwardly at the quick change of heart. "You wouldn't need a Nanny then, would you?"

"We'd get a dog-minder, I don't know, we'd sort something out. It would be perfect though, just the two of us. Of course, when we meet later for those drinks, you can see him and find that out for yourself."

"We're heading away from the city, Gen, it's unlikely you'll see him tonight. In fact unless I hear anything to say he's in custody when I call in later, you probably won't be going back to the city for a couple of days."

She put her legs back to the floor and pulled her chair back upwards slightly.

"It was a mistake. We'll be back later, I feel sure of it." She told him confidently. "Besides he was going to ask me to marry him tonight. I could just feel it. A woman knows these things. You don't have a girlfriend, you wouldn't know what it feels like."

"I never said that I didn't have a girlfriend."

"But you said..."

"I didn't say a thing, you came to that conclusion all by yourself."

She turned back towards him. If body language told him anything this meant she was now very interested in the conversation again. She kicked off her shoes and bent one leg underneath the other as if she were getting herself get comfortable to watch a movie.

"So, tell me about her. What's she like?"

It was another pointless exercise. There was no girlfriend, there hadn't been for a very long time, longer than he cared to admit.

"I thought we agreed I didn't talk about my personal life."

"You agreed that. I didn't agree to anything. So spill." She grinned like a Cheshire cat.

Casey cocked a grin and, for the purpose of the conversation, created a girlfriend. "Well, she's beautiful. In fact she's stunning."

"What's her name?"

"Isobel," he answered quickly grabbing the first female name he could think of.

"Where did you meet her?"

His mind worked rapidly trying to think of convincing answers to satisfy her curiosity

"In a bar."

Genevieve played with a tendril of hair. "Hair colour?"

He looked at hers. "It's similar to yours actually, maybe a little darker."

"Long?"

"Yeah."

"Curly?"

"Straight."

"Why haven't you got any pictures of her in your apartment?"

He shrugged. "We don't have that kind of a relationship."

"How about in your wallet?"

He tapped his head and continued, "she's in here. I can't forget what she looks like if she's in here, can I?"

"So she doesn't carry a photo of you?"

"I don't know. I didn't give her one so I guess not."

"What does she do for a living?"

"She's a florist."

"How does she feel about your work looking after other women?"

"It doesn't bother her. It's my job."

"But it's a dangerous job. You said you'd take a bullet for me. You could be killed."

"Yeah, but it's a job like any other. Anybody can get killed at work, you should see what they put in burgers these days."

"Point taken," she grinned. "See, it doesn't hurt, does it?"

"What doesn't?"

"Talking, exchanging personal information. In fact its kind of levelling. I know something about you and you know all about me."

He nodded. "Why don't you get some sleep, it could be a while before we get anywhere."

Genevieve agreed laying back down on the seat stretching out her body again and creating shapes so sensual with her hips that Casey was barely able to concentrate on the road. An hour later she awoke with a jump when he pulled the car over to the side of the road which overlooked the valley. The short barrier was the only thing stopping him from tumbling over the top.

Now the sun was going down, the city illuminated. Casey breathed in the air. It looked heavenly from up there.

Genevieve pulled open her purse and quickly dialled the familiar number.

"Glen," she whispered, "yes, its me. I don't know, up in the hills somewhere, we're heading for a motel. He's outside right now so I can't talk long. I don't think I'll be back in time for drinks. He's a bodyguard and they think you're some kind of killer," she giggled quietly. "I know, it's ridiculous but he won't listen to me. Anyway I'll try to call you again later, darling. Love you," she said, blowing kisses down the phone.

Casey turned back towards the car, and leaned inside just as she threw her phone back into the purse. She pulled out her compact and began to dab her nose.

"Good sleep?"

"Yeah, I was dreaming some really weird dream." She told him hoping it was be a reasonable excuse for her breathing hard with the excitement of talking to Glen.

"It happens."

"Why did we stop?"

"I needed a break, check out our status. I don't think we're being followed." He leaned into the car. "It's getting pretty late. I think we should find somewhere for the night."

"How do you think that man is?" She asked putting away her compact. "Was he badly hurt?"

"Pretty bad. He'll probably be in hospital for a couple of days."

"It was my fault wasn't it? If I'd stayed where you told me to, he wouldn't have been hit."

Casey sat back inside. She was right, of course but making her feel bad wasn't the way to go about dealing with it.

"It comes with the territory. Don't beat yourself up about it. We put ourselves on the line, we know what the job's about."

"So how long have you been doing this body-guarding thing?" She asked. Casey laughed at the question. "What's so funny?"

"Would you believe this is my first day?"

"Seriously?" she watched him nod. "Bummer! How do you know if you are good at it?"

"You're still alive aren't you?" he came back quickly. "But I've been in the protection business a long time. You should get out and stretch your legs for a few minutes. I don't know how long it'll be before we hit a motel."

She took his advice, put on her shoes and opened the door. Sliding her bottom around to release her legs from the car, Casey's eyes were pinned to her rear, round, petite and beautifully compact inside the tiny shorts. They really left very little to his imagination. She stood and elegantly sauntered around the car leaning against the trunk throwing her head back allowing her hair to hang like a willow tree branch lit by nothing but the setting sun. Casey watched unable to take his eyes from her.

"You should come back out here, the air's great," she smiled. "The hills are fantastic this time of day." Shadows created by the setting sun threw out bright oranges and tans, while the valley's mist hovered majestically over the tree tops. "It's so quiet up here, come on," she called again. He shot a glance at the valley then back at her before walking towards her, coyly placing his hands inside his pockets. "Peaceful isn't it?" She watched him walk slowly towards her. "Don't be shy, Casey."

"Shy? Is that what you think, that I'm shy?"

"Sure, aren't you?"

"Not particularly."

"But you're so serious all the time. Isn't that just another way men like you act when they're so shy?"

"I'm just following orders is all. I can be loud with the best of them but I'm at work right now and I need to concentrate."

"But you're so quiet, I'm doing all the talking," she admitted. "It's nice to get to know each other a little bit don't you think. After all, if I'm supposed to be guarded by you then I suppose we ought to know a little about each other."

It appeared she'd been studying him as much as he was her. She turned leaning over the trunk staring at him as he stood with his arm on the roof. Her neckline invited attention.

"I know Isobel isn't real," she said smugly

"Wh-what?"

"I told you before, I'm a woman I know these things. I can just tell."

"Of course she's real."

"How long have you two been dating?"

"Er..." he hesitated. "Just...well...we've only..."

"Casey, darling," she reached out touching his cheek to console him, "it's okay not to have a girlfriend." Suddenly he felt as bashful as a small child, vulnerable as if he'd been found out. A flush of colour filled his cheeks and he turned away to face the valley again. What was with this woman? He hadn't blushed since he was a sixteen year old kid at the Prom. "I'm sorry. I didn't mean to embarrass you. I just thought we should be honest with each other. I was saving you the embarrassment of telling me later. You'll find someone though. Good looking guys like you always do."

She was giving him dating advice? A shallow-minded rich kid whose own boyfriend seemed to have a contract out on her life? Casey tried not to laugh at the irony.

"We should get moving." He told her gazing over the precipice, "like I said, we don't know how far the next motel is."

She moved closer reaching out to his bare arm. The suddenness of her contact made him giddy for a moment. He spun around grabbing her arm for safety as she pulled him back towards her. The feeling of her body that close tempted his mind from the job. She leaned forwards, smiling, looking down at his thin pink lips, sure he stopped breathing for a moment.

Grabbing hold of what little control he had left, pushed her away.

"Let's just get moving, shall we."

"Casey..."

"Miss Dicing, just get back in the car."

"No, Casey, come back." She pulled him back towards her, spinning them both around so she leaned against the back door with Casey flat against her body. He put out his arms against the car so as not to allow his weight to crush her and pulled back.

"Gen..."

She put out both hands grabbing his t-shirt pulling him closer and then, without any indication of her intention, she kissed him, a full on hard-mouthed kiss. Her hot body against his was unexpectedly satisfying. He could feel the heat from her skin through the thin fabric and in an instant made him hot from more than just a blush.

He stood perfectly still, as though he were some inexperienced dummy from tenth grade. Had he been given time to prepare he would have touched her hair, breathed in her scent, those soft red curls of hers that tangled themselves around his heart and secretly enticing other areas too. It was a long time since he had been spontaneous; he had almost forgotten how to be.

A wave of desire ran through him but before it could intensify she pulled away. Too quickly, he regained his composure.

"What the hell was that for?"

"I don't know," she shrugged casually. "I guess I wanted to see what it was like."

"And?"

"And," she shrugged again, "now I know. Why don't we watch the sunset from here?"

"What?" He tried to forget the brief moment of passion and concentrate on the situation.

"We can find a hotel later, first I want to watch the sunset."

"This isn't a damn game! We don't have time to do that. We're in a very dangerous situation. Don't you understand? Would you please get back into the car?"

Her lips tightened and her attitude returned. "I don't want to."

"I've been driving for hours and dodging bullets, just get your butt back in that car."

"Are you losing your temper with me, Mr Bodyguard?" Her lips took on a grin all of their own, one of satisfaction that she seemed to have taken him so close to losing control. "Or what, Casey, what will you do? You can't make me, can you? You can't forcibly put me into the car?" She goaded, "That would probably be against one of your rules and I know it's against mine!"

The idea was tantalising to say the least, he'd like nothing more than to hoist her upper-class, self-indulgent butt into the back seat and leave her there. Before he could react a car approached. Immediately he turned to identify the oncoming driver, automatically reaching for his breast pocket, but he wasn't wearing the jacket any more and his weapon was under his seat. As the car drew nearer, it slowed down and the driver, they both clearly saw, was Glen. Casey's heart sank. He had allowed himself to become preoccupied and unprepared.

He ran to the front seat feeling underneath for his weapon and quick as a flash stood up again pointing it at the car. Unbelievably, Genevieve was walking over to the driver's side of Glen's car. If anybody deployed their weapon right now she would unlikely survive it.

"You won't believe the day I've had, Glen."

Casey took hold of the gun firmly, using the roof to steady his arm and watched the scene in front of him. If anybody was to raise their weapon he would have a clear shot first. Glen got out leaving the door open behind him.

"Get in the car," Glen shouted.

"Can you believe he thought you were trying to kill me! Ludicrous wasn't it. Personally I think it's a testosterone thing but..." Before she finished her sentence, the other man in the car, whom she didn't recognise, pulled out a gun and aimed it at Casey. "What's going on, Glen? Who's this?"

"Get inside the car," the other man called to her. "Now!"

She looked around at Casey, standing rigid waiting to shoot back at Glen and his passenger.

"I don't know who you think you are, Mister, but I don't take orders! Glen I asked what the hell is going on."

"Get inside the damn car, Gen." Glen's tone was cold and ruthless. She'd never heard him speak like that before. She adopted the pose she'd used with Casey, hip to one side and hands firmly on them.

"No, Glen! I don't think I want to. How dare you speak to me like..."

"I didn't ask what you want," he shouted into her face. "I just said to get inside the damn car!"

"No, I've changed my mind," she told him flatly. Turning back towards Casey she began to leave but Glen grabbed her arm pushing her against the car, turning her over and crushing her breasts onto the hood. He thrust his weapon into her neck

"For Christ's sake, woman, when I tell you to do something, I expect you to do it!" he bawled into her ear.

Casey moved closer knowing full well another weapon was pointed right at him but this was what the job was all about, protecting the client.

"Put down the weapon!" He shouted, "Let the girl go!"

Glen leaned over her, kissed her cheek hard then hit her face with the butt of the gun.

"You should have run when you had the chance." This wasn't the Glen she knew and loved. What the hell was going on?

"Put down the weapon or I *will* shoot." Casey repeated.

Just then Genevieve quickly caught him with the heel of her shoe between his legs. He doubled instantly, dropping the gun which she kicked underneath the car and ran back to Casey as quickly as she could. Shots fired behind her over and over until she could not be sure if she'd been hit or not. Screaming, she launched herself inside slamming the door behind her. Keeping her hands over her head, she hoped the noise would stop soon. It sounded like thunder, like that day.

"Get in!" She screamed, "get inside now!"

A moment later Casey was in the drivers seat, the engine squealed and the tyres smoked as they sped out of the parking space leaving behind a cloud of dust.

Chapter Six

"What the hell is going on?" Genevieve screamed. Casey's driving wasn't cool and calm any longer as he drove from the scene like a maniac. "You're hit! You're bleeding! We have to get you to a hospital. Oh my God, you're *bleeding*!"

Casey looked in the rear view mirror, then at his bicep which spewed blood over his t-shirt. The smell of sweat and fear lingered around them. He looked back into the mirror again, his breath rapid as he slammed the wheel with his palm.

"God damn it! God *damn* it, why the hell don't you just do as you're told?"

"What?" she asked defensively. "What did I do? I didn't shoot you, did I? It wasn't me!"

"No, you're lunatic boyfriend's henchman did!" He looked at his arm again. It wasn't bad, it was just a surface wound but it still stung like hell. A scratch, he would say, despite the pain it caused him. The bullet had sliced through his skin and out the other side but seemingly unstoppable blood seeped out and dripped down his arm.

It wasn't the first time he had been shot, neither the last he would wager, but the inconvenience of an injury was more than he needed. She was right though, it would need attention and soon. While he knew he could continue, he could do without losing too much blood.

"Have a look in there, would you?" he gestured to the glove box with his head.

"For what?"

"See if there's a cloth or something, something to soak this up."

She leaned forwards and opened up the compartment.

"There's nothing. What should I do?" she looked at her own clothes for something she could use; a sleeve, a cuff. There was nothing. She wasn't a nurse, she didn't 'do' first aid and she certainly didn't 'do' blood. The sight of it alone was making her feel woozy.

"What's in there?"

"A CD case," she reported with disappointment lacing her voice. "There's a box but I don't know if…" she took hold of it but before she could do anything with it he grabbed it from her, still staring frantically in the mirror behind him and the road ahead. At any moment Glen's car could appear from behind.

On the plus side – if there was a plus side - he wasn't seriously injured but Glen didn't know that. From his perspective Casey was a wounded animal about to drop at any given moment. Like any predator, Glen would use that to his advantage.

"It's a first aid kit," he told her. "Open it. Use the bandage inside. Anything, just stop the bleeding. I need to drive, we can't stop and I don't want to pass out through loss of blood."

"Oh my God," she gasped, "can that happen?"

"Not if you hurry."

Allowing the gun to fall to his legs, he wiped his forehead from sweat smearing blood across it.

She took the bandage from its wrapping and dabbed it pathetically against the wound eager not to cause him any more pain. Casey winced.

"I'm sorry, I just don't know what to do. I've never had to do anything like this before. We've always had people do this sort of thing for us," she smiled weakly. She couldn't decipher his expression but her own thoughts told her how bad that sounded. "I know it's lame. Not that we've ever had to deal with *this* kind of thing before but…" she stopped herself before she sounded worse. "You look like you're in pain, does it hurt? I mean, I know you've been shot, of course it hurts, but…"

"Just unwrap it and fold it around my arm," he ordered, ignoring her panic. "Apply pressure to stop the blood and we'll be fine. I'd do it but I can't stop – I don't know how far behind he is. I don't want to give him time to catch up."

He drove as if lunacy had taken control. It would be a miracle if Glen did catch up with them at this rate.

Genevieve unfolded the bandage and rolled it around his arm carefully. She could feel his powerful muscles inside. He was all man, of that she was in no doubt. As she came to the last of the bandage she tucked the end into itself and turned around to look behind.

"Are we okay?" she took a quick peak in the side mirror, "I mean they're not there, are they? Did we lose them?"

"Yeah, for now. I'm hoping that kick you gave him will slow him down a little."

"It was pretty hard."

"Good," he smiled. "That was quick thinking. Well done."

"What about that guy with him?" she wondered, dismissing the compliment. "He can still drive."

Casey faced her. He was dirty, bloody and sweaty. "I got him."

"You got him? What does that mean, you got him?" She stared at him as if he'd taken away her only Christmas present.

"I got him. I shot him."

"You shot him? What, you mean like dead?"

"Yeah."
"You killed him?"
"Yeah."

She looked down at the gun on his legs. "Oh my God, you mean you murdered him?"

"Hey, honey, it was in self-defence," he came back quickly. "It was either him or me and I don't know if you noticed back there but he took a shot at me first."

"But you killed another man?" she repeated, holding her hands up to her face covering her lips, her hands trembling trying to absorb the information. "You *killed* him."

Casey looked her over as she sat in shock. She appeared to have run through a rainfall of bullets without receiving so much as a scratch. Unbelievable.

"This is like some kind of bad movie," she said softly, unaware she even said it aloud. "It's not happening, not really." She hid her face, shielding her feelings.

It wasn't the first time he'd killed someone in the line of duty. Self-preservation and his training had saved them both. She was clearly shocked by the news and as much as he wanted to hold her now, comfort her, he had to drive.

Just drive.

"How did he know we were there?" he said rhetorically. "I just don't get it. Maybe he just got lucky." He shrugged. It hurt and he winced again.

Genevieve looked down towards her bag. She'd told Glen exactly where they were and if that wasn't bad enough she had stalled Casey with that moment of supposed mock passion. She swallowed dryly and felt sick with it. She could have gotten them both killed with her stupid manipulation. Casey was already injured. This was getting all to real, too much to cope with. She wasn't prepared for a life of running from bad guys. This wasn't the movies. Silently she stared out of the window watching the sun make its final decent.

An hour had passed. No words had been exchanged. Casey was getting tired of the road now the light was all but gone and Genevieve had fallen asleep after crying quietly after the shock had taken hold. He guessed she thought she was doing a pretty good job of hiding it but he knew.

Tunnel vision was next if he didn't stop soon. He peered over, red smears on her top - his vest - were as evident as was the dried blood wiped over his arm. It would be obvious to outsiders that they'd been involved in something dubious. They'd have to sort out a cover story if they didn't want to receive any unwanted attention. Wherever they stayed tonight must be low-profile, somewhere they wouldn't ask any questions.

Somewhere like...

"Hey," he woke her, jerking her smooth thigh gently which felt more than a little good in his grip. "There's a place up ahead. We can stop there."

"What? What's going on? Where are we?"

"There's a motel up ahead. We can stop there for the night. You hungry?"

"Yeah." She pulled her hands around her bare arms shielding out the air conditioning which had turned her arms cold while she was sleeping. Now the sun was down, a chilly night ensued.

"Good, me too."

He hadn't eaten since the evening before. Too excited this morning to take breakfast before starting his new job, now his stomach was ordering him rather than telling him to eat. And with the loss of blood, he was fading fast.

Neon signs, outside the cheap, somewhat dismal looking motel, flashed rhythmically. Green, blue, green, blue, its routine mesmerising. Casey pulled into an available space and turned off the engine and Genevieve opened the door inhaling the night air into her lungs, which, in turn, woke her.

"Listen," he said. "We're covered in blood. If they ask any questions leave it all to me and follow my cue. You got that?"

She nodded obediently, her face obviously tired with remnants of make up making her look worse for wear. The two left the car and walked slowly into the reception as Casey pulled on a long sleeve shirt to hide the blood.

An overweight man in his thirties with a pony tail nodded from behind a desk. Greasy strands of escaped hair hung down either side of his face resembling a head full of seaweed.

"Can I help you?"

Genevieve kept a step behind Casey lowering her face from view. The last thing she wanted to be was recognised since she was known most places she went. Most times she more than enjoyed the attention but now was as far from a paparazzi moment as she could ever hoped to want.

"Yeah, need a room for the night. You got one?"

"Double?"

"Yeah."

"We've got one available. I need a credit card and you need to sign in," he handed over a pen and clipboard to Casey.

"I don't have a credit card, you take cash?"

"Sure." He watched Casey signed in then looked over the counter at Genevieve's legs, feasting on the, working his way upwards very slowly licking his lips.

It was clear the receptionist didn't even notice the blood with the view he was getting. She was used to getting looks from men all the time, it was practically what she lived for. This man, however, made her skin crawl. She crossed her arms and took a step back behind Casey.

"Room three, Mr and Mrs," he looked at the form with half a smile, taking back the book and replacing it with a room key. "Rodriguez. Okay. Whatever. Room three, out the door and third on the left. There's a diner across the way if you want to eat. Vacate the room by eight in the morning."

"Charming man," she said under her breath as they got outside, "I'll bet even Antonio couldn't do anything with *that* hair. He wouldn't touch him with a barge pole!" She shuddered. "Creepy!"

Casey grabbed the bags from the trunk and opened the door to Room 3, turning on the light with his elbow. As Genevieve walked inside, she gasped. The bed was draped in an off-white throw, the walls, floor and furniture a neutral shade of brown and the place smelled old and damp and looked more than a little unwelcoming.

"Oh my God, you're not serious? This makes the safe-house look like a show home! Don't these people have staff? Correction, don't these people have staff who work?"

Casey kicked the door shut with his foot letting out an audible sigh. He set the bags on the bed, his wound throbbing continuously, wondering if she was about to turn into the spoiled-brat-from-hell all over again. He really did not need it tonight.

"And only one bed," she noted, her eyes wide with curiosity. She tip toed towards the bathroom about to peer inside. "Do I even want to look in here?" She stopped, turned to see his reaction and grimaced. "I guess if I imagine the absolute worst it can only be better, right?"

Casey took a long blink befitting the day they'd had and sat at the side of the bed raking his hands through his hair, his wounded arm resting calmly at his side. The pain seemed worse now, as if it were an aching toothache with its constant pounding.

Genevieve switched on the bathroom light. "Oh dear Lord! You wouldn't believe it if you didn't see it."

"What now? Not up to your normal standard?"

"I don't think it's even up to Mr Blob on Reception's standard! Come look at this. It's perfectly hideous!" She stalked back into the bedroom catching a glimpse of her figure in the mirror as she walked past.

"Casey, we can't stay here. We'll be in hospital for weeks with some horrible disease."

"We have no choice. It'll do for the night."

"But..."

"But nothing, it'll be fine. Right now I need to get cleaned up, eat and sleep." He looked her up and down dismissing the beauty in front of him and seeing just the long dirty day they had endured. "And so do you. In the morning we'll take a drive out, find somewhere else."

"But..."

"I take it the shower works okay," he went on, tilting his head to his wound, "'cause I've gotta get this cleaned otherwise we'll be in worse state than we are now." He peeled off his T-shirt letting it fall on the floor and walk into the bathroom.

"Is it okay?" she watched as his body moved with long strides. His arms were well built - no wonder he bled so much, there was a lot of them, she noticed, making it hard to take her eyes from him.

"The shower or the wound?"

"Both, I guess." She followed him, hoping to see something more of him but using the excuse to check the shower. He turned the dial and let the water run for a moment.

"Shower looks fine to me. I've spent time in worse places."

"Really?"

"Yeah."

"Why?" she grimaced. Casey smirked. She tagged at the bandage, impressed by his muscles. Sure she'd seen men undressed before, Michael, her father, Glen. But Glen wasn't built like this. Casey, she guessed Cassandra would say, was a hunk. "Should I take the bandage off?"

"Yeah. We need to get a clean one. Have a look in the cupboards while I'm taking a shower, would you?"

"Come on, you're kidding!" she laughed, "they barely have a TV set let alone medical supplies. This isn't exactly the Sheraton!"

He smiled. "Okay, we'll have to wash this one out then. I'll take a shower first."

She began to unwrap it, slowly, almost seductively, glancing up at his thin pink lips every few seconds remembering how they tasted before and secretly wishing she could try it again. If Glen hadn't turned up with his henchman when he did, who knew where the kiss might have led. She cursed herself for thinking that. Not twenty-four hours ago she was not-so-silently preparing her engagement plans to the infamous Mr De Salle.

But kissing Casey had been too quick. There was no time to savour the moment as she'd hoped. No time to touch his hair, his skin, taste his lips, or breathe in his scent. No time at all.

His chest hair blew gently under her breath, his nipples hardening at her touch. A round pink scar lie between his nipple and the arm she was tending. It was the one he'd received during her previous rescue. She glimpsed it and looked away trying not to recall that time. As the bandage unwrapped from his skin, blood soaked into the fabric.

"Ugh! Looks pretty bad. Is it supposed to look like that?"

"I guess."

"You don't know?"

"I tried not look at the other ones. Been shot a few times but didn't sit there gazing at 'em all day."

"But..." she looked back at the scar on his upper chest.

"But what?"

"You were a cop."

"Yeah, but I didn't make a habit of getting shot every five minutes! That one I didn't see at all, it was covered when I woke up and stayed covered until I left hospital."

"Oh, I thought you'd have gotten shot a lot more."

Casey grinned. "What did you think I was, a moving target?"

"No, I just meant..."

"I was a lot better cop than you think," he frowned. "Good ones don't get shot often and I *was* a good one." He didn't mean to emphasise it in the past tense but when it left his lips that was exactly how it sounded.

"I'm sorry. I didn't mean to..."

"Look, I'm tired. I just need to get cleaned up and unless you want to watch me take a shower..."

She didn't respond straight away, her mind entertaining thoughts far beyond the realms of their professional relationship. He stood in front of her, unzipping his fly, very slowly.

"I-I guess I'd better leave you to it then." She swallowed, gave an embarrassed giggle and left him alone in the cubicle taking with her the bandage to the basin for washing.

She put it under a stream of cold water, rubbing it hard with her fingers trying to remove the blood. There was so much of it that the white basin took on an eerie effect as if she had just committed a murder, her hands red with Casey's blood. The whole scene made her shiver. Casey had taken a life. She found it all so surreal and to think it was such a far cry from her situation this morning when she awoke with butterflies hoping for Glen's imminent proposal.

She wiped the soap over the bandage trying to gather a lather but it was no use. It was cheap soap, it didn't even smell good and she didn't even have any in her bag she could use. God only knew what she would use when she showered.

The mirror above the sink displayed a reasonable view of the shower cubicle behind her. She watched discreetly for a glimpse of his outline and savoured the vision. Oh yes, he was all man!

Pretty soon the mirror steamed up obscuring her view. She rinsed the bandage numerous times beneath fresh water and wrung it one last time before placing it over the edge of the sink.

She heard the shower stop and went back into the bedroom leaving him free to dress in private. A few moments later he came out dressed in nothing but the towel, his skin still dripping, his hair roughed up through towel drying. His arm looked angry as hell.

"Does it hurt?"

"Yeah, a little."

"What does it feel like?"

"Like I got shot in the arm!" he said bluntly. "It stings."

"Well," she held up the bandage, "I got it cleaner, but I don't know how clean. I don't think there's anything else we can use in here."

He took a smaller towel from the rack and covered the wound.

"It'll stop bleeding soon. I had to open it to clean it."

She winced. "That sounds gross!"

"Yeah, it was but it isn't going to just go away and we don't have time for me to get it infected."

"How do you feel? You said if you lose a lot of blood you could get woozy."

"Yeah that's right. I should be fine after I've eaten and slept."

She wrapped the bandage around the wound tying it into a neat bow.

"There, that should do it. Soon as we can, we'll see a doctor."

Casey looked apprehensive. Situations like this, there was no telling when or if that was possible.

Genevieve sat on the bed looking up to the ceiling. Cream and beige water stains marks the ceiling above her. It was likely this place leaked in the winter, and was evident it hadn't been decorated in some time. She wasn't even sure if Mr Blob knew what tasteful decoration was. This place was dreadful. She missed her apartment and wondered when she'd see it again.

Her slim body oozed sex appeal, sending out unintentional invitations for company. Casey looked away and sat down, his back to her, drying slowly in the room's stale air. He needed to think about their situation not her body, as tempting as it was.

"I'm sorry you got shot," she admitted quietly. "I didn't know that guy, you do know that, don't you?"

"Yeah, I know. Situations like that, there's no time to think, you just react. Someone's pointing a gun in your direction, you don't stop to ask them what's going on before you point one back, you know?"

"But he could have killed you."

Thankfully this time it was just an injury to his arm, but next time who knew. Casey nodded.

"Yeah, he could've."

"It's incredible. Surreal really."

"In the line of duty and all that stuff. I just can't work out how they knew where we were. I was pretty careful. I was keeping look-out, I don't think we were followed."

"Didn't you say they may just have struck lucky?" She suggested, hoping he didn't ask the words outright if she had anything to do with it. If he did, she wouldn't be able to lie convincingly. Hopefully he would accept the suggestion.

"Yeah, LA's a pretty big place though, it was *very* lucky. Unless…"

Gen's heart beat quickened. "Unless what?"

"Nah, nothing. Just got an over-imaginative mind today. I guess with all that's happened, you know."

She breathed a small sigh of relief.

"Doesn't it worry you? I mean the fact that your life could be over so instantly. We could be dead, right now."

She moved onto her side staring at his back as he sat at the end of the bed, her face supported by her hand. Tiny moles over his back caught her eye and a few scars were scattered but nothing like the ones on his chest, face and the one that would undoubtedly damage his arm. He looked like a walking war monument.

"Yeah, sure it does. But that's the risk you take in this kind of job. 'Protect the client with your life'," he said as if he were reading it from a handbook. "If you're not prepared to die for your client, then you're in the wrong job. Period."

"What kind of man puts his life on the line for somebody else every time he goes out to work?"

"This kind," he tipped his head. "But at the end of the day it is just a job."

"I'm sorry but I just cannot comprehend how one person can willingly give up their life for another and call it *just a job*," she said huskily, raising herself to her knees. "I mean it's not like you've just nipped to the store to buy a bottle of Champagne is it?"

"First of all, I'm not willingly giving up my life. I took this job to protect the client and, as fate would have it, that client just happened to be you. If, by doing my job, it means dying then so be it, at least it won't have been in vain." *Like Dan*, he thought instantly. "Secondly," his eyebrows rose, "do you honestly *nip* to the store to buy a bottle of Champagne?"

"Truth is, no I don't. I'd get the store to bring it to me," she answered firmly with a small smile as she raked her hands through her hair. It didn't take her a moment to spring from caring and considerate back to Hollywood Brat. "And generally, I don't do the food store thing. It's really not my scene. Glen has people and so do I. When this whole stupid thing is over and everything's back to normal, you might actually get a chance to meet him and see him for the dream-boat he actually is."

"Man!" he sighed, got off the bed and unzipped his case. Inside, beneath the clothes were magazines of bullets. "I'll never understand women!"

"And what exactly does that mean?" He didn't answer. "What are you doing now? I thought you needed to rest."

"Ammo," he said quickly. "I need ammo."

"For what?" she peered through the window, suddenly concerned at their location. "Did you hear someone?"

"No." He filled his weapon, placed it back into the holster and tucked in beneath the case. "Just getting prepared. Job like this you never know when you'll be thankful for preparation."

"Job like this? I thought you said it was your first day."

"I did. It is. But I was a cop for a long time. I know how these things go."

"Please believe me, Casey," she smiled at him as if she owned the words she was about to say. "Glen De Salle isn't some hardened criminal like everyone's making him out to be. He's a dear, sweet gentle man who was about to propose to me. I've spent eighteen months finding that much out. Do you honestly think I'd be with a man who wanted me dead? He's not a dangerous man, not really."

"You still don't get it do you, Gen?" he impressed, "even after he aims at you on the highway, even after he throws you on top of the hood and hits you with the gun butt and even after he shoots clean through my arm, even after all that you still can't see any bad in the man, can you?"

She recalled the events well. The bruise on her jaw would show tomorrow but for now it was just an ache. An ache, she told herself, that she wouldn't make into a big deal. Not for Glen's sake.

"It's some big mistake, that's all. What would I be doing seeing a – a -," she threw her arms in the air as she got off the bed, "I don't even know what on earth I'd call someone that was trying to kill me!"

"How about a killer? And I'm glad that you've just realised that he was."

"No, no, you misunderstand. Glen wouldn't do that, he just wouldn't."

"What do you mean, he wouldn't? He just did - three times! How many times is he going to have to do it before you realise what he is?"

"It's just so not like him. I don't know what's going on, really I don't."

"That much is obvious. Listen, if I don't eat and sleep soon, I'm going to be less use to either of us than the dead guy I left on the road."

Genevieve shivered at the thought. "What'll happen to him?"

Casey shrugged without interest. "With any luck the vultures will feed off him."

"That's cold, Casey."

"That's life, Gen. You start playing that kind of game, you're going to have to deal with the consequences."

He continually surprised her, shocked her even. One moment he was brash and gung-ho, the next caring and sensitive and now callous. He was as much of a mystery to him as she guessed he was to her.

"Why don't you take a shower and I'll go find us some food."

"A shower? You want me to get naked in there?" her face told him everything. "I could catch something and die from it."

"Great, then we can all go home!" He pulled on a fresh T-shirt holding the towel around him. "You'll be fine. What do you want to eat?"

"Anything."

"Sure?"

"Yeah," she nodded, "anything low fat, low calorie, low..."

"*Anything* it is then," he left without waiting for more additions to the list.

Alone, she tip-toed into the bathroom with such caution as if expecting a big bug was about to kill her and gobble the evidence. She switched on the shower hoping only water would fall out and not cockroaches or something equally as horrible. It looked fine when Casey used it, but then, if she were honest with herself, she didn't so much as look at the shower as him inside.

Stepping into the cubicle, she dropped the towel from her body onto the floor and unconsciously looked up towards the shower rose, taking some comfort from the fact his naked body had been in there just seconds before.

Mould had grown around the holes and she shuddered.

"Ugh!" she shut her yes quickly at the sight. The thought of mould against her hair was a horrifying thought but the warm water against her skin was oddly welcome.

When she got out of the shower, she grabbed the only towel left on the rail. It was larger than the one Casey had used and covered her bare body satisfactorily. Considering the state of the rest of the room, the towels were in pretty good shape.

She had wet her hair but without any shampoo available, it hung around her shoulders like soaking rats tails. She walked back into the bedroom patting her hair dry with the towel he'd left.

"Oh, you're back!" she exclaimed suddenly, eyes wide in surprise. She had expected to be alone.

Lying on the bed, TV set on softly, he was chewing on a hamburger. It smelled good but didn't look particularly low calorie, low fat or low anything but it bellowed low class in a big way.

"Got you a burger with fries, that okay?" he said, mouth full of food. She grimaced. "Hey, you did say 'anything'," he added. "Besides, it's pretty good, course only if you don't look at it, but right now I could eat just about anything."

"I suppose it will be ok. Listen, I don't have anything else to wear other than the clothes I came in. I've never been away like this before. I'm not in the business of running away from bad guys, I'm not really sure what I'm supposed to do. I usually have bags and cases with me and..."

"Sleep raw," he said without taking his eyes from the TV screen. He didn't need to look at her to know what her response would be.

"So, what's going to happen about the...um...arrangements?"

"Arrangements?" he looked up inquisitively.

"The sleeping arrangements," she gestured to the bed, "there's only one bed."

He glanced at her. "Yeah, so, how's that a problem?"

"Well..."

"It's okay," he smiled weakly, " I'll take the floor."

"I couldn't ask you to do that, you've been injured. You need a proper bed to rest on."

"Fine, then I'll take the bed and you have the floor."

"What?" she blinked, "I can't sleep on the floor!"

Casey laughed. She might have been genuine about showing concern over his injury but her own wants were never far behind.

"Listen, we're both adults here. I'm not going to try anything and I'm pretty sure you're not either. Why not both use the bed and get a good nights sleep? I'm beat and I'll bet you are too."

"But I have nothing to wear."

"Jeez, you never stop with that one do you! If you're worried about us *touching*," he raised his eyebrows, "you can take my shirt if it makes you feel better."

"Won't you need it?"

He pulled it off and handed it over without further thought. She took it holding it against her walking back into the bathroom to change. When she came back, Casey glimpsed sight of her, white panties with his T-shirt over her torso. He felt himself harden at the thought, pulled his gaze back to the TV and thought about Glen De Salle and the situation they were in.

With that thought in his head, it was much easier to focus.

Chapter Seven

"I can't believe people eat this stuff!" Genevieve pawed her way through the carton containing the burger and fries. "It's not food, it's waste!"

"Well, it's all we're getting tonight and you need to eat something." Casey stuffed his mouth with fries. "Got to keep you're strength up. We don't know what tomorrow will bring. If it's anything like today, we'll need all the help we can get."

She sat at the foot of the bed, Casey at the head end, picking at the fries.

"What will we do if Glen finds us again?"

"Keep on running. My orders are to keep you from the city and from him so that's what I intend to do."

"Even if it means our lives."

"Hopefully it won't come to that."

"You know I didn't imagine today to turn out anything like this. I was going to have a romantic dinner tonight with Glen, get my hair and nails done, have a facial and massage and put on this beautiful little black number I got last week. It was all going to be so perfect."

"Yeah?"

"I was going to graciously take my seat, order my favourite meal, sip Champagne with him and when he offered me the ring, I had this big speech planned." She took one of the fries and nibbled at it. It smelled appetizing enough but tasted like nothing.

"You've been expecting it for some time then?"

"I've been working towards this for months. I was going to tell him how wonderful our life was going to be, how lucky I was to have him and that I loved him so very much. I was going to tell him that I would make him the proudest husband any man could be, that I'd be there for him no matter what."

"That's some speech."

"It was all going to be just so perfect." She sighed staring at the vision she'd created in her head and in a flash it turned into a frown. "But instead I'm sitting here in your shirt, eating God knows what in some God-awful motel I've never even knew existed!"

"Hey, you know you could have done a lot worse tonight."

"Yeah? Exactly how could it *be* any worse? My life is practically over."

Casey laughed. "You could be having dinner with the guy on reception. He seemed to enjoy the view if I recall."

"That creep? Nothing in the known universe could force me to have dinner with him. Did you see how disgusting he was? Ugh!" she shivered.

"And I thought you enjoyed male company?" he laughed. "Seriously, though, we've been through a lot today. We'll need to get some shut-eye."

"Oh God, how did my life go so wrong so quickly?" She took off the towel from her head releasing tangled red locks around her shoulders.

"I think it went pretty well all things considered."

"How on earth did you work that out?"

"Neither of us are dead." He threw a French fry into his mouth. "You might look at it that way."

"Are you always this optimistic?"

"No, actually I'm not."

"This is new for you?"

"Maybe you bring out my optimism."

"I'm so pleased I was here for this. I'm so pleased you've found optimism in your life just when mine got flushed down the toilet!"

Casey ignored her sarcasm. "I just think that when you consider we've been chased out of town, had shots fired at us, Weston's down, not to mention my arm hurts like hell. I don't think we've got too much to complain about. We're still alive and that is the best and biggest thing we have to focus on."

"Great," she shook her head, "I feel so much better now. I don't feel at all guilty because I was thinking of myself. Jeez, you know how to manipulate with the best of them, don't you? That's usually my job. I guess I suck at that too. I suck at finding good, trustworthy men, I suck at keeping them and I suck at life in general!" She sighed, then added, "Oh and while we're on the subject, lets not forget the fact that I suck at respecting security."

"You suck at depression too," he told her, "you think far too much of yourself to really believe half of that."

She raked her hands through her mangled red curls and fell dejectedly onto the bed next to him. "Oh God! I hate myself," she cried melodramatically. "I'm such a bad person!"

Casey laughed aloud unable to hold it back any more.

"Come on, you're not a bad person. You're just going through a bad time right now. It happens to everyone."

Genevieve looked up, her face covered in damp hair, her pout bigger than he'd ever seen and her green eyes genuinely filling.

"Who? Huh? Tell me, who?"

"You?"

She scowled. "I don't know what I ever did that was so wrong for all this to happen."

"You didn't do a thing. Some things we have no control over at all." He said thinking of his therapist's words. It was true but it didn't make it any easier to digest. He inhaled sharply then placed a handful of fries into his mouth. "Eat your food."

She sat back on the bed and fingered her meal. She had eaten almost all the offerings but didn't feel any better for it. Instead a nasty heavy feeling stayed in her stomach, indigestion she guessed. Too much fat and salt she suspected. How on earth did people eat this stuff all the time? She threw the carton in the trash and sat on the edge of the bed again.

"My father would have laughed at me finding myself in this situation, you know."

"Really?"

"Yeah, he's probably looking down on me right now giggling at my expense. He always thought I was too big for my boots. I guess he was right. I've always had all these big ideas about how my life should be. We were so alike. Neither one of us would stop before we had our dream in our hands."

"It's pretty unusual these days for a young woman to have her biggest dream be to be married, especially one as beautiful as you."

Did she blush at his remark? Casey was sure he noticed a pink hue in her cheek.

"Is it? I thought it would be any little girls life long hope to be able to marry the man of her dreams."

"Well, sure but not to make it her life's ambition."

She listened, interested at his words. "I've imagined ever since I was a little girl that I'd have the most beautiful white gown encrusted with diamonds and a golden tiara. I wanted a huge bouquet and a long veil covered with petals to match the bouquet just like you see in the movies. I was going to be married in a big old stone church and have a dozen bridesmaids and a pageboy."

"And your father was going to pick up the check, was he?"

She smirked at the probable cost. "Well, he would have, if that's what I'd wanted."

"Do you think you will still want all that?"

She laughed. "The way it's going, I'll probably end up with a simple ceremony, a tiny posy and an off-the-rail dress! So much for my big ideas, huh?"

"I find it interesting that your idea of marrying the man of your dreams involves a lot of what your going to wear and absolutely nothing about the groom." He sniggered. "Don't women see past the frills?"

She tipped up her chin. "What do you think my ambition should have been then?"

"You didn't answer me." The look on her face said she wasn't going to either. Casey got the message. "A great career, something like that. Something where you could use your intelligence, help people, make a difference."

"I do all those things already. I give a fortune to charity."

"There's more to helping others than throwing a few hundred bucks their way. Don't you think you could use your qualities some other way than just posing for pictures or trying to wear Glen's ring?"

"But it's all I've dreamed of for months. Glen is everything to me. All my friends know that, all my family, everybody. It's the only thing that I've deemed important for so long now, I can hardly think of anything else."

"Maybe you've spent so much time trying to force one particular part of your life into action that you've forgotten about the rest of the world?" He watched her face fall again. "Don't get mad, I just mean you're obviously a very smart woman, and let's face it, Gen, you already know you're beautiful. I'm just saying don't waste the best part of your life over a crazy guy like him."

"Am I hearing this correctly, Casey? You think of me as intelligent and beautiful?" she sidled back up to him, dismissing the other comments.

"Sure I do. I'm a guy. I'm only human."

She smiled, revelling in the thought. Content with that thought, she laid down on the bed and stared at the ceiling. "Of course, you're not the only man who's ever thought that. I get plenty of male attention. There's not a week that goes by without some guy off the street telling me as much."

"And I'll bet you love it too."

"Course," she covered her forehead with her arm. "What woman wouldn't? Women love to be adored and admired. I'm no different there. My father used to say I was strong willed and that I would always get what I wanted. I guess that fits with my longing to marry Glen."

He turned on his side to face her, his wounded limb lying limp over his hip.

"I just think you could do a whole lot better than him."

"What are you suggesting?" she asked bluntly. "Someone like you, you mean?"

"No, not at all. I'm the last guy I could see you with."

"Why?" she seemed disappointed. "What's so wrong with that idea?"

He laughed. "What would be right with it? Think about it. We're very different people, you and I. We'd expect different things from life, *very* different. You wouldn't cope a day without a camera in your face and I wouldn't last a day with it."

Genevieve lay silent. Maybe he was right. She did adore the publicity but if she were truthful there were days when she could do without the constant intrusion. Somewhere deep inside her she entertained the idea of living in the suburbs, somewhere incredibly ordinary with no interruptions, nobody but the ones she chose and definitely no cameras.

"How about your father?" she asked. "Would he laugh at this situation?"

"Maybe, I don't know."

"He was a police officer too, I remember you saying. Has he been gone a long time?"

"Yeah."

"What happened?"

"He cornered a guy in a drug store. This crazed out junkie just pointed the gun and shot him dead," he admitted casually. "His partner said it was quick. That's something, I guess."

"How old were you when it happened?"

"Still a teenager."

"How do you get over something like that?"

"You don't. Being the only child of doting parents, you soon realise how easy life is taken away from you. Dad was there one minute and gone the next. He was a good cop though, I guess he was just a little slow that day."

"How did your mother take it when you told her you were going to be a cop?"

"Pretty hard," he laughed. "She didn't speak to me for a month! I guess it was hard for her to imagine life without me too if it all went belly-up. Getting that two in the morning phone call is no picnic. It was understandable but I just had this desire to protect life and try to put things right. I still do."

"Mr Rescuer, huh?"

"I don't know about that."

"I do."

There was something in her expression, the slight upturn in her lips that told him she thought of him that way and he liked it.

"She got over it eventually," Casey nodded. "She understood what it was like for me. I just think if it is possible for me to make a difference in somebody's life, then I should do it. I'm glad she got that before she passed. Dan was exactly the same as me, we were always on the same page. Everything fell into place most of the time. Then," he shook his head vacantly, "it all went wrong. Nothings been quite the same since."

"I suppose you and I were destined to meet if you think about it." Her green eyes gazed up at him. "If it wasn't in the storm drain, then now." She closed the gap between them. "Dear God, Casey, you're such a good person, why the hell couldn't I have met a regular guy like you first?" Her words were real, that much he could tell. "In that drain, you risked your life for me and today you risked it again. Why do you keep doing that, I'm not worth it. I'm just a stupid girl with a stupid knack for getting myself into stupid situations."

"I think you're a great person, Gen. Don't beat yourself up." He said gently.

"But I've been so awful to you. I'm awful to everyone."

"Yeah, you are," he told her, "but you can change if you want to."

"Why don't you hate me? You should hate me, you know."

"Who says I don't?"

She moved her hand up to his jaw and pulled him nearer, their faces almost touching. He smelled masculine and clean and she inhaled him deeply, wanting and needing more of him.

"Oh, Casey," she purred.

Too close, you're getting too involved, he cursed himself. *Control, stay – in – control!* He wanted to pull back, stay away from her lips. But it was too hard.

She looked in his eyes so intently, she could see herself in there. Her chin puckered slightly as if she were about to cry.

"Please don't hate me," she whispered. "I didn't mean to –."

"I don't," he shook his head. "I really don't."

"Then kiss me."

"What? Why?"

"Just kiss me. Tell me it's all going to be okay, that this whole mess is going to go away. Please, just tell me that," she pleaded. "If you tell me then I'll believe you."

"It will be fine, I've already promised to protect you and I will," he reassured.

She sighed peacefully. "Kiss me, Casey."

She'd entangled herself around his heart and brain. He couldn't think clearly, just the sight of her like this and her closeness was all he could think about.

"You don't mean that," he smiled sympathetically, wondering how long he could hold back from the invitation. "You're in love with someone else, don't forget that."

For a moment she had to think who that was.

"With Glen? I thought I was. I mean I am but..."

"You're just confused. It's been a hard day. Life throws us curves all the time. The trick is to see them coming and deal with them. You're doing fine."

"I meant it though, Casey. I want you to kiss me, please."

"Gen...I can't..."

Her eyes pleaded. "Don't make me beg."

He brought his face forwards until his lips touched hers. The warmth between them was pure and wanton. If only he could take her in his arms and show her just how much he needed the comfort she could offer. He wanted to but he daren't. The unknown was his enemy. It had been a while since he had been with a woman. What if it went further, what if he couldn't - or didn't - want to stop himself? The softness of her skin and the scent of her hair was almost more than he could cope with.

Too soon, the kiss was over. She looked at him and moved to the other side of the bed.

"Casey, thank you for rescuing me."

He didn't ask for clarification. Whether she meant in the drain, today or emotionally, he wasn't sure. He moved down the bed, turned off the TV and light and closed his eyes.

Chapter Eight

Sleeping in the same bed as Genevieve Dicing wasn't all it was cracked up to be. Casey lay on one edge holding himself onto the bed with his good arm while Genevieve's idea of a good nights sleep was to sleep spread eagled using ninety per cent of the mattress for her own comfort

She faced away from him all night; two spare pillows lying longways between them acting as a physical barrier despite their earlier embrace.

His arm throbbed and kept him awake, that and the thought of her touch. It was a long time since he'd receive anything as pleasant. The thought of it tightened him again. She was a great looking woman and one able to manipulate anyone to her way of thinking at the drop of a hat.

Unless he was falling under her spell, he'd swear she was genuine.

He tried to comfort her, make her feel stronger, better about herself but he'd have to be more careful next time. She wouldn't get anything other than professional sober reactions from him from now on, the kind you'd expect to get from a bodyguard.

He swung his bare legs from the bed, pulled on his jeans and shirt and quietly left the room. Glancing at his watch it was still this side of midnight. He could call Baker and see if there was any change in the situation. A quick call would tell him where he stood.

He really could use a doctor's opinion over the wound, although he was unlikely to get anywhere near a hospital tonight. If he had the supplies, he could take care of his arm himself.

The phone booth by the reception office reflected the neon sign advertising the motel. Casey wandered through the parking lot, his shirt unbuttoned bearing his chest in the night's breeze. It was welcome, chilling him enough to stay awake. He threw a couple of coins into the slot and dialled the number. It rang twice.

"Baker."

"It's me, Pitt. What's happening?"

"Still nothing. Staying low is the only advice I can give you right now. Use it well. You okay?"

"Yeah, we had a problem earlier though. I don't know how it happened but De Salle found us. He took a shot at us."

"Is she okay? You hurt?"

"I took a bullet." He looked at his arm. "But it's just a scratch. She's fine," he confirmed. "I could use a hospital though."

"No, don't do that. Can you deal with it yourself? There's a first aid kit in the car."

"Yeah, I found it."

"But you lost De Salle?" Baker needed reassurance.

"For now. It got a little messy."

"It happens. Action on your first day, huh?" he laughed. "Cool, just hang in there, Pitt. We're doing all we can this end."

"I'll call sometime tomorrow." Casey said and put down the phone.

He walked into the reception to see Mr Blob sitting alone with just a small TV for illumination and entertainment. The TV was hooked up to the counter and showed a re-run of I Love Lucy. He seemed happy enough despite the appliance being totally devoid of sound. Casey watched for a moment until his presence was obvious.

"Yeah?"

"You got any medical supplies around here? I need a bandage or something." He gestured to his arm as the man craned his head to look.

"What happened?" he smirked. "You try something and the girl took a swing at you?"

"Something like that."

He nodded, still staring at the screen though Casey was sure the smirk was for his benefit and not Lucille Ball's. "So? Do I look like a doctor?"

"I just need a dressing," he pressed. "You got anything like that around here?"

"Your girl's cute."

"You noticed that?"

"Hard not to. Don't get many pretty ones like her up here. Seems classy too."

"She is. So," Casey prompted, "you got a med kit?"

"No, I don't."

"Nothing at all?"

"No," he said flatly.

Casey stood silently, eyes back on the screen again. "I thought places like this were supposed to have basic supplies."

He shrugged nonchalantly. "So sue me."

"Anywhere else that might have something I can use?"

"The diner. Or the bar."

"The bar?"

"Yeah, a couple of miles away." He pointed his finger towards the door. "They might."

In the force, he and Dan were used to Joe Public being less than helpful but this guy seemed just plain thick.

"You've been a great help!" he said. "Thanks, I'll try them."

"You do that. Oh, and tell your girl I said hi."

He left the office and headed back for the room. As he went in, Genevieve was still asleep. Just by her being in the room, it smelled ten times better than before. By the looks of it she'd not moved an inch, her curvy frame adding an interesting and defining line to the sheets. He walked to the bed and leaned over.

"Hey, Sleepy, I've got to go out for a while."

She turned over to face him. "What's going on? Is Glen back?"

"No, nothing like that." He gestured to his arm, "I've got to get this wrapped up. There's a bar a couple of miles away so I'm going to see if they have anything I can use."

"Should I come?"

"No, you'll be fine. Nobody knows where we are. Keep the door locked, I won't be long."

"But what if someone comes?"

"No-one will."

"But if…"

She looked frightened sitting up in the bed staring at him with that forlorn look of hers. Casey blinked hard. There was something vulnerable about her, something about her childlike state that made his imagination run wild and the thought of Mr Blob checking on her while he was out blurred his mind.

"Okay, maybe that's not such a bad idea, but hurry up."

She threw her legs out of bed and caught him watching her.

"Well, turn around then!"

Casey rolled his eyes and turned. She took hold of her shorts and tied the shirt up with a knot in the middle of her chest while Casey thrust his weapon down the back of his jeans pulling his long sleeved plaid shirt over the top to cover it.

"Why are you taking that? You're only going out for a bandage, do you really think you'll need a gun."

"Hopefully not," he said honestly.

Finally the two drove out of the parking lot.

"Are you still in pain?" she pulled her legs to her chest, her hands holding them close.

"I'm okay I just need to take care of it."

"Should I drive?" She yawned, "You know, so you can rest it."

"I'm fine."

Three miles further on, the lights from a bar shone out like a beacon. Motorcycles lined the way outside leaving just enough space for Casey to park the car.

"Stay here, I'll just be a minute."

"I'm not staying out here all by myself. I'll come in with you."

"I don't think that's such a good idea, Gen. Stay in the car."

"But what happens if someone comes?"

"They won't, I'll be just a moment."

"No, Casey, I'm not staying here alone. You're supposed to be protecting me and you said you wouldn't let me out of your sight and now you're going to leave me out here all alone? *Anything* could happen."

He laughed inwardly. This was rich! It had taken him the best part of a day to convince her that she needed protection and now here she was ordering him to do exactly that. He looked at her long legs which invited attention with every inch.

"You're right, but since there's likely to be a few guys inside with a bellyful of booze, it might not be the best place for you. I actually think you would be safer out here."

"What? Why?"

"Genevieve," he looked down at them again, emphasising his point, "you're a smart girl, think about it."

"I don't get scared by men looking at me. I don't care. I want to stay with you."

The look in her eyes told him she wasn't going to budge on this one. He sighed and nodded reluctantly.

"Fine. Just stay close and don't provoke anyone, don't say a thing and keep a *very* low profile."

"Me? Provocation?" she unfolded her legs and opened the door. "As if I would."

Casey walked around the car keeping her close. As he opened the bar door the crowd instantly stared at him, then her.

"Keep walking, stay close," he said softly over his shoulder. "Don't attract any attention."

He felt ridiculous asking that of her; the girl was a walking centrefold! She put out her hand, touching his hip searching for his hand, which he promptly gave. Holding it tightly, she felt his body's heat transfer to her skin and silently lapped it up reminding them both of the closeness they shared earlier.

"Hi, what can I get you?" the bartender asked, a tall man, with blonde curly hair. He looked a little older than he dressed but he was a surfer by day by the looks of it. A cord around his neck held onto a sharks tooth and his tan told Casey he spent a lot of time near the beach. He looked every inch the part. Postcards behind the bar depicted scenes of the ocean; girls wearing bikinis with perfect white smiles, girls wearing nothing with bigger smiles. Behind them the Jukebox screamed out and behind that stood the pool table.

"I was hoping you'd have a medical kit," Casey said.

"Pal," he frowned, "do I look like I'm running a medical centre. I sell beer not bandages. Now you can either buy a beer and something for the lady or you can leave."

"If I buy a beer, can I use your kit?"

"I guess," he shrugged.

"Beer then, please. Make it two."

"Jodie!" he shouted in the doorway out the back, "bring down the med kit, will ya?"

"Someone hurt, Jed?" Jodie hollered over the noise of the customers.

"How the hell do I know, just bring it, will ya?"

"I hope they ain't bleedin' to death out there 'cause I already cleaned up today!"

"Hell, woman, nobody ain't dyin' out here. Fella needs it is all," Jed nodded. "Box'll be down in a minute." He grabbed two beers, pulled off the tops spilling the froth over the bottle neck onto the bar. "What *do* you need it for? You don't look sick, either of you."

Casey threw down a couple of notes on the bar but said nothing. He handed a bottle to Genevieve and took the other one swigging it instantly. It was better than the burger and way better than the sour taste he'd had in his mouth all day.

"I don't drink this stuff," she told him quietly, "I've never drunk beer in my life. Why on earth would I start now?"

"You don't have to drink it, just make it look like you are." His eyes darted around, gathering up the scene in front of him. "Don't call any attention to yourself. We don't need any trouble." Nobody seemed to be looking at him but almost every set of eyes were on her body. "Remember, keep a low profile.

It was hard to do when you were built like a supermodel.

"Don't they at least have any wine?" Genevieve asked, staring at the beer bottle in front of her.

Casey swigged and smirked. "Do they look like the kind of place that sells wine?"

"So what did happen?" Jed asked, wiping the bar from spillages.

"With what?"

"The kit. You hurt? Or is it the lady?" he looked at her entire length then back up to her face. "Looks plenty fine to me!"

"It's me," Casey interrupted quickly. Genevieve might not mind the attention but Casey was beginning to find it just a little disconcerting. "It's just a graze, nothing too bad."

"If it ain't nothing too bad what do you need the kit for? We don't want no trouble here, Pal."

Casey was silent.

He didn't need any unnecessary attention. Getting the kit and leaving was all he intended to do, but the fact he hadn't answered fully was attracting a lot of attention. Jed and his customers edged the bar and waited for an answer. Suddenly, it appeared the whole of California wanted to know their story!

"I – I just…"

"Here you go, honey," Jodie handed over the box just in time. "What's the problem." She sidled up and hung over the bar, her low cut top doing nothing to hide her assets. They were as fake as her blonde hair. She smiled like she was twenty despite being nearer sixty.

"He won't say," Jed put in.

"Won't say? Well, why don't I just take a look at whatever it is for you, honey?"

"I don't need any help. Thanks all the same."

"Everyone needs a little help every now and then. Why don't I see if I can't kiss it better?" she grinned. "I don't bite. Well, not usually but always on request!"

It was not her bite he was afraid of, it was leaving Genevieve alone with the rabble in there.

"It's just my arm. It's nothing, really."

Jodie looked down at it but it was still covered by the shirt. She stared at his face then up to the customers. She could tell he needed some privacy.

"Why don't I take a look at it out the back."

"I really can't stay. I've got to get moving," he told her. "Can't I just take the box with me?"

"No, honey, you can't."

"I'll pay."

"Listen, if you're worried about your girl, she'll be fine out there. Come with me and let me take a look at it." She eyed his face, then his body and a grin plastered onto her red lips. Insistently she took his injured arm and pulled him firmly out the back into the hallway. He had no choice but to go, she was squeezing the wound. "Honey, don't you go worrying about anything. I'm going to take good care of your arm, let me see it." She pulled off his shirt, unwound his bandage and threw it in the trash. "Well, this ain't no scratch. What did you think you were going to do with this? Pretend it never happened?"

Casey craned his head through to the front. Whatever happened he couldn't have Genevieve out of his sight, not for long.

"Don't worry about her. She's in good hands. The boys will take care of her," Her tone was intended to reassure him but it didn't. "This is from a bullet, ain't it?" Casey remained silent. "Listen, you don't have to be shy with me. I've hung around joints long enough to know a bullet wound when I see one. Came clean out the other side, didn't it? You were a lucky guy. If that was just a few more inches to the left you'd be standing in front of me right now a dead man."

The thought of her words made them both smile a little, easing the moment.

"It's fine, really. I just need it cleaned and covered."

"Yeah I can see that and I'll do it for you too but I'm going to take my time 'cause I don't get many lookers like you coming my way, so you better make yourself comfortable."

"I appreciate that but I really need to get out of here."

"I'm sure you do," she nodded, staring at his face again. Casey swallowed. "You look familiar. I reckon you look kinda like that young guy on the news they've been searching for."

"What guy?" he smiled casually. "What'd he do? Rob a bank?"

"They reckon he's some ex-cop whose gone a little crazy. They said he kidnapped some woman. Didn't take a lot of notice of it if I'm truthful. Just remember seeing a cute young guy on the TV and that was all, but you look a lot like the picture they showed."

"Do I? That's weird, huh, that two guys can look so similar?"

"Ain't it?" If she was joking, she had the best poker face he had ever seen.

"Probably some mistake," he told her. "Cops make 'em all the time."

"Mistaken identity, you reckon?" She wiped around his wound with iodine making him wince.

"Yeah, I guess."

"What about the girl?" she asked.

"What about her?"

"Say, hypothetically," she posed the question, "if a member of the public had information about a girl in that situation, what should they do? Call it in?"

"Depends," he shrugged. "It might be that it was a very different set up than how it looked."

"Yeah, like how?"

"Well I guess you can tell a lot about a relationship just by looking at the people. For instance, if she looked okay, you know happy, not anxious, not signalling for help or trying to escape then I guess it'd be a fair assumption that she was fine."

"I guess. What about afterwards, though, out of public view, behind closed doors."

"Nobody knows what goes on then, but my guess would be if there was a problem then she'd looked jittery, nervous, maybe try to make contact with someone." He nodded, hoping his message was getting through.

"What would you do, kid?"

"I'd study her for a while, then if I was sure I was wrong about the assumption I'd let them be." He looked out again at Genevieve. She seemed to be fine and was even sipping beer from the bottle. "Chances are she was okay. Like I said, a lot of people look alike." He looked Jodie in the eye. "You wouldn't want to make a mistake like that, would you, you know, get innocent people in trouble for nothing?"

"But, say if you were wrong and something happened to her, how would you live with yourself?" The new bandage was wrapped firmly and fastened with a little tape. Casey put on his shirt and swigged his beer.

"I'd have to be certain that she wasn't in any danger before I'd made that assumption. Once I was sure, I wouldn't have any problem sleeping."

"Your girlfriend's pretty."

"Yeah, she is."

"She looks like she ought to be an actress or someone with that body. How long you two been together?"

"Couple of weeks."

He watched two men from the pool table approaching her. She nodded and even giggled before she walked to the table with them. Casey craned his head to see where she was going but from his position it was hard.

"Don't worry about them, they're good boys. They'll take care of your girl."

"I'm sure they will." He looked down at the dressing she wrapped around his arm.

"So, will I see you in here again?"

"It's unlikely. Thanks for this though, it was good of you."

"No problem, sugar. You just take care of yourself and that pretty girl out there."

He craned his head again. He could just see her lifting the bottle to her lips again. For someone who didn't drink beer she was certainly eager to drain the bottle.

"You want my advice, honey. You two make a cute couple, you should marry her, and quick."

Marriage? Did she just say marriage?

"Wh-what?" he almost choked on his drink.

"She's too pretty to be single. Marry her and be done with it," she suggested as if she were his Agony Aunt. "You ain't going to find anyone prettier and if you don't marry her someone else sure as hell will. She's got to be the prettiest thing I ever saw in this place. Looks like a China doll, and, 'course, the fact you're smitten with her stands out a mile. Yep, marry her, that's what I'd do if I were you."

The problem was, until Jodie mentioned it, marriage to anybody – let alone Genevieve Dicing - hadn't even crossed his mind.

Chapter Nine

Casey laughed aloud. Jodie joined him, unsure exactly what she was laughing about. Marriage, in her mind, wasn't a laughing matter. She had been with Jed too long for it to be considered amusing anymore.

"Thanks for the advice." Casey nodded casually. "I'll keep it in mind."

Jodie took a last look at his arm. "I still reckon you ought to get that checked out properly."

"I'll try. Thanks for your help."

He walked through to the bar, Jodie closely in tow, obviously watching how Genevieve acted around him. Casey walked over to the pool table just as she was about to take a shot with one of the men standing behind her. Dressed in faded blue jeans and a black leather jacket, a cigarette between his fingers and a bandana around his neck, he closed in behind her. Her long bare legs were slightly apart and her soft round rear stuck out inviting attention. The pool cue lay straight through her hands as she took aim but not one of the men were looking at that.

"Honey," Casey called. "It's time to go now."

She looked up seeing him wink immediately. She followed his prompt.

"No, not yet, I'm just taking my shot, watch this. I'm good at this."

"Come on, Sweetie, we've got to get back. It's late."

"Lady said she wanted to take her shot first," her opponent told him. Folded arms lay across his leather jacket with a black T-shirt underneath with a faded skull and crossbones. Casey wasn't short but the man towered above him and was twice his width too. It was pretty clear they were the riders of the motorcycles parked up outside.

"Look, I don't want any trouble. I just want to get my girl back home."

Genevieve took her shot and the ball rolled down the hole. The guy behind her roared.

"Take the next one for me too. My lucks changing now this little doll's here."

She smiled happily, took another couple of swigs from the bottle and leaned over the table again. This time the man behind her took in the fullness of her butt with his eyes. Casey watched, half his mind on the job the other half feeling irritation at the thought of her audience eyeing her so intently.

"I said it's time to go, honey."

"And I told you she's taking a shot first," the man said again. "I've got a hundred bucks riding on this game, man," Genevieve's partner told him.

"Just relax, will ya? Go get yourself another beer or something and come back later."

Just before she hit the ball, he placed his large tattooed hand over her bottom and squeezed it. Genevieve hit the cue through surprise more than judgement but the ball still went into a pocket and again the man cheered heartily.

"Okay that's enough!" Casey took her arm and pulled her away. He wasn't going to stand by and watch some thug pawing her. "It's time we left."

"You ain't listening are you, pal?" her partner said. "You deaf or something or maybe you're just stupid?"

Casey shook off his hold. "Look, I told you I didn't want any trouble."

"Well you came to the wrong place then, 'cause that's all you're goin' to get here!"

The opponent marched up to him grabbed his wounded arm beneath the shirt sleeve. The pain was so intense he almost passed out. Suddenly a fist landed in his jaw pushed him backwards to the bar knocking over a stool and leaving him on the floor. Genevieve looked around, stunned and shocked. She put down the cue and tried to run to him but her partner pulled her back.

"Boys, that's enough!" Jodie called out."

"We ain't finished yet. Red, you got another shot to take."

Genevieve shot around to face him. He was huge but it didn't bother her in the least.

"You hit him!" she yelled into his face, "you hit him!"

"Yeah, that's right." he took another puff of his cigarette blowing it into her face. "He'll be fine but I won't be if I lose my hundred bucks! Take my shot."

"To hell with your money, how dare you hit my...my...boyfriend!" she spat, pulling away from him.

Casey attempted to get to his feet by way of grabbing the nearest bar stool. He wriggled his jaw, hoping everything still worked. Jodie looked over the bar at him. Both Casey and Genevieve showed concern for each other just as a couple would.

"You okay, honey?" Jodie called.

"Fine. Never felt better!" he waved a hand in the air and staggered to his feet.

"Hey, where you going? I want her back here to take my shot."

Casey took hold of her firmly so she wasn't tempted to go back but a moment later her pool partner stood in front of them barring the way with the cue in his hand.

"I said I want her back to take another shot," he said deliberately

"And I told you I didn't want any trouble. We're leaving."

Genevieve squeezed his hand in hers, the feeling of contact with an ally was paramount with threatening eyes upon them.

"You want me to smack you again, boy? Is that it?" He pushed the cue out in front of her. "Get over there and take the shot, Red."

"No!"

"Pete," Jodie called, "leave them be, honey. I'll take your shot for you. Maybe I'll be better luck."

"I want *her!*"

Genevieve pulled her hand free from Casey's until it flew hastily with the other one indignantly onto her hips.

"Listen, I'm not some piece of meat to be ordered around, Mister! Maybe I don't want to take your shot, maybe I want to leave. Had you thought of that?"

Casey swallowed hard. *Oh man! Here we go again!* He just knew how this was going to work out and chances were it was going to hurt. If he could talk his way out of it at all then so much the better.

"Look," he interrupted before it got way out of hand, "we're just passing through and now we're leaving so if you can just step out of our way, we'll be on our way and nobody will get hurt."

"You threatening me?"

"No," Casey laughed half-heartedly, "most definitely not!"

"Then get over there, Red and take my shot."

"No, I won't. I don't want to."

"I didn't ask if you wanted to, I told you to get over there and do it - now!"

Her body language told him she wasn't having any of it but he didn't get it.

"Pete?" she reached up and tapped his shoulder. "Is that your name? Then, Peter darling, why don't you just leave us alone? Go back to your little game and play nicely, won't you? There's a good boy."

The smile at the end of her speech added to his increasing aggression, but the fact that she had the audacity to pat his shoulder too sent tension all through Casey's aching body. This could only end one way. He had seen enough bar brawls to know when he was in deep trouble. One time came to mind when Dan had 'borrowed' another man's girlfriend for a kissing competition. That ended badly too!

Man, oh man!

As she brought back her hand, Pete grabbed it by the wrist.

"Why you little minx! You talk to me like that and think you can just get away with it?"

"Come on, man, let her go. We don't want any trouble, we just want to leave, okay?"

Genevieve's eyes were open wide, shocked at how the situation went from placid to aggressive in seconds.

"For people who don't want any trouble, you sure know how to start it." Pete said. "Take the damn shot!" His nostrils grew bigger with each word.

"Fine!" she blurted out, seizing her hand back and grabbing the cue with the other. "If it means that much to you, then fine!"

"Honey..." Casey began, then stopped as she stormed off back to the table.

"You want me to take the shot? Let's do it then, shall we?" she leaned over the table, the bar as quiet as the Jukebox could let it be. Her long legs looked like cues of their own and her small rear stuck out in a right angle inviting more eyes on that than the shot. With her chest lowered onto the table too, it only added to the effect.

A wolf whistle came from somewhere in the bar through the smoke-ridden atmosphere and caught her attention. She aimed the cue at the ball and deliberately hit it against the side of the table. It bounced off and hit the black ball sending it down into the pocket. The game was over, Pete had lost his money.

"Oh man! What the hell did you do that for?" Pete squealed. "You lost me a hundred bucks, you little..."

Pete's partner grinned like a Cheshire cat, smug and ready to collect his winnings.

"Oh, I'm sorry," she sauntered back to them exaggerating the sway in her hips, swinging the cue in her arm. "Does that mean you lost?" she goaded. "And to think of all the hard work we'd put into it. I had no idea!"

Casey shook his head in disbelief. Now was not the time to try it on and keeping a low-profile was clearly not in her repertoire tonight. He gave up – what was the use?

"You owe me a hundred dollars, Red. I ain't letting you out 'til you hand it over." Pete put out his hand and barred the exit once again. She looked at him, arched her eyebrows and moved her hair back from her face.

"Do I look like I have a hundred dollars on me?" She said flatly. "No, of course I don't. So I guess we know what the answer is then don't we? Hmm? Goodnight Peter darling, it was wonderful to meet you."

"What?"

"I said no." She repeated. "I owe you nothing."

"Give it to me now!"

"Come on, honey, let's go," she nodded ignoring Pete and attempting to push past him. Pete leaned down, grabbed hold of her body and swung her over his shoulder. She screamed as Casey tried to pull her back.

"Hey! Put her down!"

Pete swung her over the table top onto her back, pushed between her legs and bore down on her.

"A hundred bucks - now!" he shouted into her face. "Or I'll take it in kind."

Genevieve was angry, scared and confused. Surely he didn't mean – he couldn't! How had it all happened? She could not work it out. What had she done wrong?

Casey tapped Pete's beefy shoulder. "Excuse me?"

He turned around as Casey flung a heavy fist into his jaw, turning him around against the table and between Genevieve's open legs then forwards onto the floor. Now he had bruised knuckles as well as an injured arm. From the size of the man it was clearly a lucky shot.

"Man, you got trouble now, boy! Big trouble!" Pete's partner warned.

Jodie and Jed attempted to simmer down the customers by offering them more beer but got little response. A crowd grew around the table just as Casey picked up Genevieve's cue to defend himself.

"Dash!" Pete called to his friend, "watch out!"

Dash and Casey danced around each other, cues in hand as if they were about to begin a fencing match. Each took a swing at the other, Genevieve kicking at Pete as the crowd grew excited at the entertainment. Dash's cue broke in half as it hit the table then was thrust back into Casey's face wounding his eyebrow. Casey returned the jolt whacking him around the neck stalling him for a moment before throwing a punch into his stomach.

He threw down the cue and turned to Genevieve. Pete was back on his feet holding her down, ordering the money from her.

"I don't have any money!" She yelled, "so get off me, you overweight imbecile!" She brought her knee up just like she did with Glen.

The expression on Pete's face was sufficient that she had done her job. She wriggled from underneath and off the table just as Casey took her arm.

"Quick, come on," he shouted.

The two ran from the bar and back to their car. Casey turned on the engine, skidded around and onto the road and drove toward the motel

"Jesus, what the hell were you thinking? Do you know you started a bar brawl back there, what the hell did you do that for? Didn't you think we were in enough trouble already?"

"Me?" she faced him. "Me? How did *I* start it? I wasn't the one who wanted to go to a bar to get his arm seen to! You should have gone to a hospital in the first place."

"We were supposed to be keeping a low profile. Going to a hospital was not an option. And talking of low profile, do you even know what that means?"

"How dare you!" she spat, "how *dare* you! I have more to lose than you. How dare you say that to me?"

She pulled her legs back up to her chest and stayed silent until he got back to the parking lot outside the motel. The motel's illuminations were off but a light outside their room lit the way.

She stormed out of the car and waited for him to unlock the room door. As she went inside, she instantly grabbed the cover from the bed and held it to her

"I'll sleep on the floor, Mr Pitt! You take the bed. Enjoy it, I hope you die in your sleep!"

Casey closed the door behind him. There was no point in talking to her in this mood, besides he hadn't a clue how he'd done anything wrong. In his eyes it had been she who caused the commotion, he simply protected and defended her from the first moment.

Fumbling with the keys, he watched her settle in the corner on the floor. He caught her eyes twinkling as she pulled the cover over her face, a mass of red curls over-spilling the top of it.

What a day, and now, what a night. His arm still hurt, and now he had a cut above his eyebrow courtesy of Dash - whoever the hell he was - and his knuckles and stomach throbbed too.

He walked into the bathroom and switched on the light to check out his new injury. It was bleeding but it wasn't too bad, another scar no doubt, he was collecting them he told himself, but it would be fine. Everything would be fine. He splashed cold water on it, cleaned it and switched off the light.

Sitting on the edge of the bed, he pulled off his boots and took out the gun leaving it on the night stand. Swinging his legs onto the mattress, he breathed deeply taking in the room's mustiness and rubbed his eyes.

Why she had decided to sit on the floor to sleep was beyond him but he was learning not to ask questions when he figured she did not know the answer either.

"Goodnight." He didn't expect a response and was right not to.

Half hour passed but the room wasn't as silent as he hoped it would be. Every few seconds he could hear Genevieve sniffing. It was clear she was crying but he hadn't a clue why. Maybe it was the events of the evening or that she was just getting the fact Glen wasn't the nice guy she thought he was.

A while later he stepped out of the bed and, with just the moonlight lighting the room, he went over to her. Crouching down in front he pulled away the blanket a little. A wet face peered up at him, locks of hair plastered to her cheeks.

"What's up?" he took a strand, wiping it back from her face. "What's the matter?"

"Nothing!"

"But you're crying."

"No, I'm not," she sniffed. Casey smiled. Even when she was being a tough guy she really wasn't.

"Then why do you have tears running down your face?"

She sniffed them back. "I don't."

"Come on, what's wrong?" he asked. She allowed a few more tears to fall but said nothing. "Come on up onto the bed, it's more comfortable than the floor."

"I can't."

"Why not?"

"Because if I come up there you'll have won," she cried.

"Won what? And when did we start scoring points here?"

"I hate you, Casey Pitt!" she pouted. "I hate you!"

"Why? What'd *I* do?"

If he thought she was going to answer, he was sorely mistaken. She let him help her up, still covered in the blanket, and he lay her on the bed. It was pointless trying to talk with somebody who didn't want to listen when all he really wanted to do was lie next to her and hold her in his arms.

"Get some sleep," he told her, "we could have a long day tomorrow.

He wondered about Manny's condition and whether Baker had dug up anything new since the last phone call. Chances were the men were in bed with their wives and not thinking about their situation at all.

Casey, on the other hand, didn't have that luxury.

Instead he was sharing a bed with a beautiful young woman who hated him and hoped he died in his sleep. He hoped he didn't since he had a job to do first and dying wasn't part of it.

Chapter Ten

Four in the morning brought with it a bout of insomnia. Stirring from a particularly unpleasant dream in which the pool cue had been firmly lodged inside his bullet wound, courtesy of Dash, Casey awoke.

At seven, when the sun was well and truly up, so was Casey. He'd headed out to the diner to get breakfast. On his return he opened the door kicking it shut with his boot. The noise stirred Genevieve. "What time is it?"

She shielded her eyes from the sunshine but turned over in the bed groaning something incoherent about the light. She'd slept in the shirt and shorts from the night before but her body cried out for a bath and her mouth for a toothbrush. Lavender and Chamomile essential oils would be wonderful for a bath and she'd happily accept a massage with Charlotte's fine hands, if that were even an option. Hell, even a quick manicure from her would be good.

She recalled her chipped 'frosted peach' nail, the serious lack of an engagement ring on her finger and the current situation and groaned.

"It's just after seven." His deep voice was bright, if somewhat strained through fatigue. The previous nights action in the bar was unexpected and it had been some time since he had spent the night in a strange bed.

Genevieve pulled the cover back over her face and groaned again.

"Seven? It's too early to get up, I need more sleep."

"Not a morning person, huh? Well, me either," he smirked. "How about that, we have something in common after all. And there was me thinking all we had was your ability to get yourself into trouble and mine to get you out of it."

He stared at her, thinking about his appearance. The unforgiving discomfort of a blackened eyelid didn't put him in the best of moods but his arm felt better. He just hoped Jodie understood his underlying message last night.

"You can't stay in bed forever, Gen, we need to get moving. You've slept enough."

"I need more."

"You can sleep in the car."

"Can't we just call Glen and ask him what's going on?" she mumbled from under the covers. "I have my cell phone in my purse. It would only take a moment."

"Touch that thing and I'll kill you myself," he shot her a cold look, one she didn't need to see to know was there. "Besides, are you honestly saying you *want* to speak to the man? Are you nuts?"

He ripped the cover down quickly sending her hair in different directions with the breeze and left a coffee cup and bagel on the table next to her.

"Yeah, that's it I'm nuts. I'm here with you when I should have been back home last night celebrating my engagement." The tone in her voice told Casey she was just as sick of the situation as he was. "Like this is all my planning! As if I wanted to go on some adventure with Action Man and ruin my life."

"No, instead you decided to take on a guy fifty times bigger than us both!" He stretched out his muscles recoiling at the collection of wounds he'd received. "I guess you can't have it your way all the time."

She reluctantly pulled herself up puffing up the pillow behind her. Taking a sip of the coffee and a bite of the bagel, she wiped her face with the back of her hand.

"I hope this is low fat," she said. Casey ignored her. "All I want is a decent nights sleep and a bath, and would it be too much to ask for a toothbrush?" she whined.

"You can use mine."

"I'm not touching something that's been in your mouth," she shrank back from the thought. "I'd rather go without."

"Fine, then do that."

She huffed then bit at her bagel. "When are we leaving?"

He pulled the net curtain to one side and looked out of the window. It was a little overcast but the day was bright. Wearing Jeans, a white vest and an over shirt, he looked every inch the Action Man she'd suggested. The light shone on him highlighting his fair hair making it appear blonde. His stubble had grown a little more too adding to his already rough 'n' ready look. She watched him as she ate. If it wasn't for his obvious stubbornness over almost everything that came out of her mouth, he'd be quite something, she thought.

"We'll take a drive as far out as we can. I'll call in, see if anything's changed. If luck's on our side they'll have caught up with your boyfriend and his henchmen and we can all go home. This sorry mess will be a thing of the past."

"And if not?"

"Then we get to spend another exciting night together." His eyebrows rose. "What fun, huh? I can hardly wait."

"Fantastic!"

"Honey, it's not of my making."

"No, of course not, Mr Pitt. Nothing ever is."

"What's with the sudden attitude?" he asked, "I thought we'd acquired a rapport."

"Rapport?" she laughed in her throat. "I think it's best this way. When I get back I plan to pick up my life exactly where I left off."

"Meaning?"

"I am going to become Mrs Glen De Salle if it kills me."

Casey suppressed a cynical laugh. "You know it might well come to that."

"I *will* marry him, you know." She turned her head and huffed. "I've spent a lot of time making it happen. Despite what he's done, and I'm sure he had his reasons," she quickly added in the man's defence, "but it's still going to happen. You can bet your bottom dollar on that."

"Really? Yesterday I recall you felt a little differently. Besides, I think you're marriage might be a little one sided with your husband in jail."

"He won't be going to jail – he's done nothing wrong."

Casey tipped his head. "He took a shot at you, remember? Or has all that pampering made you conveniently forget?" She narrowed her eyes and sulkily pursed her lips at him. He continued. "I guess we'll find out when we get back, won't we? Now get moving, we've got a lot of ground to cover."

"Where exactly are we going? Have you even planned a route yet or are we supposed to just drive around aimlessly for another day?"

"That very much depends on what Baker says. I'd like to think that as soon as I call him he'll tell me some very good news and we can finally say bye-bye to each other."

He left the room pulling the door hard behind him.

He hadn't meant to sound quite so abrupt but the woman was pressing all the wrong buttons today and that made him mad as hell. She was as ungrateful as he was accommodating but it didn't seem to make any difference. He headed over to the phone booth, the air cool against his face, and dialled.

"Baker's line."

A different voice answered. A little concerned that somebody else was in Baker's place, Casey cagily answered.

"Can I speak to him?"

"Who is this?" The voice was deep but not as deep as Baker's and sounded slightly apprehensive.

Casey frowned. "Who the hell is *this*?"

"Smith."

"Well, Smith, I want to talk to Baker!"

"Is this Pitt?" He asked. Casey didn't respond. "Pitt, there's been a change here. Baker's down. They got a call late last night. De Salle's men broke into an apartment down town, some tip off or something. They completely tore it apart. Someone reported a disturbance and the cops came. Baker went to investigate but they caught up with him. I don't know too much else just that his car rolled over and he's in the hospital. I've taken over."

"Is he going to be okay?"

"I don't know."

"How about Weston?"

"I don't know that either, I just got here."

Casey tried to think. Why would they break into an apartment, what was the point? Was it even connected to them? If it was Genevieve's place then what would be the point of that either, Glen probably knew pretty much all about her anyway unless he got impatient and went looking for her money.

"Where was the apartment?"

"That's the strange thing," his voice was strained as if he genuinely knew very little about the situation, either that or he was covering something up.

"What?"

"I got the impression it was pretty relevant. Hold on I'll get the address." Casey heard a bunch of papers being moved from one side of the desk to another. "1135 Pine Avenue, Newport Beach. Does it mean anything to you?"

"Jesus!" he gasped.

"What?"

"That's my place!" his heart pounded. Confusion and anger took over.

"Man, I'm sorry. I've literally just come into all this. Give me some time to get some information together. All I know though is you have to keep Dicing away from the city."

"I am."

He was low on funds and was going to mention as much but somehow that didn't seem important now he'd learned his apartment had been trashed. Everything he ever owned of any importance was in there. Personal effects, family photos, pictures of Dan and Casey on the beat together, photos of his parents. Now it was all gone

"Check in later. Hopefully, I'll have some information for you."

Smith hung up leaving Casey with the receiver firmly in his hands. After he put it down, he closed his eyes and inhaled deeply. As if on auto-pilot he punched the side of the booth over and over.

This situation was getting crazier by the minute.

What had started out as a simple body- guarding job was turning into something much worse. This was a nightmare. It was all going horribly wrong and he felt utterly powerless to stop this roller-coaster he'd found himself within.

Maybe there was a way out of it, maybe there wasn't. If Dan were alive, the two would sit over a beer and talk it through but since those days were no longer, it was all he could do just to stay alive another day.

Why trash his place, what were they looking for? And who was Smith? Could he be trusted? Casey had no choice but to trust him, nobody else was available and everyone so far mixed up in it had been 'taken out'.

He recalled his last moments at the apartment. They changed clothes, took supplies and left their baggage on the bed. Maybe De Salle's men had jumped to conclusions and word got back they'd been intimate. Glen wasn't likely to take that news well.

Genevieve would be waiting for some news; he'd have to be very frugal with what he knew so as not to scare her. The past had told him how some women coped with danger. Some thrived on it, others fainted at the thought. He didn't know if she was the type who would thrive but he knew someone who might. He thrust his hand into his pocket and took out his wallet for a phone number.

Inside, he noticed, there was barely a hundred dollars left. They could hardly get to an ATM without being traced. Baker hadn't given him much more to start with. He had only fifty dollars with him when he left his place. He hadn't been expecting to take a few days out in the mountains when he left for his first day at work.

He picked up the phone again, punched in the number from his wallet and tapped his index finger along the top of the phone as it rang.

"Hey there, I can't get to the phone right now but please leave me a message and I promise I will call you straight back. Thanks for calling."

Hearing that voice again after so long made the hairs at the back of his neck stand on end. He closed his eyes. Things were not going well so far today. He hung up and tapped in the number again. The same message spoke loud and clearly in the same voice as though it were toying with him. This time he left a message.

"Cathrynn, it's me. I need you. I - I need some help real bad."

He put down the phone, blinked his eyes tight and sighed. He swallowed and looked down at his hand. It was trembling. He didn't think that call would take as much out of him as it did.

He pushed open the motel room door and drank the last of the coffee on the side. Genevieve was still in bed. She'd gone back to sleep

"Get up, we've got to get moving!" He pounded his fists on the bed over and over. The violent vibration didn't only stir her, it woke her completely.

"Stop it!" She whined, "go away!"

"We have to move out. Now!"

She pulled the cover from her face and winced at the light.

"Can't we do this later? All you keep doing is waking me up."

"And all you keep doing is pissing me off! Sleep in the car. We have to get moving."

"God, I hate this," she groaned into the pillow, "I never get up this early unless it's for Antonio."

"Well, Antonio isn't here right now so you're just going to have to get used to the fact that you and I are here to stay until your boyfriend is safely behind bars!"

Her face peeked up from under the cover. "You don't think they'd really do that to him do you?"

Casey didn't answer. He checked the holdall, inside he still had a few clips left, but no extra cash. Things were getting desperate.

"Did you call that Baker guy?"

"Yeah."

"And?"

"And nothing. Come on, lets get moving."

She sat up, holding the cover to her body despite already being clothed.

"There's no new information?"

"Not yet."

"Then why do we have to get moving quickly? Is there something you're not telling me?"

He snatched the covers from her hand and pulled her from the mattress until she was on her feet.

"We don't have time for a discussion. We can talk in the car. Let's move."

"Casey, you're scaring me. What's going on?"

He took hold of his hold-all, placed his weapon in his waistband and opened the door.

"We don't have time for this. You've got two minutes to make yourself decent."

"Or what?" she questione.

He didn't even want to think of a threat that didn't involve her being slapped silly.

"I'll be waiting in the car."

Once they were on the road, things were quiet again. With Casey thinking about their next move and Genevieve wondering how she would cope another day with a chipped nail and no facial, the two sat in silence

Her legs stretched out in front of her, peach shoes kicked off under the dash board. She rolled the dial at the side of her seat and lay it back a little more, wiped her hands through her hair, now a frizzy mop in dire need of a good wash, and settled down. Casey watched from the corner of his eye and at the same time tried to concentrate on the road ahead when all he wanted to do was get back to his old life with his old partner and do the job he was made for.

Things made sense back then, not too much sense, but more sense than now and they were fun too. They'd rarely be given a case they didn't solve, the two spending their leisure time mulling over clues. For a long time Dan's family had been like his own.

"How long do you plan to drive?" she asked, her eyes closed.

"I don't know," he shook his head, "maybe two, three hours. You should probably get some sleep."

"I was trying to back there," she bit hard into his words, "But someone keeps waking me up! What's the matter anyway, you seem very moody today."

Casey glared. "Nothing."

"Well, it might be nice if you didn't get so moody," she scolded. "It's bad enough I haven't showered, we might be on the run but I don't see any point in looking bad as well, do you?"

"There was a shower in that motel room, you could have used it."

She opened one eye. "Don't even go there! I wouldn't have expected a dog to use that thing."

At the corner of his eye he noticed her lifting up her hand. Was she checking her fingernails again? It was pretty hard to imagine her looking bad at all, the woman simply didn't have that quality in her. Long smooth legs, which seemed to go on forever, crossed one over the other making her even more appealing. He looked away, planting his view entirely on the road

"God only knows what Antonio or Charlotte must've thought when I wasn't there. I altered appointments and I didn't even show up. I can't imagine they'll ever forgive me for that."

"I'm sure they'll get over it."

"Oh, hardly. I won't be lucky enough to have them just pop out to me again. Once you upset people, they never forget it you know. You don't know what its like in my social circle," she told him. "Sometimes it can be just awful. Of course I wouldn't expect you to understand."

Here it was again, her patronising tone was back. Casey didn't need it right now. Thinking about the practicalities of their situation, their lack of money, the lack of information he was supposed to go on, the news about Baker as well as Manny and all this on top of a job of which he hardly even knew the ropes and now he was supposed to trust a man he never even knew existed. It was the craziest time he'd ever known. If Dan were here now, he'd say it was his kind of fun!

"Do you think that Antonio or Charlotte would have informed the police of my absence?"

"They were probably only too thrilled you didn't show up!" he said softly, unaware if she even heard.

"I was just thinking about Cassandra," she went on. "She was supposed to be joining us for that drink too." She suddenly sat up and reached into her bag. "I'll bet she's been trying to get in contact, why on earth didn't I think to check before?" She switched on the cell phone and waited.

"What the hell are you doing?" Pure horror covered his face. "Switch that thing off!" His free arm grabbed at it but she held it further away.

"What are you - stop it, leave me alone! I don't have to do anything you say, Mr Pitt. I jump though hoops for nobody. Do you understand, nobody."

"How about if your life depended on it, huh, would that make a difference?" he yelled. "I'm trying to keep you alive here and we know next to nothing about why we are even here."

Still edging for it, he pulled the steering wheel to the side of the road, creating a cloud of dust near the edge. The turbulence threw them both about inside causing the phone to spin out of her hands and onto the rubber mat beneath her shoes.

"What are you doing, you'll get us killed!" she hollered. "Are you crazy?"

"Me? You're the crazy one. Switch that thing off or I'll show you some driving you'll never forget!"

"You don't frighten me, Casey Pitt," her tone languished in self-importance, "I've been around the block enough times to know which people are full of hot air and which are the ones *worth* knowing."

"Excuse me?"

"You heard! You think just because you are some big almighty bodyguard person sent to protect me – which, I might add, I didn't even ask for - that you own me or something, but you're wrong. Nobody owns me. Nobody makes me do anything I don't want to do. *Nobody!*"

"How about Glen De Salle? Does he own you?" he snapped. Without a moments hesitation she grabbed his hand and bit the back of it. Casey yelled. "Why you little…!"

Pulling the car to the side of the road violently, he took the keys out of the ignition and got out. She watched him, totally oblivious as to his actions. He stood still, one arm on his hip the other raking his hair. A second later, leaning over the hood, both hands stretched out in front of him, he lowered his head and then, without warning, he slammed his fists onto the hood with anger and yelled. It shook the car making her jump inside.

His head was still down when she opened the door and stepped out.

"What on earth was all that about?"

"You bit me! You little minx! You bit me! Look!" Her teeth marks were very clearly indented in his skin.

"And that was worth nearly turning the car over for?"

He exhaled hard, looking up at her with a flushed face. "Just leave me alone to think for a minute. Just get back inside the car."

Dismissing his orders, she walked back up to him and leaned on the hood. Her long legs again sent to distract him. She looked into his face and saw anguish.

Something was definitely wrong.

"You need to think 'cause I bit you? Damn it, Casey, you need to get out more."

"I said leave me alone."

"And I asked what all that was about?"

"I told you to get back in the car."

Something about the look in his eye told her this outburst had nothing to do with her assault on him.

"Oh, could it be the big protector has *feelings* after all?" she pushed, over dramatizing the words in physical inverted commas either side of her head.

"Stop it, Genevieve. I'm in no mood for your condescending tone right now, okay?"

"I just-"

He slammed his fists on the hood once again, this time she saw a scowl on his face.

"Lady, I'm not kidding around here. Get back in the God damn car!" he shouted.

Genevieve shrunk back. Casey Pitt wasn't the robot she thought he was. This man actually had emotions - big emotions - and right now they were beginning to frighten her

"No, I won't!" she shouted back, trying to hide her fear. "What the hell's gotten into you?"

"Nothing!" He said, convincing nobody. "Everything's fine! Everything's just fine and dandy!"

Losing it in front of a client was never a good choice. It showed weakness. That wasn't a good thing with anybody, especially in a situation with a woman who was convinced she was at the top of the food chain and he wasn't even fit enough to live life at the bottom.

Control. He had to get back his control.

"You don't seem fine. What's happening? Is it Glen? He's on our tail isn't he?" she asked. "It wouldn't surprise me, you know, he's a very determined man. He always has been. I think it's quite an appealing quality, actually. Apparently he gets it from his-"

"Shut the hell up, lady!" he yelled. "Just shut up!" His fingers white at the tips. If he'd had claws he would have scratched the paint work.

"What's the matter with you?" she barked, her voice carrying some distance. "Has something happened?"

"No, forget it." He took a breath to calm himself. "Just – just forget it, okay?"

"How can I forget it? You're freaking me out here! What am I supposed to do, just pretend everything's okay while you go ballistic on me? I have a would-be fiancé trying to kill me and my only source of protection just took a nose-dive! What the hell's going on with you, Casey? Just talk to me."

"It's nothing, okay?" he grabbed her shoulders in his hands and shook her. "You got it?" Looking into his icy cold eyes she could see something was very badly wrong.

"Please, just tell me. Maybe I can help." For a split second she thought he might, maybe he could trust her long enough to explain what was going on inside his head. Then it was gone. "Casey, what's wrong?"

"Just," he released her shoulders and walked away from her, "get in the car. I need to think."

"Why? Where are you going?"

"Look around you, honey? Do you see any place to go?" he howled. "Just leave me alone for a minute."

"It is Glen isn't it, he's done something hasn't he? I just knew it, he's coming isn't he? He's going to-."

"Shut the hell up!" he spun around back to her again. "I can't think with your incessant talking!"

She surrendered a nod and moved off the hood. Eyes wide to his outburst she went back to the car like a reprimanded child.

It was true of course. Michael, her brother, used to say as much when they were teenagers. She'd talk so much for so long about absolutely nothing, that he'd scream and shout and work himself into a frenzy before slamming his bedroom door behind him. She always knew she got to him and every time she was secretly amused by it though she'd never let on. Michael would undoubtedly get his own back somehow, the rivalry between the two had been overwhelming at times.

Casey turned around, his back towards her and leaning on the hood. With his face in his hands, he inhaled back his anger. This was working out badly. He hadn't let his temper out or frustration show in a long time. Not since...

"You are coming back, aren't you?" she called out the window. Casey didn't respond. He leaned up straight, rested his open palms on his jean-clad thighs and inhaled deeply. "I only ask because according to my phone, I have a half dozen missed calls."

"I told you already," he called back, his voice much more in control and level. "Turn that thing off and put it away! I don't want to see it out. They can trace us if it's on."

"Okay. It's off. See, look, I'm putting it in my bag. It's gone."

Perhaps it was best to go along with his suggestions. Besides, apart from the occasional odd show of anger, he probably knew what he was doing, she told herself.

He was a cop before all this and he must've been good at it. He better had, she hoped, both their lives depended on it and she didn't have a single clue as to what to do next.

He leaned off the hood and walked around to the door. Sitting inside, he switched on the engine and they moved off. Silence prevailed once again.

She didn't dare speak and he simply chose not to, but the silence was deafening. She pulled her seat back up, leaned forwards and switched on the radio. Casey promptly switched it back off. She glanced at him and switched it back on once again and took a long blink when he turned it back off.

"Why not?"

"I told you. I need to think."

"And you can't do that with music?"

"I prefer quiet."

"Yeah you said that before but being quiet is so dull." She pulled her legs up tucking one underneath her as though she were about to take a Yoga session. "You want to talk?"

"No, I don't."

An awkward silence filled the space between them.

"You want to listen to me talk?"

"*No*, I definitely don't!"

"Why don't you tell me what's going on?"

He turned to face her and asked sarcastically, "Gee, wouldn't this be classed as talking?"

"Fine, fine!" she sulked.

Silence reigned for a further two minutes. Two agonising minutes. She looked outside the car. She looked inside the car. She stared at her nails; mildly angered by the missed opportunity Charlotte hadn't had. Boy! That girl would be cursing her now. Her name would be mud all over California. Genevieve raked her hands through her hair until the silence finally broke her.

"Look, this is driving me nuts! I hate silence. I hate not talking. I hate-."

"Do you hate being killed? Baker's down," he blurted out.

"What? Down? What does that mean, down?"

"He's in the hospital."

"Why, what happened?"

"I don't know exactly but there's a new guy on the case, says his name's Smith."

"Smith?"

"Yeah. You know him?"

"No, of course not. Why would I?" She asked, "Do you?"

"I started this job a day ago, how would I know him?"

"Then how do you know we can trust him?" she asked.

"I don't."

Genevieve swallowed. "And this is what the tantrum was about, a new guy on the job?"

"My apartment," he sighed. "It was trashed last night."

"Trashed?" she repeated. "You mean someone broke into it?"

"Yeah."

"Well, you're insured aren't you?"

"Gen, that's not the point! Jeez, don't you ever think about anything else but money?"

"No, I didn't mean - well, did they find out who did it?"

"Kind of."

"Who was it?"

"Acquaintances of the infamous Glen De Salle."

"Glen? What would Glen want with your apartment? He doesn't even know you."

"I guess he does now." The news silenced her for a moment, an amazing achievement in itself.

"I don't understand. How did he find it? He didn't follow us there, did he?"

"I'm pretty sure we were alone but I guess he has his ways. Guys like him always do."

"No, not Glen. I don't accept that. I can't believe he'd do something like that. Despite the gun thing – which, incidentally, I didn't even know anything about - he is actually a good kind man."

"Right, yes, a good kind man without a conscience. Listen, I'm getting a little tired of hearing how fantastic this guy is, okay?"

She dismissed the comment, holding her head haughtily.

"Well, tell me why would he want to trash your apartment?"

"How the hell do I know what goes through that guy's mind?"

"Well, was there anything there of any value? I mean it wasn't a huge place or anything was it." She turned to face him, his blue eyes were steely cold and insulted. "I'm sorry," she quickly added hoping to diffuse it. "What I meant was-."

"You saw the place, you know what I have." He shrugged, "or what I *don't* have anymore. Everything I ever owned is gone, pictures, personal effects, everything. It's all gone."

Genevieve dropped her head. "I'm sorry."

"Me too, I don't have a lot but what I do have means a lot. *Meant* a lot." He corrected.

"Do you think he saw our clothes on your bed? Maybe he thought the worst and got mad," she wondered. "Well, look on the bright side. You don't know how bad the place was so there could still be some things left. You may be able to salvage something."

"Right."

He'd pretty much resigned himself to the fact it was all gone. Hearing a suggestion that there might be something left was intended to be uplifting but it didn't feel like it.

"I suppose if he did have the place turned over, then it means he knows a lot more about you."

"Way more!"

"You sound weird. Was there something in particular you didn't want him to know?" she asked uncomfortably.

"Nothing I want to talk about right now if that's what you're getting at."

"Okay. I understand. I'll keep quiet. I promise. I won't say another word. If I do you can -." He stared at her with exasperation. "Okay, okay," she zipped her fingers across her lips, "not another word."

He was hiding something, though, that much was clear.

Chapter Eleven

The evening had come in quickly. They'd spent the day on the road, stopping only for rest breaks and a little food, something to which, it seemed, she had a total aversion. Casey would make her eat tonight, even if he had to hold her down and force it down her throat. There was no way on God's green earth she was going to give him some stupid story about fat grams. He wasn't going to have her become even more of a liability by collapsing through starvation.

After spending the previous night holding himself from the floor through lack of space from his bed-partner, Casey decided what little money they had left would be spent on two single rooms at the next motel. That way at least he could expect a decent nights sleep. With a room just next door there was little she could do in the way of attracting unwanted attention.

They pulled into the parking space outside the motel office. 'Under New Management' boasted the sign outside. The girl behind the counter looked presentable; something they hoped rubbed off on the rooms this time.

"Hi," she sang in a chirpy upbeat voice, "Mr and Mrs- ?"

"Er," Casey looked behind him. Genevieve seemed as unimpressed at being referred to as Mrs Pitt as she was when she discovered her current beau was making an attempt on her life. "Can we have two separate rooms please," Casey smiled, "but next to each other, if possible."

"Of course. Please sign in there," she handed the book over and offered him her pen which she took from her long shiny brunette hair piled up behind her head. "I'll need a credit card."

"Can I pay cash?" The same questions were bound to arise day in day out. The sooner this thing was over the better and they could both get back to their regular lives.

"Sure, are you passing through?" she stared up at Genevieve for a moment and paused. "Hey, you're not the girl they're looking for are...?"

"Oh, Jeez," Casey laughed aloud, pulling her close. "Honey, it's happened again. We've had this all the way through our vacation. Can you imagine how embarrassing it gets?"

"I'm sorry," she smiled, taking in their private joke. "You both just look so much like them."

"I know. It's unbelievable really. But rest assured," he laughed again, placing his arm around Genevieve's waist, "we're not them. We're on our honeymoon actually."

"And you want two separate rooms? Some honeymoon."

Casey's heart sank, he hadn't realised.

Thankfully Genevieve jumped in. "He snores so bad after...well, afterwards, I just want a restful night for once. You know?"

"That's how I got this," he gestured to his blackened eyelid. "I guess I was too loud, she hit me in the night!"

"Oh, I didn't!" Genevieve was horrified at the suggestion. Casey quickly grabbed her again laughing.

"Just kidding with you," he winked. "Just kidding."

The receptionist laughed, seemingly convinced at their rough play. Casey handed back the book in which he signed 'Brown' twice.

"Where can we get something to eat?"

She gestured behind her and grinned proudly. "We have small restaurant out the back next to the pool."

"A pool?" Casey perked up. "You have a pool?"

"Yes we do, Sir, and guests may use it until eleven. Have a great stay."

He picked up the room keys as Genevieve followed him out.

"You hear that, Honey? They have a pool."

"I heard and you can stop with the 'honey' now too."

"You don't sound thrilled."

"I'm not particularly."

"Why not? It's a pool!" He open the door to his room and tossed the other key over to her. Before she answered he looked up at her expression. "Oh, I get it," he smirked, "let me guess, you have nothing to wear?"

"Exactly. Besides I certainly wouldn't go swimming at a place like this." Before she turned her key to go inside, she turned to him again. "Honeymoon, huh? Don't flatter yourself! I'm going to get some sleep." She closed the door and left him standing there.

"Fine, fine," he turned his own key, "whatever you want, your Royal Highness, more like a right Royal pain in the -."

He walked inside and saw the place was more comfortable than he could have hoped. Blue and cream wallpaper clad the walls, the bed was clean and tidy and the room even smelled nice. He pushed the door behind him and looked inside the bathroom. Even Genevieve couldn't find something wrong with this, could she? The white bathroom furniture sparkled, a small basket of soap and shampoo sat at the side of the basin, and the towels were big, soft and fluffy. It was much more pleasant than the last place. Heck it was almost more pleasant than *his* place!

The *pool.* Oh yes, don't forget the pool. He pulled open the curtains and looked outside. A cool blue pool, shimmering in the setting sun, beckoned.

"Oh, yes!" he smiled. "Oh, yes indeed!"

So what if Genevieve didn't want to swim. Who cared? She didn't have to. It'd be quite nice to spend some time without her constant chatter, her grumblings and whining for a change. If Glen De Salle hadn't been shooting at him, Casey would've offered the guy the medal he had received for bravery *just* for putting up with her this long!

He pulled off his shirt, stood bare-chested and moved his shoulders around and up and down. His arm didn't hurt half as much now the idea of swimming entertained him. Getting it wet wouldn't be a good idea but he didn't care one iota. Tonight was about relaxation.

He unzipped his fly, wriggled out of his jeans unable to hold his eagerness back any longer and opened the back door. Course, Genevieve was right, he had nothing to wear for the pool either but he wasn't going to pass up an opportunity to relax in there. There was nobody else around anyway, he'd get away with his boxers. Who'd know?

He placed his key by a towel and stood at the side ready to dive in. The smell of chlorine filled his nostrils enticing him further. As he went in, the loud splash brought Genevieve to her window. She stood discreetly behind the net curtain and watched him rise to the surface. Hard muscular arms wiped away the water from his face. He blinked a couple of times, the setting sun shining in his blue eyes, fair hair now flattened against his skull. The soft tanned skin on his neck and shoulders caught her eye as he shook his head, his heavy breathing emphasised by the pool's acoustics.

A moment later he swam beneath the surface, powerful arms taking his body deep and out of sight.

It didn't bother him that the bandage on his arm was ruined now, or that his wound would take longer to heal, or that the cut to his eyebrow was soaking wet. All that mattered to him was that he felt free, unchallenged and calm, peaceful even.

There was time to think, time to reflect, time to breathe.

Genevieve came away from the window and lay on the bed. If nothing else, she would be able to get some sleep tonight without constantly being told what to do every five minutes.

She'd been quite impressed he asked for two separate rooms. She could walk around the room naked if she so wished without having to worry he'd say or do something. But it was quiet without him, even if he wasn't a big talker. There was nobody for her to boss around, nobody for her to take constant jibes from. She half wished he'd chosen a double room now just for his company.

Apart from their obvious differences, he wasn't a bad person and he did have her best interests at heart. So what if he was being paid for it, you didn't get anything in life without paying for it. But he was a totally different kind of person to Glen. Casey was the kind of guy she would have flirted with at the mall when she and Cassandra used to socialise down there.

He didn't have a lot of class, but sometimes you didn't need that if you had a personality instead. He did have the look, the smile, and the warmth though.

Genevieve smiled. Cassandra would definitely have found him alluring. He did have a great body and, like Glen, he was also attractive. She stopped herself with that train of thought, but it wasn't the first time she'd thought of Casey in that way. Not by a long shot.

Her head ached from being on the road for so long. She felt as though she were still moving. All she wanted was to sleep. No, scratch that, all she wanted was for Glen to stop this stupidity and let her get back to her normal life and sleep in her own bed, feel her own covers against her skin, listen to her music system and get back to normal. And, of course, show off the enormous rock on her finger.

She would have been out with Cassandra today choosing her wedding colours, flaunting the ring to anybody who dared ask. Of course, she'd charmingly accommodate them especially if the paparazzi were around. She'd elegantly hold her handout, display her long slender fingers and frosted peach coloured extended nails. There was little point in having these attributes if you didn't show them off, she'd always thought. Besides, with her figure and looks, she was practically a walking work of art and quite proud of it too.

She closed her eyes, hoping the aching would soon cease. She could still hear Casey swimming about outside, up and down, back and forth. Half of her wanted to get in there with him, show him how exactly un-uptight she could be. The other half of her knew if she let him know that much, whatever else happened after that, Glen would never want her back and she couldn't let that happen.

Glen was everything. He had the class, the background, the money, the reputation. Casey was rough and hard and...

"God, why did you have to be so damned attractive?" she said aloud to the swimmer outside. "Too cute," she nodded. "Too God damned cute!"

And having him take on the role of her protector too made him even more exciting.

She had convinced herself that the whole Glen thing was just a sick mistake. Despite the fact he'd thrown her around and been generally obnoxious, he was still Glen. Glen De Salle, wealthiest bachelor in her social circle. It would still be worth putting up with a few indiscretions if it meant being married to him.

She suddenly opened her eyes. A thought crossed her mind. Casey wasn't here to shout at her now, she could use her phone. At least she could talk to Cassandra, find out what she knew about the situation. She leapt from the bed, pulled open her bag and grabbed the phone. Switching it on she waited for a few second for any messages to come through. The six missed calls she saw earlier was now up to eight. She tapped down to find out the sender and Cassandra's name came up every time.

'Return call,' the phone suggested. She tapped the 'okay' button and the phone rang.

"Pick up, Cass," she murmured, "pick up." The phone had been switched to voice mail but she didn't want to leave a message she wanted to hear Cassandra's voice, hear the relief in it at her safety.

She scrolled down the screen and saw Glen's number. What was stopping her from dialling it? She could speak directly to him, find out what this idiocy was all about, ask him what had gone on at Casey's apartment, and, more importantly, did Glen still love her?

Of course he did! She folded up the phone and switched it off. Why would she even have to ask such a lame question? Why wouldn't Glen still love her? He was her everything and she was to him. Wasn't she? Calling him felt wrong, a betrayal to the man swimming outside who had endured personal injury protecting her.

She threw the phone back into the bag and walked to the window again. Casey was sitting at the side of the pool, arms spread wide either side of him supporting his weight as though he owned the place. He looked happy, peaceful, and clear-faced.

She sat at the desk nearby, resting her chin on her hand as she stared out to the pool. She really would like to have joined him and if she was honest with herself, to laugh with him too, play even. It might have been fun if she could just bring herself to get into a pool again.

I'm trapped! I'm going to drown!

Genevieve awoke abruptly as her head fell from her arm. She'd been dreaming. Thank God. It wasn't real this time. How long had she been out? Her heartbeat was speeding and she pulled her hair back from her face and looked outside. Casey was gone.

She had no idea she'd been tired enough to sleep. She went into the bathroom and splashed cold water onto her face. She was still a little bruised but it wasn't too bad, besides her hair could cover up a multitude of sins through its sheer volume.

She picked up the remote control throwing herself back on the bed where she should have stayed in the first place, then maybe she wouldn't have had that recurring nightmare.

Her therapist said it would stop just as soon as she accepted what had happened and moved on. But it was too big to simply forget and accepting it seemed too much of a challenge. If she simply put it to the back of her mind and ignored it then that was a lot easier to cope with.

She felt cold. The thought of the water in the drain that day had haunted her again thanks to that dream. She shivered and pulled the cover from the bed around her body. It smelled better than the previous room's soft furnishings. This one reminded her of her childhood for some reason. She breathed it in flicking through the channels before stopping at a news item.

The volume was off but she clearly saw a picture of herself staring back. Shocked, she looked at the screen then at the handset trying to work out which button increased the volume. She found it in time to hear:

"…This is the second abduction for the Hollywood socialite in just over two years. A source has said that the kidnapper is, ironically, the detective who rescued her the first time in Washington DC. The source also indicated that the now retired detective, who's been named as Casey Pitt, has 'a history of depression and unpredictable behaviour which was, in fact, the reason behind his retirement from the force'. The source also suggested that Pitt has kidnapped Miss Dicing in a desperate act of revenge for the death of his partner, Detective Daniel Chandler. Miss Dicing could be in very serious danger and the police ask the public to not approach this man but if seen, to contact them immediately."

Casey's picture covered the screen alongside Dan's then flashed away. No wonder the girl on reception thought they looked similar – it was so obviously them! The news report continued.

"Information received from the Virginia Police Department indicated that while Pitt did, in fact, retire on medical grounds, his state of mental health was considered to be good. It was also said that he was a decorated officer."

Another reporter took over, this time she had Cassandra and Michael next to her.

"Miss Cassandra French, Genevieve Dicing's best friend since childhood, and her brother Michael Dicing are both with us now. What can you tell us about the abduction, Miss French?"

Cassandra looked frail, her normal giggly demeanour was gone and a withdrawn face replaced it. Her long dark shiny hair was untidy, dull and looked just as uncared for as Genevieve's.

"I was so shocked to hear about it. She's such a darling, why anybody would ever want to hurt her, I'll never know." The reporter took the microphone back and asked her if Genevieve was watching was there was anything she'd like to say to her. "Oh yes, Gen, if you're watching. I'm praying you're safe. Please come home soon."

"And Mr Michael Dicing, the late Vice President's son, how has it been for the family since your sister's abduction?"

"A nightmare. Things like this aren't supposed to happen at all but this is the second time she's been kidnapped. I only hope Pitt is captured and dealt with accordingly."

Genevieve watched in horror at the sight of them all

"How has your mother been through all of this?" The microphone was pushed up to his lips and the camera panned into his face.

"My mother is beside herself. In fact, we've decided to put out a reward for anybody who can lead us to Pitt and provide a safe return for my sister."

"And just how much is that reward, Sir?"

"Ten thousand dollars," Michael sniffed as if holding back tear.

"Thank you." The reporter went on. "There you have it. Ten thousand dollars to the person or people who help bring Miss Dicing home safely."

The channel picked up another news item quickly, discarding Genevieve's feelings. She exhaled dropping the remote. She was in shock. Casey *had* kidnapped her after all? Isn't that what they were saying? *Abducted?*

They'd mentioned a history of depression too. Was that why he was worried about Glen finding out? Admittedly she had suffered with it herself shortly after the first kidnapping but Casey? He seemed so strong, so in control.

It must be true, that must have been why he lost it earlier. Cassandra looked awful on the TV and seeing Michael had sent a chill right through her. Unanswered questions flew through her head, spinning around like an out of control carousel. Exactly how manic was his depression supposed to be? If he was kidnapping her, would he kill her? Exactly how dangerous was he? Did she need to protect herself from him, was that it? Maybe she should think about 'borrowing' his gun to defend herself. Maybe she should just get on the phone and call Glen to come get her. Maybe...

She trembled inside the covers

This sorry mess started off as a misunderstanding, or so she thought, and now with the news report firmly in her mind, she was the victim of yet another kidnapping. Why now? Why her? When was it all going to end?

A moment later someone knocked on the door sending her into the air with a jump.

"Hey, you decent?" Casey called. "You want to get some dinner?"

Her eyes darted around the room. What could she use to defend herself now she knew he really was kidnapping her? She could maybe throw her bag at him but that would likely do more damage to the bag than him, and it cost a pretty penny.

There was a book on the side of the desk, a telephone directory or was it or a bible? She'd seen it briefly when she awoke. She couldn't recall, but whatever it was, it looked hard and heavy. She could launch that at him, that would probably cause some damage, slow him down.

"You asleep?" he called out.

She moved back to the desk and carefully took hold of the book, holding it solidly in her hands.

"No."

"Come on then, I'm hungry, let's eat. We can get a take-out."

"I'm – I'm not hungry. I'll take a rain check if that's okay with you. You go, though," she told him. If someone saw him out getting food, surely they'd remember the ten thousand dollars and call him in. It would only be a short time later they'd find her. "I'll see you in the morning."

"What? Are you kidding? No, it's not okay with me. You need to eat, we both do."

"I'd rather not, I'm – I'm too tired to eat."

She crept up, quietly moved the wooden chair which stood beneath a picture and placed it beside the door. She stood on top holding the book high above her head ready to bring it down on him with force should he attempt to kick the door in. That's what violent men did, right? Kick doors in, besides, he'd been a cop, hadn't he? You saw it all the time on the TV, cops kicking in doors to gain entry when a simple, 'hello – anyone there' would have been perfectly sufficient!

"I'm not buying that! Get your butt out here now." Despite his words, his tone was surprisingly jovial. The swim must have alleviated his tension.

"I'm not coming out, Casey, you might as well just go alone."

"What's going on in there, are you okay?"

"I'm fine," she said closing her eyes in hope he'd leave her alone. If she'd had a hand free she would have crossed her fingers for luck too. Suddenly the handle rattled and her heart sank to her toes.

Oh my God! This is it – he's going to break in! He's going to kill me!

She grasped the book so hard it turned her finger tips white. He might have got this far in kidnapping her but now it was going to be different. She could bring down the book over his head, kick him like she had with Glen and make a run for it. That was Plan A. Plan B was…well there wasn't a Plan B just yet, the fact she had a Plan A was something to be proud of. With a bit of luck on her side she wouldn't have to worry about a Plan B.

"Then open the door."

"No."

"Why not?"

"I've got… a headache, that's all."

"Yeah, you're probably hungry. Come on, let's move it."

"No!"

"What is it?"

"I can't open the door!" she groaned silently. "It's…um…broken!" She knew it sounded lame, she even rolled her eyes, but she couldn't think of anything else.

"Okay, stay back."

"What? Why?"

"Because I'm coming through."

"*What?*" She'd hoped the excuse would send him away not present him with the challenge to come crashing through. Oh, this was ridiculous! What was it with men and challenges? "No! No, I'm fine! Just go to dinner and I'll see you in the morning."

"I'm hardly going to leave you stranded in a room alone all night without food. Now is the door jammed or not?" He rattled the handle again.

"Um…" she tried to think clearly, get him to leave her alone. Her arms were aching and uncomfortable with the book held high, blood was quickly running out of them leaving them cold and shaky.

"Look, move out of the way, I'm coming in."

Before she could think of any other excuse to give him, Casey came crashing through just as she brought the book down hard over the back of his head.

He fell to his knees with a loud gasp. His rear end pointed towards her proving a good target for her foot so she jumped off the chair and kicked him, hard. He fell to the floor, holding himself trying to catch his breath.

She ran for her bag, grabbed it and headed for the door.

Chapter Twelve

"What the...?" He pulled himself to his knees grabbing her leg and pulled her to the floor with him, lying over her.

"Get off me," she yelled, "get *off* me!" her nails tore at his face and she kicked him as she struggled beneath his strength. He pushed her flat to the ground, straddling to keep her restrained.

"What the hell was that for?" Thick thigh muscles held her legs and hands on her wrists. He peered down at her face, her hair sprawled out behind her. Wide green eyes stared back in what could only be described as complete fear. She was trembling under his weight, her breasts heaving under his vest. "What did you think you were doing, hitting me like that?"

"Don't kill me! I know what your doing, Casey Pitt! Don't think I don't. I saw it all on the TV."

"Saw what? What the hell are you talking about?" he winced at the pain shooting through his head.

"You!"

"What about me?"

"You're kidnapping me!"

"What?"

"I saw the news. You have a history of depression and – and – and you are crazy or something and you're kidnapping me! There's a reward out for my safe return too."

"What the -?"

"What is it that you want, huh? You know I have money. How much do you want? Twenty thousand? Fifty? A hundred? My father left me a fortune, his mother left it to him. You can have it all just don't kill me."

Casey pulled up resting his palms on his thighs, releasing her arms momentarily. She didn't move.

"I have no idea what you're talking about," he said calmly. "But if you suggest anything like this again, I swear I'll whip your ass so hard you won't be able to sit down for a month - and *then* I'll kill you!"

She stared intensely waiting for his next move. Sure he was a manic depressive with a problematic history...or something...the news was fairly fuzzy on the details and, in her defence, she'd come in only half way through. But he *was* dangerous, wasn't he? She'd seen him kill a man after all and he shot at Glen too.

Glen really was trying to rescue her, the bullets were meant for Casey all along, not her. She knew one thing for definite though, she was in danger and if she didn't get away from him soon, she'd be dead.

"Let me get this straight, you watched some news item and decided I was kidnapping you, is that it?"

"They said it, not me. Them," she admitted, gesturing to the TV set with her eyes. "But it's true. I can tell it is. They said you're doing this because you blame me for David!"

"David?"

"Or Dean or Don or…"

"Dan?"

"Dan, that's it, Dan! You abducted me because you want to get back at me for getting Dan killed! They said it," she sped through the sentence as though it was her last breath, "on there. That's what they said."

He gazed at her with confusion, even looking at the blank television screen in case it was able to further shed some light on this drivel he was hearing.

"What on earth…?"

"The news report," she went on, "they said…"

"Yeah, 'cause they never embellish stories do they?" he added cynically. "Oh come on. I can't believe you'd really think this. I put myself through hell and high water to get you to safety and you have the audacity to accuse me of kidnapping you to get revenge?"

She tried to struggle from underneath his legs but his hands sprang firmly back to her wrists holding her in place

"I seriously can't believe this. Ok, I get that you're a self-centred air head and that all you care about is the colour of your nails, what to wear and some stupid over-sized rock you want De Salle to put on your finger, but to honestly accuse me of this? Come on, Genevieve, surely you know me better than that by now."

"But they said it. I saw Cassandra on there and Michael. They're all missing me. They're not going to say something like that if it wasn't true, are they?"

"You don't think that maybe Glen and his men are putting about this little story do you, that maybe the news hound on this case couldn't resist the idea that if you had been kidnapped again that it was going to make great news?"

His face grew closer. She could smell the chlorine from the pool on his skin, and his maleness. Was this what they meant when they said she could be in serious danger? Was it for her life or her heart? A gun might defend her body but what could protect her emotions? Maybe she should devise a Plan B right about now but her mind was filled with mush at the sight of him being this close. She was captive on so many levels.

"I – I don't know what to think," she uttered, her voice small and confused.

"Well, I'm not kidnapping you - you should have worked that much out by now." He licked his lips and stared into her eyes. His grip was hard, raw, a little rough, but it also felt good, solid.

Sure, she looked feisty and could take care of herself – at least verbally - but right now she was underneath him, totally at his mercy and completely vulnerable. He could try anything and she'd be able to do very little about it but, she questioned silently, would she even want to?

"But the news..." she started again.

"Forget the news."

"But they said..."

"I already told you I'd take a bullet for you. Hell, I already did and you've even seen your boyfriend take a shot at us and you *still* have the nerve to accuse me of kidnapping you? Why the hell would I go through all that if I wasn't trying to protect you?" Finally he grinned, white teeth framed by thin pink lips surrounded by an unshaven jaw. "You know this would be funny if it wasn't so crazy."

She swallowed silently. She could comment but there seemed little point.

"Incidentally, what would be my motive?"

"Money?"

"I don't want your money. I've never even mentioned it, have I?" he asked. Genevieve shook her head. "It's you who hasn't stopped talking about the damn stuff ever since we met. What else?"

"I don't know."

"Right," he nodded smoothly. "So we're agreed then? There's nothing you could give me that I could possibly want?"

A hopeful look appeared in her eyes as she allowed herself to think of one other think she had he might want. She'd already made a reference to her lack of sexual experience when they were changing in his apartment. Maybe she could somehow 'offer' herself to him as a plea bargain to get out of this mess.

"No," she said softly, "I suppose not."

"Nothing at all," he added again as if it made a difference. He moved away to get to his feet and she closed her eyes covering them with her hands, hiding her obvious emotional relief that he wasn't about to kill her after all.

What a mess! What a nightmare! Who to believe?

His response was so convincing but then there was the news, wasn't that convincing too? She wept under her palms. Not only did she feel idiotic to suggest the kidnapping in the first place but now if it wasn't true she still had to endure Glen and his attacks on them. Either way it was terrifying. It was all such a bad dream, she was so confused.

Casey stood to his feet looking down at her body lying pathetically on the carpet. "You okay?"

"No, just go away and leave me alone," she sobbed from behind her hands. He leaned over extending his hand and pulled her to her feet

"Come on, let's get some dinner. It'll all seem clearer with some food inside you. Not a lot, I'll admit but…"

"Don't you get it? I don't know who or what to believe anymore!" she barked. "First I'm convinced you're kidnapping me in the cab then you tell me Glen's up to something and I begin to believe you, then I see the news report and they're telling me point blank that you *are* kidnapping me and now you say you're not!" she cried, tears welling and falling down her pale freckled cheeks. "I don't know what the hell to think or feel or who to believe or anything anymore!"

"It's all going to be okay," he pulled her close, hugging her and stroking her hair. "I won't let anything happen to you, I promise. You've got the best protection going.

"Protection from what?"

"Glen."

"How do I know that's the truth? Who's going to protect me from you?"

He stared at her, trying to see it from her point of view.

"I know it all seems confusing right now, but you've got to believe me. We'll work it out. Hell, I worked as a cop for long enough to know nothing is ever as it seems." He took her to his chest wrapping his arms around her, stroking her jaw with his thumb. He was warm and soft. If he was a kidnapper, at that moment, she didn't care. Just having him hold her was enough to fill her with comfort.

But it was all so mystifying.

"I've never lied to you, Gen. You have to believe me."

"Why would I need protection from Glen. We've never even slept together, he's never so much as laid a finger on me. He's not a violent man."

"My guess is he's into something a little bigger than we know. I don't think it's exactly the kind of thing that he'd want to chat about over drinks."

"I don't believe it. It's all so surreal. I don't even know what the truth is anymore. How do I know this isn't just another story?"

He held her head in his hands and she stared up at him, her green eyes dripping tears like raindrops.

"Why would I lie?" he asked. He wiped her tears with his thumb. "Tell me, why would I?"

"I don't know. I really don't."

"I've never hurt you, have I?" he asked, his tone gentle. "If I was kidnapping you, would I have taken care of you like I have? I've never purposely put you in danger or pulled a gun on you. Surely that should tell you something. Even in the storm drain I..."

"No!" she stopped him firmly. "Don't talk about that day, I – I can't take anymore right now. I can't think about it."

"Hey, come on, take it easy, Gen. We've had a rough couple of days. Give yourself a some time, it's a lot to take in."

He inhaled the natural scent from her hair and felt the heat from her body. She needed him, his strength, his hold but this was getting way out of control. Comforting her was one thing but the reaction she had on him was quite another.

"Why don't you stay in here and I'll go get some food. If you promise not to throw anything else at me when I get back, I might even bring enough for two!" he joked. "And after that, relax, take a bath and get some sleep."

"But what about the police? They're going to be looking for us. The reporter said for people to call it in if they saw us. Plenty must've by now. The girl at reception recognised us. If you go out there you might not come back."

Casey took a long blink and shrugged.

"Then I guess we hope nobody's been watching the box. We've still got to eat whatever happens. Lock the door behind me and don't open it for anyone. I'll be ten minutes. If I'm not back by then use this to protect yourself," he said handing her his gun. "Oh, and Gen," he added, "remember who the bad guy is, okay?"

Chapter Thirteen

Genevieve sat on the base of the bed staring at her watch. The second hand on its diamond encrusted face - another gift from Glen on her last birthday - ticked by unbelievably slowly. As each of the given ten minutes went, her heart beat alongside.

Holding the gun in her hand, emphasised the seriousness of the situation. The metal heated her fingers and, at the same time, the chilling sensation of fear filled her very being. She closed her eyes, hoping and praying Casey would return with something as innocent as dinner and not an abundance of police restraining him in handcuffs. She felt an obligation to him, as if his life was in her hands now.

She imagined him in front of her now, police surrounding the motel, and Casey looking as desperate as a snared animal. The thought brought her close to tears

What if it all went pear-shaped, what if Casey did not return? Sure the journey would be over but this man had saved her life numerous times. Between a mad gunman over two yeas ago and showers of bullets from Glen's weapon, she was more than a little amazed she hadn't been seriously hurt. It was miraculous when she thought about it.

And it was all down to Casey Pitt, her protector, her bodyguard.

When this was all over, which route would her life take? Would she agree with the news report, go back with Glen De Salle and live her fairytale dream life she'd wanted so badly for so long or would she take Casey's side, tell the world how he kept her safe and cared for her despite her constant harsh words and disrespect?

Hardly able to think clearly, she opened her eyes to see her hands trembling. The gun was her power against him if she chose to believe the news item or her only protection from Glen if Casey was right. Deep down, deep in her heart she had come to realise she *wanted* Casey to be right.

Ten minutes was surely up by now, she told herself glimpsing at her watch again, but she'd been too hazy to recall what time he left. She could leave, now. Right here and now she could walk out of the motel room, phone the police and go back to the city back to her life. But something was stopping her. Her gut told her if she left him it would be a huge mistake. Leaving Casey alone would be an error of judgement. Or would it?

Maybe the same thought had filled Casey's head. Maybe he'd gone already and that was why he was late back. Maybe his excuse of getting dinner was simply a ploy now the news item had told her the truth and he'd used the time to sneak away into the darkness. Maybe she was as free as a bird and didn't even know it, that he'd given himself up, he was unarmed after all. She held the evidence in her hands.

She stood, swallowed hard and walked towards the door. Focussing from her position through the window, she couldn't see police car lights in the darkness, no people surrounding the place and no trace of him at all. Was their car even still out there or had he used it to make his swift and silent escape?

She looked at the door and turning the handle slowly. She held the gun ready to use like he told her. She'd never shot one before, nor had she even held one but she'd learn quickly especially if it meant a choice between life and death. She wasn't afraid of shooting – just killing. She could probably maim but she couldn't take a life, at least she hoped not.

Cautiously, she pulled the door open to look for the car. The warm air outside filled her lungs and then Casey appeared from nowhere armed with dinner.

"I thought I told you not to open the door!" He scolded. "And unless you're thinking of using that thing, it'd be a good idea to point it downwards. I don't want to be shot again thanks."

She gawped at him, still shaking, tears threatening to fall.

"Where were you?"

"Getting dinner, you knew where I was." She slapped his bad arm making him wince. "What the hell was that for?"

"I thought you'd escaped or something!"

"Escaped?" he asked, arching an eyebrow. He edged her backwards and kicked the door shut with his foot. "That was an interesting choice of words. Care to explain where that train of thought came from?"

"I thought you'd taken the chance to get away. I looked to see if the car was gone and you'd set me free."

"Set you free?" he smirked, taking the food from the bag and laying it on the bed behind them. "You mean as opposed to keeping you prisoner, perhaps? Oh, Gen, I thought we'd covered that one." He fumbled with his back pocket, took out his wallet and opened it up in front of her face. "Look, see this? I'm Casey James Pitt, retired DC cop."

"Yeah, like the news said." She looked at the ID. Of course it said nothing about the cop part but it confirmed everything he had already told her and gave the bonus information of a middle name as well. It was a cute picture too, she noticed. "But that proves nothing."

"I left the gun with you, didn't I? Why would I do that?"

"Maybe it was a ploy."

"A ploy? You still think I've got some grand scheme plotted against you? I'm actually quite flattered you think I'm that smart," he smiled. She didn't respond. "You're getting way too paranoid, do you know that? You know me, Gen, you remember me from the storm drain. I haven't changed much in two years. I was a good guy then and I'm a good guy now. I don't blame anyone for Dan's death but me and the scum who killed him."

"You don't blame me?"

"Why would I?" he gently cupped her face. "You didn't pull that trigger."

"Neither did you."

"No, that's true, but I was in a position where I could have prevented it. We were there to rescue you. You were not to blame for any of it."

"But if I hadn't been kidnapped in the first place, if I hadn't got my father to call off the suits with my tantrum, neither of you would've been there and ..."

"Hey, you can beat yourself up forever with talk like that. Believe me, I've spent a long time doing exactly that and let me tell you, it gets you nowhere except a few dozen rows of flowers in a rooftop garden and whitewashed walls."

"But the news report said..."

He looked directly into her sad, confused emerald eyes.

"Gen, please listen to me. I *do not* blame you for anything," he said deliberately. "What happened to Dan is something I guess was meant to be. I'll never get over it and it's pretty much screwed up my life but I don't hold a grudge against you. If I had a grudge with anyone it was the guy who did it and he's already dead. We had orders to find you and we did. Dan got killed, I got shot and you got out. But we did our job, end of story."

"That sounds so casual, so clinical. I remember it differently." She sat at the end of the bed, Casey next to her, their hands entwined and their supper forgotten.

"Go on."

"He took me, right off the street, you know. I was going to Cassandra's place. I tried to scream but he had his hand over my mouth. He was so big I couldn't move. I didn't understand what was happening. First I thought it was Michael joking around but this guy was too big and didn't sound like him so I knew something was wrong."

"How did you get to the drain?"

"By van. I think he hit me. The next thing I remember was being pulled out and dragged into the drain." Casey listened intently, holding her trembling hands. "It all seems like it happened yesterday, it's still so clear. I'm truly sorry about your partner. If I'd have known how it was going to turn out..."

"Me too," he shook his head. "I can never make any sense of it. When you're in the force you know you can go as easy as that but I guess we got a little complacent that day. I can tell you of a million situations that could've turned sour but that day, I just didn't see it coming. We were like glue, Dan and me. We'd been partners for a long time, knew exactly what each other was thinking, knew when to act, when not to. I guess we'd used up all our nine lives."

"I honestly believed you both died. When they found me, they took me out first so I never got to see what happened to you. It was hard enough coping with what had happened to me without seeing you and Dan shot too. I just couldn't get it into my head that someone could just take a life like that, in cold blood. And the water was so cold and the storm so loud. It was like a bad dream but I couldn't wake up from it."

She trembled in his arms, her face softening into a smile with a memory from the past. "I just couldn't think straight but I remember you tried to calm me down. You kept asking stupid questions, my name and then if I was dating."

"And I remember you were scared as hell but what I didn't tell you was that I was too."

"You were? But you seemed so confident, so in control."

Casey tilted his head. "That's the job. When you've got a pretty young girl who's scared out of her wits and you've got to get her out alive you have to think quickly. It was all I could think of at the time. Keeping you alive was everything. It still is."

"I thought you were incredible to do what you did. I thought you'd think I was some crazy rich kid, and if I started telling you that I thought you were some kind of angel or a hero to your face..." Casey listened. "My mother practically forced me to see a therapist right after and I remember telling them that this guy who saved me was amazing, like I had some mad crush on you. I remembered you to be much older. I told her this guy promised he was going to keep me alive and he did."

She saw his eyes sparkle.

"I told her I thought you'd been killed, a life for a life kind of thing, like someone had to die that day if I was going to live." Her chin puckered a little. "I remember telling her that I was glad it wasn't me. I felt so bad saying that like I was a disgusting person for thinking that way."

"Everyone thinks like that when they're in a bad situation. Death makes us all glad we're alive. It's how it works."

"When you knew Dan was dead," she asked, "did you thank God you were alive?"

"Actually, no." His thin lips tried to smile as if it were a joke. "I wished I'd died right alongside him. And I still have days when I wish that was true."

"And now?" she asked. "Now, are you happy you're alive?" She leaned up to his face and kissed his lips so softly it was as if a fairy had touched him.

He nodded. "Yes," his voice was no more than a whisper. "Yes, I'd have to say I am happy to be alive right now."

She was thankful at the thought. "I guess I shouldn't tell you stuff like this, huh?"

"You can tell me anything you want, Gen, anything at all."

"I know I'm no picnic, Casey, I guess I act the way I do because it's some kind of defence mechanism. If I act shallow it's only because I don't want to get hurt again."

"Who does?" he said. "Nobody wants to be hurt, in any way."

"I'm sorry I was such a bitch to you before and I just wanted you to know that in case...in case we don't get out of this."

"Hush," he told her. Curling a knuckle under her chin he stopped her from continuing. "I don't want to hear talk like that. We're going to get out of this together. Bad things happen to good people but I have a feeling things will turn out for the best. If Dan's watching over me at all, I like to think he'd help us out of this if he could."

"Did the police counsel you, you know, afterwards?"

"Yeah, it was pretty hard," he admitted. "Not the best time of my career."

"Is that why you left the force?"

He nodded. "I couldn't do my job anymore. They said depression set in and I'd became a liability. The worst thing was, they were right. Nobody wants a partner they cannot trust. I could understand it though. I'd have been the same. When you're in a tight corner, you don't want your partner to be running the other way, you know?"

"Is that what the TV meant about manic depression and unpredictability?"

"I don't know where they got that crap from. I'm no danger to anyone, unless someone's pointing a weapon at me, then I'll get pretty cranky but I think that's only fair! After it all happened, I took off and started fresh in LA. It seemed the right thing to do. I got a new apartment not far from the ocean, I saw new faces, and had a fresh start. I took a while to get my head together."

"Then you planted your garden?" she said, fitting it all together in her head. "It's pretty."

"Thanks. It's supposed to be calming. I don't know how calming it is, I never take much notice. I don't really remember planting half of them," he admitted. "Then one day I got talking to a guy in a bar who was looking for people like me, ex-cops, as bodyguards. I met up with the guy and the next thing I know I'm driving a cab and you're sitting in the back. Life sure does throw you some curves."

"I know exactly what you mean," she smiled. "In therapy I didn't want to re-live any of it. I hated every minute and I just wanted to forget it all. Like putting it all at the back of my mind and going shopping was the answer. Then we started getting reporters phoning, 'would we like to share the story with them' and 'we'd pay more if we went with this one and not that one'. People don't care what happened to you so long as it makes good reading," she told him.

"That's the sadness."

"My mother told me to ignore them all but Michael kept saying it would be a good thing, take the money and move on and my father just seemed to get more and more involved with his work. I guess he couldn't cope with it either. It was a couple of months later he died of a massive heart attack. The stress was just too much."

"I'm sorry. It's pretty hard when you lose a parent. Did you do the interview?"

"Yeah, I tried to keep everyone happy."

"Except yourself?"

She laughed. "Funny isn't it? I'm pretty stubborn generally yet as soon as something like that happens, I'm trying to make amends with everyone because I felt so guilty putting them all through it and all because I didn't want to have security that day. I felt like *I'd* killed my father!"

"But you didn't."

"Anyway, I gave an interview, they took some photos. They paid just like they said they would but I didn't care about that. Michael took care of that side of things for me. He's always been good like that."

"Then you met Glen?"

"A couple of months later, yeah. Michael wouldn't get off my back about going out. He said I should get back into the social scene quickly and practically forced Cassandra to dress me up for a benefit. You know the rest." Casey stared silently at the floor. He looked preoccupied. "What is it?"

"I was just thinking that's all," he smiled. Behind him was the unopened brown paper bag he had brought back with him. Inside was a couple of tuna and salad bagels. "Here, eat this," he told her. "You'll feel much better afterwards."

"Real food?"

"Well, I thought it might be a little more appetising that another day old burger. There can't be many fat grams in this."

Genevieve smiled back at his consideration and took a bite. "You got a medal, didn't you?"

"Yeah."

"I guess that was back at your apartment, huh?"

"Actually no. I didn't want it so I gave it to Dan's family. I thought it was better for them to keep it."

"I'm sorry I didn't go. My mother went in my place."

"I remember. I met her briefly. She's a nice lady."

"I couldn't face seeing you again. I was so sure you'd died and I didn't want to see you again 'cause I knew it would bring it all back. I wasn't sure I could thank you and not break down."

"You know breaking down isn't a crime." He told her, "we all do it some time."

"Yeah, I know. Did you have anybody to see you receive the medal?"

"I had a friend show up."

"Isobel?" she asked coyly, taking a bite of the bagel.

"No," he laughed. "You were right about her. She doesn't exist."

"I know." She smiled, "I'm pretty good at things like that."

"And yet you're having a hard time seeing if I'm telling the truth." He said. "Go figure."

"I think I know who's telling the truth, Casey."

"You do?"

"Yeah, I think I've known for a while. I guess I just didn't want to face up to it."

"You know it's all going to be okay, don't you?"

"I hope so," she said, "I don't want to die."

"Me either," Casey told her. "And if it has anything to do with me, you won't."

Chapter Fourteen

Genevieve checked out her bathroom, twisted the hot water full on and waited. Casey left for his room when the two agreed to get an early night. If it came to it and they had to up and leave during the early hours, they could be ready.

Arms across her chest, she caught sight of herself in the mirror. The one thing she wanted above all else was a bath but, by the look of her straggling hair, tired skin and dirty clothes, she needed a facial, pedicure and manicure just as badly.

Casey had given her a fresh T shirt from his bag and she could barely wait to feel its freshness against her flesh. If they hadn't left the city in so much of a rush and visited her place instead of Casey's she could have at least grabbed a few clothes and a case full of toiletries. Still it wasn't to be and now she had to make use of the facilities this place offered. She looked idly around the bathroom for something to put underneath the rushing water. Why couldn't places like this have aromatherapy oils on tap!

At least their relationship had gotten better these past few hours. They were both softening and, under the circumstances, maybe it was a good thing. If this was to be the end then she would rather spend it without conflict if at all possible. He really wasn't that bad after all and he was right from day one, he really did have her welfare at heart.

She sighed arching an eyebrow as she stood staring at her reflection.

"How do you get yourself into these situations, Gen?"

Her mind drifted back to Casey. He'd begun to grow his daily stubble: she noted the follicles growing through the first night they were together. Glen, she remembered, didn't look half as appealing with a beard as her bodyguard, but then he was quite a different kind of man altogether. If Glen grew even the slightest of beards he would have had it shaved off quicker than Genevieve could order a skinny decaf latte with extra hazelnut syrup.

Glen wasn't rough and ready, he was sleek and sophisticated. Someone you'd happily take home to meet Mother; the one man you could rely on in life for security, money and love.

Well, security and money anyway.

Genevieve sighed hard. Marrying Glen had been her first and foremost thought for the longest time now. Even Cassandra mentioned it more than once that if Genevieve had thoughts of other men then she'd happily entertain Glen instead. He was undoubtedly a good catch with his black hair, brown eyes and European background. What French descendent wasn't a good lover? Not that she knew anything about his love-making, that part of their relationship had never been discussed or practiced. The odd peck on the cheek and stroke of her hair – all for the cameras – were all that she had experienced.

She wasn't even sure she could actually imagine Glen making love to her. She could imagine him in her bed and even touching her skin but the actual act? It didn't seem right. Glen was far too perfect and clean to get down and dirty. In all the time she'd been with him, they'd never become close or intimate. Not that she didn't want to, she just wanted their wedding night to be perfect. He was exactly the type of man for whom she'd been saving herself. Tall, dark and handsome, he was everything a girl could want and so very much more, Glen De Salle had it all in abundance.

It was true though, whichever way she sliced it, Casey Pitt had presented himself to her as a bodyguard and her protector and the thought of him becoming much more was very enticing. In all honesty, why wouldn't she be turned on by him?

It was human nature to be attracted to the opposite sex, and he was a very good looking man. Although, after their heart to heart earlier, 'goodlooking' seemed to be gross understatement. The man was downright sexy and the more he occupied her thoughts the more she wanted him to. But there was so much more to him than just the attraction.

When this whole sorry affair was over, she'd likely tell him 'goodbye, good luck and thank you for keeping me alive' - that was if he did keep her alive. Maybe they'd stay in touch but it didn't seem probable given her lifestyle. They'd pose for the camera after the obligatory news report then it would be hugs and air kisses all round. That was her life and there was no point in thinking it was going to be any other way and God only knew where Glen would fit into this mess afterwards.

She wiped the mist from the mirror. Her reflection had hardly changed as she stood motionless waiting for the bath to fill, red hair cascading down her back and framing her face.

The tub was almost full despite the very severe lack of bubbles inside. She pulled off Casey's vest and wriggled out of her shorts. Her panties were still white, thank goodness, even after days of wear. The thought made her cringe. Honestly, what on earth would her mother say about that? It was hardly the epitome of one of Los Angeles' biggest socialites! Oh, if the press got a hold of this one. That titbit of information would be enough all on its own to ruin her!

She let her panties slip from her fingers into the wash basin and filled it with warm water, the soap cube sinking to the bottom. She didn't cherish the idea of wearing them for another day without a quick wash. If she could find a maid service it would be something but Casey's idea of lying low sadly included taking the cheapest motel rooms around and maid service wasn't on offer. She wrung them until they were just damp and hung them on the heater.

As she stepped into the bath water, she inhaled deeply. The heat of the bath was welcome as the water soaked her skin. This was as near to a sauna as she was likely to get – if ever again - and even if she just soaked for ten minutes it was something. Her body would thank her afterwards.

She lay down, letting the water lap against her skin, breathed in the humidity and closed her eyes. Her mind began to wonder: what was Casey doing right this moment? Was he on the phone talking to Smith? Maybe he was in the bathroom too, taking a shower or lying naked in the tub like her. She recalled the memory of his shower the first night they spent together and the view she had from the mirror. She swallowed, licked her lips and inhaled again imagining the soap washing over his muscles.

This was ridiculous!

She was just his client after all, nothing more, nothing less. What would be the value of getting into a relationship with him anyway? None. They were definitely from different sides of the tracks, he father would have said had he still been alive.

"Mark my words, Genevieve Dicing," he said one cold winter's day when the two of them walked in the snow, "any man who takes you on will get more than he bargained for! A strong mind is a good thing when its mixed with the right company. You've got so much of me in you it'll be a brave man who take you on. Either that," he added whimsically as an afterthought, "or he'll be the stupidest man alive!"

She'd quite liked the idea that Glen De Salle was going to fit the role of strong-hearted man rather nicely but with the events of the last few days she wondered if she could ever feel the same about him. It was, after all, his power that attracted her to him in the first place.

It had been the way he would snap his fingers in a restaurants and have everyone running around after him as if he owned the place. What woman wouldn't have been captured by that power? What woman indeed?

She toyed with the idea that maybe Glen's influence was on par with Casey's strength and determination. They were two powerful men in two different ways. And Casey certainly was a determined man, brave too. Days of dodging bullets, putting up with her moods and being treated like a second class citizen. Oh yes, determination to get the job done was definitely his strength.

Maybe right now he was lying on the bed, TV on and remote control in his hand. Or maybe he was asleep, dreaming of days gone by, of missions that had gone to plan, one's that didn't include the protection of an emotional red-head who liked nothing better than to complain about 'unsuitable attire for one's abduction'!

The water soaked her hair, the heat massaging her scalp. She shuffled her body until her ears moved under the surface. Tiny bubbles leaped to the top popping instantly and the sound of her pulse vibrated through the water. Despite the surroundings, it was a pleasant and relieving experience to bathe.

Casey's face appeared in her mind again. His blue eyes, unshaven chin and spiked hair caused her pulse to quicken, she could hear it beneath the water. Oddly she felt guilty. To whom? Glen? What did he care? Wasn't his only mission these days to kill her, that was becoming all too clear now. She came to realise that the very first time he pulled out the gun he *was* actually aiming for her but she still found it difficult to understand why.

If she listened to Casey in the first place, would they even be on the run? She couldn't answer that but knew if they didn't stop running soon they'd probably end up driving half way across the country.

Any type of guilt now should be felt by Glen, she decided, not her. She'd shown him loyalty and love and in return received pain and fear.

Maybe Glen didn't have a conscience as Casey pointed out. Maybe he was totally void of all emotions and just a darned good actor. He said he loved her but he couldn't possibly, not when he had treated her this way. The thought crushed her insides as if they were pebbles beneath a tonne weight.

He didn't love her. He never did. It was all a show. Just for the press. She squirmed in the bath tub. To feel so sure over something that was a lie cut her to the core. It was always supposed to be Glen, Mr and Mrs Glen De Salle. She would have walked into Antonio's or Charlotte's or anywhere in California, and be referred to and known as Mrs De Salle and everyone would lap up the time they spent with her. She would have been treated like royalty. So what if it was all fake, it was Hollywood!

The humiliation of it all.

Genevieve let out her anger and the tears fell. First they came slowly and quietly then the noise ascended as she allowed herself to understand it was over. It *was* over. There would be no attendance together at functions, no tabloid press photos for the public and no 'wedding of the year'. Nothing. Glen De Salle and Genevieve Dicing were no longer the hot Hollywood couple everyone wanted to be. As with most other things in the business, it had all been an act.

"*Bastard!*" she howled at the bath water. "I hate you!" The room echoed.

She sat up quickly, the water splashing from her body, and cried into her cupped hands. Anger took hold. She took a deep breath to let out the emotion, then another crying out aloud. She bulged her fists and pounded on the tiles on the wall over and over. She felt a little better, sure her throat was sore but that was the least of her problems.

Suddenly the bathroom door crashed open. Genevieve gasped as the bath water lapped at her skin. Wide-eyed and in utter shock, she turned to see Casey standing in the doorway bare-chested, wearing only jeans, with gun held between clenched fingers. He pointed the gun into all directions looking for something, *someone* to shoot at.

"What is it?" He yelled, "what's going on?"

She gasped covering her bare breasts with wet arms. "What the hell are you doing?"

"You were screaming," his face contorted with concern. "What the hell's going on? I heard shouting, I thought Glen was here or at the very least I figured you were being attacked. You've been crying, why?"

"I was upset! For God's sake, it's not a crime is it?"

"Nobody's here?" he bent backwards craning his head out of the bathroom checking for intruders. "You're alone?"

"No!" she gestured to the water, "I've got an entire football team in here with me! Yes, of course I'm alone, or at least I was until you barged in here all guns a-blazing! You look like a God damn cowboy!"

"I was worried," he explained. "You screamed."

He was worried? Over her? Was it a real worry or just his mission calling out, she didn't know. She did know, however, that as good as he looked with an unshaven chin, he looked doubly gorgeous bare-chested. There was something erotic about a man holding a gun and wearing very little in the way of clothes. Casey looked down into the tub. His first thought was of her safety, now he could see she was okay, his attention was otherwise engaged.

"I was angry," she confessed, trying to keep it together and not let his presence distract her more than it already had. "And I *still* am so get the hell out!"

He took a moment to savour the scene, grabbed a fluffy white towel from the heater and threw it at her which she snatched greedily covering her embarrassment. Trying with all his might to stop staring and hold back his smile, he told her,

"You have to see the funny side of this."

"Do I? Get out Mr Pitt before I – I-."

"I get it, I get it." He raised his hands in mock surrender and turned to leave. "I'm out of here. No more screaming, okay? I've got an itchy trigger finger tonight and I don't want to be responsible for any accidents."

"Well, I guess that's up to you isn't it."

He left the bathroom purposely leaving the door wide open. The cool air rushed in, biting at her wet skin creating goose bumps and hardening her nipples. As he left the room she heard the outer door slam shut, she closed her eyes again holding the towel to her face and screamed into it with frustration.

"Could you *be* any more irritating, Pitt?" she yelled at the top of her voice into the towel. The tub rung with the sound of her voice and, after a second had passed, she was silent but heard his laughter from the next room. The infuriating little... Her lips were taut with frustration then, in defiance of her entire being, they upturned and she let out a giggle.

No! She was far too angry now to find anything funny. She would not allow herself, absolutely not!

Before she had the chance to reprimand herself anymore, she held the towel to her mouth and laughed hard until her belly hurt and tears absorbed into the fabric. God, that man made her blood boil.

And that was priceless.

Chapter Fifteen

Genevieve left the bathroom, a damp towel around her body, and crept into the bedroom. She was alone, of course, of that she had no doubt. Casey was listening to music next door if the noise she could hear from his room told her anything.

She toyed with the idea of watching a movie, something in which to lose herself but the thought of being surprised by another report, starring Genevieve Dicing and her alleged abductor, chilled her to the bone. This was one time being famous wasn't all it was cracked up to be. If her mother had been interviewed Genevieve would lose all possibility of reason. Not that Casey would put her and reason in the same sentence.

She towel dried her hair and put on the shorts against her bare skin then pulled the grey shirt over her head. Casey's scent lined it and her body tingled with excitement knowing he'd worn the same garment.

She heard his door slam and stood still for a moment waiting for him to come crashing through her door again but he didn't. She stood by the window discreetly watching him walk to the phone booth at the end of the road. His stride was fascinating as he crossed the parking lot. She could watch that walk all night. She hoped he was calling Smith again and hoped even more that Smith hadn't been taken out too. If Casey came back with some good news so much the better.

It was nearly eleven and she was exhausted. The light came on inside the booth and she could see his back pressed against the window. She watched as she combed her hair, piling it back behind her. She may not smell as good as usual but she sure felt a lot cleaner but a squirt from the perfume in her purse would sort that out.

The perfume was a gift from Glen. Everything was a gift from Glen, right down to the five hundred dollar hair cut she sported. All that was going to change now though, she decided. She sprayed the scent over her body, neck and wrists then in front of her and walked through the mist. Her hair would dry with the light floral scent with the absence of her usual products.

She looked back outside. He was still talking. It must be some conversation, she thought. Maybe they'd caught Glen or his 'people' – whoever the hell 'they' were. She didn't even know he had *people* – at least not like that. He turned around in the booth and she pulled back from the curtain, sat on the bed and looked for something else to do.

Automatically she glanced at her chipped nail. Somehow it seemed to represent the whole ordeal.

"Oh, God," she sighed, "how did this all happen?" she recalled the recent events and threw herself backwards spraying her hair out behind her, closing her eyes.

There must have been a beginning to all this. She remembered walking out of the mall with Glen and Cassandra then being inside the cab on her cell phone on the freeway going somewhere that wasn't home. At some strange point in the middle of all of that her life had changed so dramatically it was beginning to cloud over.

The silence of the room twinned with her rhythmic breathing lulled her into a dream like state. She played the event over in her mind. Kiss Glen, hug Cassandra, get into car. *Don't forget drinks tonight, okay?* With his sunglasses resting casually on his head, the glint in his eye told her he knew what she meant by that. Drinks equalled engagement, at least that night it did. She could just feel the celebratory atmosphere in the air.

Just the week before she and Cassandra had been casually looking at diamond rings remarking at the ones Genevieve had particularly liked. She knew Cassandra was making private notes to pass on to the prospective groom. The diamond she picked out was larger than her delicately manicured finger nail and brighter than the shine in her hair. It would be the focus of every front page in the land. She imagined the reporters, the news hounds knocking on her door waiting for her to pop out just to give them a glance of the rock. An estimated value would be emblazoned on the front pages, though she would never reveal exactly how much it cost. Speculation, after all, was often more exciting that the truth. She would give them a customary smile and courteous giggle letting them know she knew she was the luckiest girl in the world. She was Hollywood's royalty and proud to display her jewel to her subjects at any given moment.

Her dream state broke quickly, pulling her from a restful mode into a fearful one as a hand lay across her mouth and a hard body to her side. Her eyes flung open to see Casey's face so close to hers she had to squint to focus. She wanted to yell at him, to force it out of him that this was a kidnapping after all. Her confusion was such that she hardly remembered her own name these days.

"Don't scream, okay?" he said softly, she could see the anguish in his eyes. "We have to leave right now." He took his hand away a little to gauge her reaction first before letting her go.

"What's going on?" her heart pounding in her chest. "Is it Glen, did he find us?"

"No, and I don't want to give him the chance." He leaned up from her assisting her to sit. "I just got off the phone to Smith. The guy at the motel last night reported us. We have to go, right now."

"The creepy guy?" she asked, "Mr Blob? I saw him looking at me, I just knew he recognised me. Damn it!"

"Well, I guess he wanted to get his hands on the ten grand your brother put up. It was going to happen sooner or later. We're lucky it lasted this long." He threw her a quick smile. "I don't suppose it helped me walking into the bar for a first aid box either but anyway, we don't have time to speculate. Just get your stuff together as quick as you can. I'll be back here in two minutes."

"I'll be ready."

She grabbed her dry panties from the bathroom and two minutes later they vacated the parking lot as quietly as they could. With still damp hair, the chill of the night sent a shiver through her.

"You okay?" Casey looked over at her.

"Cold. It's gloomy out here. I was ready to sleep not get back on the road."

"It makes good sense to leave now. Darkness is good cover."

It was just a shame the darkness had to be so unwelcoming and unforgiving. She pulled her legs up to her chest and held them tight. He fumbled in the bag behind his seat for his shirt and pulled it out for her.

"Here, put this on."

She took it, pulling it around her. "How's your arm?"

"Better, I think. You should have come in, by the way. The water was beautiful."

"I'm not very good in pools."

"You can swim can't you?"

"Of course, I just don't feel comfortable in them anymore."

"Anymore?"

"After the drain episode, I couldn't bare it."

"You should have said something. I'd have stayed close," he reassured her.

But it was too late now. Genevieve laughed. "What so funny?"

"The way you always want to provide a solution for everything."

"It's a 'guy' thing."

"I think it's kind of cute."

"Cute? Me?" he laughed. "No, sorry, I don't *do* cute."

She watched him speak, the yellow light from the dash board illuminated the features she had come to look forward to seeing.

"Well, Casey, here's the thing. Would it be so bad if you did do cute, 'cause I think maybe you do. Really well at that."

He faced her briefly before looking back at the road.

"You wouldn't be coming on to me, would you Miss Dicing?" he asked, his tone formal. "I mean that'd suggest you were losing those prickles of yours."

"Prickles? Me?" she answered, smiling coyly. "I don't *do* prickles."

"Get some sleep," he laughed. He looked good when he laughed, she decided.

"What about you?"

"Don't worry about me, I'll be fine. Go ahead."

She didn't need coaxing. She tipped her seat back, curled his shirt around her body and hugged it close. The collar leaned softly against her nose and she fell asleep breathing in his scent.

She wasn't aware of how long she'd slept or indeed where they were but when she awoke, the car was parked in a lay-by in the middle of nowhere too dark to see anything. She glanced outside and tried to focus on something familiar but it was pretty impossible. Even her watch was too dark to read. She looked around at Casey who was lying against his window, his arm supporting his head. The only sound was from their mutual breathing until she heard an animal yell somewhere in the distance. She gasped sharply; unaware her sudden movement had rocked the car and moved closer to Casey for comfort. Without batting an eyelid he lifted his arm and pulled her close. She nuzzled into his chest, thankful for his warmth and tenderness and fell back to sleep.

Waking on and off throughout the night, Casey finally glanced at his watch at four-fifteen. He looked down at the red-headed beauty asleep in his lap. A mass of copper curls glistened in the morning light. He glanced outside, the horizon was beginning to take shape. He lifted her head and gently re-positioned her back onto her seat.

"He's really very nice," she mumbled in her sleep adding, "honestly Mom, you'll love him too."

Casey grinned at her vulnerable state and recalled her moment in the bath. Heck! This woman had a great body. She had definitely got to him but he had to stay on top of things, keep a clear head. He reached under his seat hoping for a map. Using the sunrise, he traced his finger all the way from the city into the hills on Expressway 15. According to the map, if they travelled any further east they'd be well on the way to Las Vegas.

"What's happening?" Genevieve stirred. "Where are we?"

"On our way to Vegas if we're not careful," he told her with a half grin, still tracing his finger over the map.

"Cool, lets get married!" she yawned. Stretching her arms as much above her head as the roof would allow, she smirked at her comment and absorbed his expression. "Just kidding. Don't panic."

"I think we should make our way back to the city if we can, the sun will be up soon."

"The city? Is it safe now?"

"Not exactly. You remember the call I made earlier?"

"To Smith?"

"No, it wasn't actually. I was calling an old friend. I think they can help."

"Is he a cop?"

"Not exactly and 'he' is a 'she'. Cathrynn," he said, "She lives about twenty miles outside of the city. If we can get to her, I know she'll help us."

"Oh, Cathrynn?" she nodded, trying her hardest not to sound too jealous. "How exactly will this *Cathrynn* help us?"

"She can loan us some money for a start. Without that we can't do much of anything."

"And you think she'd risk life and limb for us?"

"Uh-huh."

"And she's reliable is she, this Cathrynn person?"

"Yeah, she's a close friend of mine. She and I go way back and she's more than just reliable."

"Okay," she nodded defiantly, landing herself squarely back onto the seat. "I suppose if you really think so."

"I do. But it means heading back. Do you think you're going to be okay with that?"

"Do we have a choice?"

"Not a practical one, no."

"Then to Cathrynn's it is." She faked a smile, hoping that Cathrynn wasn't going to be too much competition.

Once the sun was up, the day showed little sign of offering anything other than heat. The temperature was rising. According to the dial, the tank needed gas soon too. He remembered seeing a sign for a gas station about twenty miles away.

"Where did you meet this Cathrynn woman anyway?" Genevieve asked suddenly, as if she'd been thinking about it for ages.

"She's Dan's sister. Cathrynn Chandler's a good person, Gen, I know she'll help as much as she can."

"And you two were an item?"

"What?"

"I asked if you two were an item?"

"I heard you, I just didn't imagine you'd be quite so blunt about it."

"So were you? I mean it's not like I should have to ask really. It's pretty obvious but I just wanted to hear you say it."

"What?" he squirmed. "No, of course not. We kind of got it together one time but I don't think you could call us an item. You seem a little hostile all of a sudden, what's the matter?"

"Hostile? Hardly, Casey, I'm fine."

"Well, those prickles are back. If I didn't know you'd better I'd have said you sounded a little jealous."

"Last night I said I liked you, I didn't say I was giving up my life for you!"

"What you actually said was that you told your therapist you thought I was amazing and incredible."

"You remembered those exact words? My goodness, Casey, you were paying attention. I'm impressed. Might there be a little ego-trip going on over there by any chance?"

"What's the problem, Gen? There *is* a problem I take it? If you're worried about heading back to the city, don't be. Nothings changed as far as your protection goes."

"Oh, has something else changed then? Do enlighten me 'cause I'd hate to have missed it."

"No, of course not. If Glen shows his face, I'll be all over you like a rash, you've really nothing to worry about."

"Well I'll be sure to thank you for your time, Mr Pitt!"

"What the hell's the matter? You were peaches and cream back there and now all of a sudden you've turned back into your old self. Life's an emotional roller-coaster with you, isn't it? I just wonder."

"Wonder what?"

"Well, could it be the fact we are heading back to the city or could it be you're a little unnerved that there was actually a woman in my life before I met you."

"Get over yourself, Casey. I generally don't go gaga for a guy in the first two minutes I meet him. Especially one's like you." She huffed and shoved her chin in her palm gazing outside. "What is it with guys? Why are you always so sure a girl is going to fall madly in love with you. You're a conceited bunch, if you ask me."

"I don't recall anybody actually doing that," he mumbled.

"Whatever!" she focussed outside. "I'm tired! Read into it what you will."

If that was anything to go by, the next twenty minutes was going to be fun. Casey put his foot down with frustration, if she could stare out the window in total silence he was darned sure he could.

As if they needed something else to bicker about, he looked down at the dash board to see a red light flashing.

"Oh, man!"

"What?" she said curtly. "Why are we stopping?"

"We're out of gas. I thought we could make it but..."

"So, we have to walk now?" she barked, her nostrils flaring at the inconvenience. "But it's the middle of nowhere, where will we walk to?" Casey pulled up at the side of the road, a dust cloud flying above. He opened the door and stood outside. "What are you doing now, taking in the damn scenery?"

"I'm thinking."

She rolled her eyes and laid her head back on the window.

"This is nuts!" she groaned. "Why didn't you notice we were low on gas? How could you let this happen? Even an imbecilic moron could keep an eye on the dash!"

"*You* didn't notice it either!"

"You are supposed to be protecting me and here we are in the middle of the God damn desert with no gas, no food and I look like crap!"

Casey turned around, his face steely and hard.

"Listen lady, I don't think I've done too bad a job so far," his voice rose with every word. "You don't see Glen on our tail, do you? You had a chance to sleep, didn't you? You look pretty much alive to me, and you certainly sound okay! In fact I haven't heard you do much of anything *but* snore, complain and whine ever since I met you!"

"You should have realised this was going to happen. You should have made provisions for it, or – or done whatever bodyguards are supposed to do. And I don't snore, I'll have you know."

"You know, I don't remember the section on Future Predictions in the 'How to be a Body-Guard' Handbook!"

"You don't need to see into the future to know we are low on gas, idiot! That's what the little meter thing on the dash is for or don't they teach you that kind of thing in cop school?"

"Wha-!" his jaw dropped and his eyes widened. Genevieve turned her back on him, folded her arms and mumbled something under the breath.

"How the hell are we going to get out of this little scrape, Mr Pitt?"

Fuming, he marched around to her side of the car, opened the door and stood in front of her.

"Well, *Miss Dicing*, here's an idea. Why don't we put one foot in front of the other and hoof our butts to the nearest gas station? Hmm?"

"That could be miles! I don't know if you even noticed but my feet have been in the same heels for ages! *I* can't walk miles to get gas that *you* forgot to get. I probably can't even walk to that tree!" she nodded to a small piece of foliage about fifty yards away.

"So take 'em off."

"What?"

"I said take them off. Go barefoot."

"I'm not going barefoot! Do you know what kind of creatures there are out here? There are scorpions and snakes and spiders and all kinds of horrible things."

"Well, I guess if you don't want to walk in those things you'll have to keep them on, won't you."

"Oh no I won't." She stamped her foot, crossed her arms and stuck out her lower lip. "I won't do it!"

"Oh, and there it is, we're back to being Miss Spoiled Brat once again! I knew it wouldn't be long with the hostilities and all. Is this what happens with Mr Fantastic is it? You just stand there stamp your feet and he runs around after you?"

"Shut up! You haven't got a clue what my relationship is like with Glen."

"You mean other than taking pot-shot's at you? I'm telling you here and now I won't stand for that kind of behaviour from anybody – not even a spoiled brat like you."

"I really don't give a damn what you do so long as you get some gas to fill up this heap. In fact why don't you go now and I'll wait here."

He pulled her roughly from the car and stood in front of her. "No."

"Why?"

"Well, there is this little thing called protection and if I don't keep you within arms length all hell will let loose and I don't want to be responsible for that. Come on, grab your things, we'll hoof it together."

"I told you, Casey, I am not going anywhere in these shoes. I'll wait in the car until you get back."

"No!"

"Don't you dare say no to me, I'll do exactly what I please! And I don't take orders from a two-bit ex-cop anyway!"

Casey took a deep breath. This was impossible. He filled his lungs with dusty air, held it for a couple of seconds mentally counting to ten just to keep his sanity.

"You're coming with me and that's all there is to it."

"I most certainly am not and there's nothing you can do that will change my mind," she huffed.

"Get moving, Gen, or I might have to do something drastic."

"Do what you please, Casey. I don't really give a damn."

Without thinking any more, he pushed her against the car and held her face in his hands. Suddenly his lips came down on her mouth with such passion and strength, it shocked her. It took her a whole three seconds to realise how good it felt before she began to respond. His body drew closer until she felt his hard chest against her breasts and his muscular thighs against her slender legs. He smelled raw, sexual and masculine. But as soon as his hands moved down her neck and up into the back of her hair, he'd stopped, stepped away and grabbed his bag from the car throwing it over his shoulder in one easy movement.

She was still faraway in a secret place somewhere inside her mind, so he bent down and threw her over his other shoulder breaking the spell immediately. She screamed at him, pounding his back with her fists until he returned her to the ground.

"How dare you do that! What the hell did you think you were doing?" she yelled.

Immediately he put her down. "Now, either you walk in those things, you walk *without* those things or I carry you over my shoulder again and believe me, you don't want to be carried over my shoulder!"

"You don't make life very appealing, do you?"

"And you don't make me want to make it appealing. Choose!"

"Oh!" she stomped her foot, infuriated. "Of all the people I have to be stranded with, it had to be you, didn't it."

"Yeah, I guess that's the way the cookie crumbles, honey. I can't honestly say I'm any more thrilled with it either." He sighed, grabbed his bag and begun walking.

"I suppose I'll walk then – you know if I *have* to."

"You have to."

She took her bag, sighed again and followed him along the dusty road towards emptiness thinking about nothing but the long walk ahead of her and that wonderful kiss he thrust upon her.

Chapter Sixteen

Thirty minutes of quite literally following in Casey's footsteps wasn't exactly her idea of heaven. Nothing was, at that moment, apart from resting, but if she'd ever had dreams of joining the army or route marching around California she would know exactly who to call for assistance.

"This is ridiculous!" she yelled out ten feet behind him.

The road side sent dust into her face and the breeze carried even more dust into her hair. She felt as if she were being exfoliated under duress! She wanted to stop and sit down. If she saw another rock, pebble, twig, or bush she would go seriously crazy.

"Get moving," he shouted. "We've got to see something soon."

"Please don't tell me that means you have no idea where we're going."

"Yeah, course I do. We're going back. I told you that already. I just hope we don't have to walk the entire way."

"You know we could call a cab. I have a phone right here, remember? All I have to do is just switch it on."

"Genevieve Dicing, I already told you, if you do that I will kill you myself."

"So why haven't you done that already? I'm sure you want to."

He stopped, turned and waited. His hands on his hips only adding to his already exhausted look. His mouth was open, taking in as much air as he could get, as dust stuck to the perspiration on his face.

"Believe me, honey, it's crossed my mind more than once."

"And yet," she jerked her head to one side, "here I am, still breathing."

"Guess that shows you what a damn good bodyguard I am then, doesn't it?"

"Or maybe it means you can't bring yourself to do it."

"I've been seconds away from doing it for a long time, trust me!"

"Then what's stopping you now?" she asked as she flicked her hair over her shoulder and stomped past him forcing him to follow her for a change.

"You *want* me to shoot you or something?" he asked, his eyebrows raising. "If I did for one thing I'd have to clear up the mess and for another I wouldn't get paid."

"Money!" She squawked. "So you *are* driven by it?"

"Certainly not in the same way you are."

She shimmied on, aware of his insult and glanced over her shoulder.

"And you can stop staring at my butt too, Pitt! When we get back I'll have you arrested for that."

She caught him out and he laughed. The only sad thing was that he was not aware he was doing it until she mentioned it. At least if he had, he would have enjoyed the moment.

"Arrested for staring at your butt, huh? Now that's a new one."

Genevieve continued walking. Either his footsteps were silent or he'd stopped. She couldn't work out which, so turned. He was stationary, just watching her.

"What now?"

"Come back here," he called.

She walked back and stood in front of him. "What?"

"It seems I am going to have to eat a little slice of humble pie."

"How's that?"

"I need your cell phone."

She raised her brow. "You want my phone?"

"Yeah." He nodded.

"What for, because if you're going to launch it into the unknown then the answer is most definitely going to be 'no'."

"I won't launch it anywhere. I want to use it."

"You're kidding me, right? You've been telling me all this time to turn it off and even threatened me if I so much as check my calls. And now you want to use it?"

"Yeah, like I said," he sighed, "humble pie. Now are you going to hand it over," he said with a twinkle in his eye and a quick movement of his eyebrow, "or am I going to have to deploy drastic measures again?"

"You're going to kiss me to get your hands on my phone?" She wanted to yell out to him, 'yeah, go right ahead, Buddy,' call his bluff just to see how she would respond but her better judgement warned her against it. "You could just ask you know."

"I just did."

"Why's it suddenly ok to use it. All this time you were worried they'd trace us and now it's ok?"

"It's no different now. I just need to make a call."

"You're crazy, Pitt, you know that? Can't we still be traced?"

"Yeah."

"And what if I say no?"

He raised his eyebrows twice and offered a sexy grin. Genevieve blushed and her heartbeat rose a notch. He hardly made it easy to refuse him.

"Good. Now we understand each other," he smiled. "Now you want to get out of this, don't you? You want to be back home in your luxury apartment socialising with God knows who God knows where, don't you?"

"You've no idea just how much."

"Great, then hand it over and this little adventure can be over."

She reached into her bag, gave it to him but half wished she hadn't. Having him kiss her in order to get what he needed wasn't such a punishment.

"Who're you going to call?"

"Cathrynn."

Genevieve heart sank. "Why?"

He tapped in her number and waited for Cathrynn to pick up. Her answer machine clicked on. Casey closed his eyes with resignation. Just as he was about to record his message, she picked up.

"Cathrynn, it's me." A relieved smile landed on his lips, Genevieve watched. "I thought you were out. Can you talk?" Casey lowered his voice a little and turned as if it were a private conversation.

"It's *my* phone!" she mouthed dramatically raising her eyes and hands to the heavens.

"Listen, I need a favour, honey. I'm still stuck up in the mountains with her. Tell me about it," he rolled his eyes. "The car's out of gas, can you come get us? Great, Cathrynn. I can't wait to see you either. I owe you big-time."

A moment later he handed back the phone and continued walking. She followed, silently at first, then, as she could wait no longer for information, she broke the silence.

"So what now? That's it, is it? Your girlfriend is going to come and get us, is she?"

"Looks that way."

"And she's going to take us back and everyone lives happily ever after. Is that your plan?"

"Well we could've been traced which means Glen will probably send a couple of guys to shoot the hell out of us but I like your way better."

"Glen wouldn't do that."

Casey peered over his shoulder. "Just like he didn't do it before, yeah I see where your logic's going with this 'cause he's such a nice guy!"

"I'm hungry and my feet are aching!"

"Really? I'm hungry and my *ears* are aching," he countered, walking faster.

It was getting closer to midday. Each time a car drove past each time the pair stood as far out of sight as they could. They just couldn't take that chance, they had come too far. The sun was hotter, the dust was drier and as much as he was there to protect her, neither of them had thought ahead to bring so much as a bottle of water.

"I don't feel so good," Genevieve stopped. "Casey, I need to...to rest." She didn't wait for his permission, as he turned to answer her she simply fell down at the side of the road as if she were a puppet released from her strings. It looked more than just amateur dramatics. He ran back.

"Come on, Cathrynn will be hear soon. Get up."

"I can't," she gasped, "I'm so tired. My feet!"

"Gen, get up."

"I can't!"

"Get *up*!" he shouted.

"If I could I would, Casey, but please believe me. I can't walk anymore," she whispered with as much energy as she could muster. "I just can't. You go, please let me stay here and rest. I don't care what happens anymore."

"I do and I'm not leaving you up here alone. Get up, Gen." He told her. She didn't respond. "Listen, if you don't get up, you don't get to live, it's as simple as that. Forget your feet, this is your life we are talking about. We don't have time for this!"

Again she didn't answer. He studied her until he was satisfied she was genuine then bent down to lift her, cradle her between his arms and let the bag hang down as he walked.

"Cathrynn," he said into thin air, "save my life."

If Casey didn't rest soon too, he'd be no use to anyone at all. He walked for ten more minutes then stopped along the road, gently lay her down and stretched his shoulders. His injury hurt but his fatigue and dehydration were far worse. In the distance he could hear an engine. This could be Cathrynn or another passer-by or even Glen. At this moment he didn't care just so long as they had water and provisions to rest for a while and if they didn't, even being shot dead right now sounded fine with him.

He looked down at Genevieve's face. Finally he could sympathise with her. She wasn't made for this kind of life. The toughest thing a girl like her should have to experience was wondering when her next facial should be. Casey shook his head and muffled a laugh.

"You're a real looker, Gen," he wheezed with as much of a grin as he could find, "but right now you look like crap!"

The engine got louder. Casey looked up to see a grey saloon heading straight for them. If it wasn't Cathrynn, at least this whole mess would be over. He reached for his weapon just in case but his energy was running low. As the car stopped, a cloud of dust flew up and a woman ran towards them.

Cathrynn was here.

"I got here as soon as I could, Casey. Oh my God, are you okay? You look awful!" She shrieked. She touched his cheek gently, bent down in front of him and studied Genevieve. "Is she okay? She looks like she needs a doctor."

"She probably does. Do you have any water?"

"Yeah, in the car. Wait here."

"No time, Cathrynn. Help me get her in there."

He put away his weapon, shared the weight with Cathrynn and got her to the car.

"I didn't really know what to expect otherwise I could have brought more supplies."

"She's dehydrated is all. Once she gets some sleep and some water inside her she'll be fine."

"I meant you. Are you okay? You've looked better."

"Me? I'm fine."

"You look like you need a hospital, Casey."

They placed Genevieve on the back seat, forced water down her throat and let her sleep it off. Casey sat in the passenger seat and closed his eyes, his mouth dry and open fighting for clean, dust-free air.

"Are you going to be alright?" Cathrynn started the engine and turned the car around.

"Yeah," he gasped, "I am now." Subconsciously, he nursed his left arm and looked inside his shirt to see his wound. Blood had seeped through the bandage

"You're injured bad?"

"I'll live."

"Casey, I had no idea you were hit. Have you had it properly looked at?"

"Kinda."

Draining the bottle of water she gave him, Casey felt it re-hydrate every inch of his body before he could speak again. He wiped his mouth and poured the water in his cupped hands, allowing it to wash over his face.

Cathrynn was concerned. "You don't look so hot."

"I'm fine. Just take us to your place."

"Alright, get some rest," she nodded.

"My head's killing me."

"Too much sun," she said, stating the obvious. "If there is anything I can do for you Casey, I'm here. All you have to do it ask." She handed him another bottle of water. "Drink this, you need it."

He wiped his eyes with his fingers, scratching them as well as stroking them. He could fall into a marathon sleep right now but there was no way he could allow himself. Cathrynn was risking a lot coming for them and if anything happened to her he would never forgive himself.

"You're an angel, Cathrynn." He looked at Genevieve limp body in the back seat. "Thank God you came."

He turned in time to see her smile. He hadn't realised how much he longed to see that again.

Chapter Seventeen

Genevieve awoke to the musical sound of a woman's laughter. She wondered if it was Cassandra for a split second. She looked around the room and realised she was no longer in the mountains but inside an unfamiliar bed with pastel pink bed linen around her. She looked at her surroundings but recalled nothing of how she came to be here. This was no motel. It had a personal touch about it.

At first, she didn't know whether to be alarmed or at ease, until she heard the sound of Casey's familiar voice. She swung her legs over the bed, sipped from the glass of water next to the bed and drained it. Her head had felt better and her entire body ached after the ordeal she had just endured.

She heard the female voice again and walked out of the room to investigate. Walking down the hallway, the scent of tea filled her nostrils as cool wooden floorboards welcomed her aching feet. Soon she saw the back of Casey's head and a flutter of relief sailed through her. Next to him and, she noticed with an arched eyebrow, was a brunette haired woman who seemed to giggle at every word he uttered.

It was Cathrynn, her senses told her, and Casey's arm rested around the woman's shoulders. Just as Genevieve took a breath to announce herself he turned to kiss Cathrynn's head. Even from this angle, she could see a glow in his eye. Cathrynn must be someone pretty special.

"You two sound chipper."

Casey turned as Cathrynn sprang from the sofa to greet her second guest.

"Hi," she smiled, "we were just reliving old times. Why don't you come and sit down. I can make some more tea."

"You look better," Casey nodded.

"I feel it."

"Cathrynn and I were just taking a walk down memory lane, we go back a long way."

"I can see that."

Casey was happy and refreshed, she noticed, even to the point of having showered. His arm had been redressed too if the slight bulge of the bandage underneath his shirt was anything to go by.

Oddly, the thought of lying in a bath didn't appeal to her now when a shower would suffice. In her dirty clothes, unkempt hair and unclean skin, she just wanted to wash the last few days down the drain and re-start her life.

"Come sit down, you must be exhausted. Casey's been telling me what's been going on. It sounds like the two of you have been on the craziest adventure. I'll make some more tea and afterwards you can clean up if you like."

Cathrynn's apartment was small but nice enough and had more of a woman's touch than Casey's had. It was visually appealing.

Genevieve took the hospitality, sitting next to her bodyguard peering around the room taking in her surroundings. She spotted a large photo on a shelf of Casey and another man, Cathrynn was in the middle hugging them. They looked so happy. Hanging over the top of the frame was a medal.

When Casey told her he had given it to Dan's family, he meant Cathrynn, Genevieve now realised.

"That's my brother," Cathrynn said following her eye line. "It was taken about five years ago at my old place." She picked it up and brought it to Genevieve, tucking the medal inside her hand for safekeeping.

"Don't let the smiling faces fool you, that weekend was a nightmare," she said. "It was like clearing up after a pair of high school kids. My own brother I could handle, but when you have his best pal there and the two of them got together, things got real messy."

Genevieve took the photo, focussing on Casey's face more than the others. He had changed quite a bit over the past few years it seemed. Her recollection of him in the drain was of a medium built man with a face that she had remembered as her saviour. It was dark, dirty and wet down there but his face didn't look half as rugged then as it did now, proving that age suited this man.

"Casey's such a dish, isn't he?" Cathrynn teased, speaking as though he was not present.

"Will you stop?" he said, with a half filled mug of tea in his lap. "You're going to make a grown man blush."

"Oh, come on, Casey, I'm not saying anything you don't already know. Men are so like that aren't they? They all love themselves really. Show me a man who is insecure and I'll show you a liar!" Cathrynn giggled.

"Your brother looks kind of cute too." Genevieve smiled diplomatically. It was true though, at least from the little she remembered of Dan Chandler before he fell to his watery death. From the picture, she could see the same sincerity in his eyes he shared with his kid sister.

"Casey and I were supposed to go out for dinner that night but Dan started with his protective big brother routine and the three of us ended up going out together. I don't know what he expected us to get up to but whatever it was, we didn't – or couldn't. He was there all night with us. They were both as stubborn as each other."

"I'm not stubborn," Casey retaliated. "Determined, I'd say."

"After my brother, you're the most stubborn guy I've ever known! Sorry Miss Dicing, after seeing Casey again after all this time, I almost forgot myself. I'll go get that tea."

"Gen," Genevieve nodded, raking her hair back. "Call me Gen."

"Despite what's going on , I have to tell you, it's very exciting playing hostess to Hollywood's Hottest."

"Hollywood's Hottest huh?" Genevieve offered a half-smile, unsure if she should accept the honour. "I don't know that I'm worthy of such a title. The press always describe me as royalty but it's all very overstated. I'm just me really."

"She was talking about me," Casey winked at them both.

Cathrynn shot him a sarcastic nod. "You're not exactly up there with the rich and famous, pal! Try Hollywood's top bachelor, that might work." She left them for the kitchen in pursuit of tea.

"I thought you were supposed to be the quiet one," Genevieve said. "You told me you were shy and reserved, outside of work of course. I've not seen much shy but reserved," she lifted her chin and nodded, "I'd say that was true."

"I was - compared to Danny. And I never said those exact words."

"Well, you were really quiet in the car when we first met," she nodded as if to confirm it for herself. "I remember that much."

"And you didn't quit talking. Even if I wanted to speak, it would've been hard."

"And you were sizing up the client, I suspect?"

"It's my job, Ma'am," he doffed an invisible hat. Genevieve laughed quietly.

That twinkle in his eye had returned only this time he aimed it at her and she liked it.

"So it was Cathrynn, then? The person you gave your medal to."

"Yeah. Danny's one is with his Mom. It seemed only right to give mine to his sister. I wanted her to have something that meant a lot."

"To you?"

"To both of us."

"That was thoughtful," she nodded sympathetically. "I'll bet she treasures it. What is it exactly?"

"The Medal of Valour," he nodded

"Wow," she sighed. He truly was brave. "And you didn't want it?"

"I felt she needed it more than me."

Before he could continued, Cathrynn's voice called from the kitchen.

"But don't think Casey's saintly, I don't know what he's been saying the past couple of days but he's not so flawless. He's a red-blooded guy just like the rest of them. But in his defence, his heart is totally in the right place."

She brought in a tray and laid it on the coffee table in from of her guests. Pouring from a teapot, she offered milk and sugar then handed it to her guest.

"But then I always did have a soft spot for you. As guys go," she looked at Genevieve, "he's one of the best. I'd trust him with my life any day of the week."

Cathrynn's slim cheekbones flattered her face. Her blue eyes had a childlike quality about them and her petite size said she was no threat whatsoever even if she and Casey were 'together' in some sense or other. With a smile on her lips, her energy and impish qualities, she gave off a feeling of being Genevieve's new best friend.

She was a lot shorter than her brother. Dan Chandler was an inch taller than Casey, Cathrynn however barely skimmed five-feet-four. It only served to make her cuter. Her glossy brown hair moved freely in a long bob style. Wearing beige cropped trousers and a plain cream vest, Cathrynn was as practical and she was petit.

"You should quit your job and go into sales, Cathrynn, you're making me sound too good. Even I might try for a date with me."

"See?" she thumbed in his direction. "What did I tell you? The guy's as conceited as any I've ever met."

Genevieve laughed. "Are you seeing anybody right now, Cathrynn?"

"Me? No, nobody seems quite right for me lately." She sat down and cradled her cup in her hands. "I've not really dated since Danny died. I didn't feel like I wanted to, you know?"

"I'm sorry about your brother."

A bright perky face smiled again, this time it was with empathy.

"Yeah me too but it happens. He was in his dream job and I can't ever imagine him leaving us any other way. He died doing what he loved best, didn't he Casey?"

"He was a great guy," Casey said, taking the photo from Genevieve. "I miss him a lot."

"Me too. If ever I was going to have a big brother, I'd choose him every time. He taught me so much and was always there for me. When I became a kindergarten teacher, he came by the school and taught the kids all about self-defence. They loved him of course, everyone did, even the parents. It was hard not to like him."

"He sounds like he was pretty popular," Genevieve said.

"He had this amazing energy like nothing was unbeatable. If they had a particularly tough case, the two of them would be at it all hours until they cracked it."

"I guess he was the brains. Course," he added with a straight face, "I was the looks."

Cathrynn picked up a cushion and threw it at him.

"You are incorrigible! But I'm so glad you're back. I've missed you so much."

It was good to see another side to him. In this informal gathering, a light-hearted banter was much needed and most welcome. Genevieve watched the two of them playing, flirting and enjoying each others company and then it occurred to her, that was something she never had with Glen.

Theirs was a very different kind of relationship: cold almost, unloving and emotionless. She had told herself she didn't require those things, status and power were much more important than love.

She tried hard to think of one time when Glen had launched a cushion at her in jest, or giggled with her at a silly school-girl joke. It simply hadn't happened. She could barely imagine him lowering himself to those standards in the first place.

She had told herself in the car she was likely going to be jealous of Cathrynn but now she was here – inside the girl's apartment – she was jealous for vastly different reasons than she had first anticipated. Casey was natural with her, their relationship required little effort, in fact, virtually no work at all. They teased as a matter of course, flirted like they were lovers and thoroughly gelled. It was simply their bond which envied her.

"I dated a couple of cops but they didn't really do it for me. Action-packed dates were a novelty one time but that grows weary after a while," she crinkled her nose. "It wasn't what I was looking for."

"And what are you looking for?" Gen asked.

"I'll tell you when I find it!" She laughed. "I guess I attract guys who are more likely to turn out as friends than dates. Take Casey for instance. Who would have thought he had a sensitive side to him, this big macho man?" She adopted a mock serious expression and waited for him to respond before continuing.

"Oh, no, please don't!" He hid his face behind the cushion. "This isn't about the Teddy bear is it? Oh no! Cathrynn, Gen thinks I'm this big tough-guy, not some…lame…" he was lost for words.

"A teddy bear?" Genevieve was all ears, her eyes open wide and thirsty for this piece of hot gossip. "Oh you've just got to tell me now."

"Okay, get this," Cathrynn said with a giggle as though she would burst if she didn't get the story out. "A few years ago, I broke up with this guy who, it turned out, was married. I had no idea, of course, or I would never have dated him. But he was a complete con-man."

"Apart from that," Casey crept out from behind the cushion for a moment and rested it on his chest, "he was totally wrong for you."

"Yeah but then you think everyone's wrong for me."

"That'd be 'cause they are."

"He's like a total big brother to me, have you noticed?" Cathrynn scowled at him then turned her attention to her guest again. Genevieve knew something of big brothers with Michael though he'd never been quite so protective except for this past few days with the reward out for her safe return.

Cathrynn continued. "I'd taken a couple of days off work and was at home feeling extra sorry for myself, crying all the time. Well, you know the kind of thing, it got pretty ugly."

"Yeah, been there," Gen smiled, eager to hear the story.

"Danny had obviously told Casey about it, so one day he turns up on my doorstep with flowers, chocolates and this huge Teddy bear. I mean huge. It wasn't just big – it was really *huge*."

She grinned widening her arms lengthways to emphasise the bulk. She glanced at Casey who was still cringing behind the cushion which made her giggle even more. "I couldn't even see him at first when I opened the door, just this huge pink teddy bear."

"What did you do?"

"Well, I did what any woman would do in that situation – I burst into tears of course!" she laughed. "I was an emotional wreck at the time. He said he bought it just to see me smile."

Genevieve was touched. "How incredibly romantic of you. And there was I thinking you were just a big hunk of beefcake."

"Tell me," Cathrynn went on, "what girl is going to look for a guy after that when she has all she needs in a friend like him. He's just a big softy at heart." The more Genevieve heard about his sensitive side, the more she softened and wanted to hear more but if the look on Casey's face was anything to go by, it wasn't going to happen easily.

"It sounds like you two have got a great set up," she said.

It was the way she said it that made Cathrynn add: "You know we're not an item, Gen, don't you?"

"Well, if you're not, it sounds like you ought to be. You two sound fabulous together."

"He's brave," Cathrynn nodded. "I'll give him that. There's not many guys who would walk into a store and buy a four-foot teddy bear. But then don't get me wrong. I don't want you to leave here thinking he's

God's greatest gift or anything. He's also arrogant, ignorant and a complete idiot too."

"That sounds more like the Casey I've gotten to know these past few days."

"They giveth with one hand," Casey shook his head, "and taketh with the other." He didn't know whether to up and leave right now or bask in the back handed compliments a while longer. "Come on, ladies, I've just been through hell and back. Give me some credit."

"No," Cathrynn finally answered the question, "we're not an item. Far from it, in fact. But sometimes you just bond so well with someone that no matter what life throws at you, you just know who you can rely on when it gets sticky. Isn't that right?"

"I came running here, didn't I?"

Cathrynn smiled. "Yeah, you did. And despite the circumstances you two are in, I haven't had this much fun in a long time. I'm just so pleased I got to see you again." Cathrynn sat back in her seat cross legged and hugged the cushion. "It has been a while, you know. If you ever leave it that long again, I'll come up with something way more embarrassing than the Teddy bear story, believe me."

"Oh, I do."

Genevieve drained her cup. "You mean there are other stories?"

"No," he quickly shook his head. "No, nothing at all."

Cautiously he looked back up at Cathrynn hoping there wasn't anything he'd overlooked. She just gave him a playful grin. He was sure she would make up something convincing even if there was nothing else to report.

"So what's your next move?" Cathrynn asked. "I can't imagine for a moment you are going to give yourself in."

"To do that would imply I had kidnapped her and obviously I didn't, I just need to work out why Glen's doing this."

"Money?" Cathrynn offered outright, sipping her tea. "Seems the most obvious thing to me."

"He's loaded already," he said. "Though I think you may be right. It's a fact of life. Danny always said once they've made their first million, they get hooked. Maybe that's it, he's addicted to money."

"You are both suggesting that my would-be fiancé *is* actually behind all of this." Genevieve interrupted. "It's quite possible someone else is and he's just caught up in it. I still find it hard to believe that the man I'd planned to spend my life with is trying to kill me."

"Of course you would do." Cathrynn smiled sympathetically. "But I've followed your life since Danny was killed and there's never been one photo when he looked genuinely lovingly at you. Sorry but the two of you just look like you're modelling for the camera."

Cathrynn's words were true if not blunt.

"We are in love. *Were* in love," she corrected.

"I know how easy it is to want to believe that, but I don't think he feels the same way about you. Sure, he's a great looking guy - *I'd* date him," she quipped noting a disapproving eye from Casey, "but when was the last time he said he loved you and you believed him?"

"He says it all the time."

"Really?"

"Really."

Cathrynn sighed then shrugged. "I don't believe him. I'm sorry, I just don't."

She quickly jumped up to grab a recent magazine with the two of them inside. She flipped open a page and the two of them were pictured coming out of a glitzy restaurant together. Genevieve wore a long blue gown glowing with sparkles and Glen stood next to her in a tuxedo. "Look at his body language. He's not touching you, not holding you in any way. He's not even looking at you."

"It was just a photo. We didn't know it was going to be taken."

"So, then if you had, you'd have looked more loving at each other?" Cathrynn pushed. "Is that what you're saying? Doesn't that seem to you to be a little forced?"

"It's complicated. Our relationship isn't like yours. We have different ways to express our love."

"How?"

"Money," Casey nodded. "They go out to glitzy restaurants, galas, that's how they carry on. It's just for show, for the cameras. It's like they're a couple of A-listers going for the 'Best Supporting Role'. She's waiting to pick up her Oscar for 'Best Would-Be Wife of the Year'!"

"How dare you!" Genevieve scorned. "This is my life you're trashing here. I genuinely loved Glen, even now, even despite what you think he's done."

"Casey, she's right, you should apologise."

"Why? I'm not sorry," he shrugged. "She needs a reality check."

"Glen De Salle has been nothing but good to me."

"Yeah, he's a model husband. What wife wouldn't want an attempt on her life every minute of the day? I just don't get it, why would anybody think the worst?" he said sarcastically.

"That's enough!" Genevieve scolded, rising to her feet. "You don't know him like I do. You can't possibly speak for him."

Casey rose too. If nothing else, Genevieve could fuel his temper in one breath.

"Honey, I had a gun pointed at me, just like you did and I have the scars to prove he's used it too. There's nothing you can say that will convince me he's not trying to kill you – or me for that matter."

"He's the nicest, kindest, sweetest man I've ever known."

"Who happens to want you dead!"

"When my life fell apart, he was there to pick up the pieces."

"Yeah, so he could kill you himself!"

"Casey!" Cathrynn smacked his thigh. "Give the girl a moment to speak, will you?"

"Speak?" he laughed, "she hasn't stopped since I met her! Gen, you can deny it all you want but the more I think about it the more I can't get the idea out of my head. Glen De Salle is after your money. That's all it has ever been about. The man wants your inheritance."

"Well, how on earth could he get it?" she asked. "We're not married yet."

"I don't know, I haven't worked that part out yet, but the point is, he is after your money and will do just about anything to get it. We've lived through the past few days finding exactly how far he will go to get his hands on it."

"Why not just marry me then? Why has it taken him so long to propose? Answer me that, Mister Oh-So-Perfect?"

"I don't know, you live with the guy."

"We don't live together, Casey, I've already explained that. We don't have that kind of relationship yet."

"You're a -?" Cathrynn stopped herself. "Sorry, I didn't mean to imply anything, I just didn't think he'd be such a gentleman that's all. Glen comes across as being extremely passionate."

"Yeah," Casey sniggered sarcastically, "the guy's wasted no time finding a way to get his hands on her cash but can't find it within himself to touch her body. Tough break, huh?"

The air crackled around them. Her hurt angry eyes seared right through him but it was too late to expect any kind of apology. She pulled her hand back quickly and slapped his face stinging his skin.

"How dare you! How dare you say that!"

"Hey, I didn't say anything you didn't already think yourself! Think about it Gen, surely you've got to have asked yourself why he hasn't tried to sleep with you in all the time you've been together?"

"I can't believe you're asking me this. How dare you speak to me this way? My private life has nothing to do with you, Mr Pitt, or anyone else and I'll thank you to keep your sleazy thoughts to yourself!"

"Yeah, that's it, isn't it?" He inhaled deeply. "Touched a nerve, did I?"

Cathrynn finally stood, but still looking up at them. "Casey, don't push it,"

"Has he even kissed you?" he asked, "and I don't mean some peck for the camera, I mean really kissed you?"

"Stop it!"

"You've been together what, a little over a year? And in all that time the most he's ever done is take you to dinner? I'm no relationship expert but this sounds a little odd to me, doesn't it to you?"

"He's a gentleman – something you'd obviously find extraordinarily difficult to fathom!"

"Or maybe he just doesn't find you attractive, Gen, did you ever think about that? God knows, you're not the easiest person to live with. Maybe the guy should have that Oscar after all - just for endurance! Apart from wanting to kill you myself, I've spent only three days with you and we've kissed twice already!"

An embarrassing and awkward moment ensued. A glance at Genevieve's face told Cathrynn that tears were imminent.

"Casey, that's enough, you're upsetting her."

"No, Cathrynn, she needs to hear this. With the paparazzi around her all the time telling the papers how fantastic her life is, I think she needs to hear a few home truths." He stepped forwards and looked Genevieve in the eye, his voice controlled. "It's all about money. It's so simple when you think about it. You're with him because you want this so-called perfect life for yourself and the only way you think you can get it is by marrying a guy who is loaded and he's with you because he's turned on by your inheritance. Take the money aspect away from it all and you're left with two empty people with nothing to offer anybody."

Cathrynn swallowed and shook her head. "Casey, be careful."

It seemed Casey was the only one listening to her, as Genevieve focussed all her anger and attention on him. As far as she was concerned, Cathrynn wasn't even in the room.

Casey laughed. "It'd be pretty pathetic if it wasn't so true."

"How dare you speak to me like this? You think you can treat me this way because you used to be some heroic cop." A tear fell from her eye and down her cheek but was quickly wiped from view. "Well, let me tell you something, Mr Wonderful, you're nothing either! I don't need your protection, I never asked for it and I don't want it. I never did. Glen is the best thing that ever happen to me and he put my life back together after you messed it up. He did it before and he can do it again."

"If I recall correctly, it was me who rescued you - *twice*! How exactly is that messing up your life?" He didn't give her a moment to answer. "And Glen *is* trying to kill you and seemingly will stop at nothing so if you don't want my protection, how the hell are you going to stay alive another day?"

"I made a mistake, Casey, I thought you were someone different." Genevieve scowled. "I guess I was wrong."

Cathrynn put a hand on each of their shoulders to calm them.

"It's come to this? Come on guys, we can sort this mess out without you two hating each other in the process."

"I don't hate her, I just think she's made some pretty poor choices along the way, that's all."

"I don't care if you hate me or not, because *I* hate you!" she blurted out. "All I've ever wanted is for Glen to marry me and my life to be perfect. I didn't ask for any of this. I don't even know why I'm here!"

"You're here because the idiot you want to marry is trying to kill you and as much as the idea is becoming more appealing by the second, *I didn't want to see you dead!*"

"Casey, calm down," Cathrynn interrupted again. "This isn't getting us anywhere. Gen, can you think of anybody other than Glen who knows how much you're worth?"

"Everyone knows how much she's worth for Christ's sake, Cathrynn," Casey broke in. "She's never out of the papers, it's all people like her ever talk about! They're obsessed with the stuff."

"People like me? What exactly does that mean?"

"It means shallow, rich kids. People who don't know what else to do with their millions but spend it on making themselves look good for the next picture."

"You're jealous!" she laughed. "That's what this is about, isn't it? You're jealous because I have money and you don't."

"You just don't get it do you. There's a whole big wide world out there filled with people who are lapping up the celebrity status the infamous Genevieve Dicing has and they're just dying to get a whiff of that massive fortune you waft around the media and you love it, don't you? They don't really want to know the real you they just want to be associated with you – for the money. You think the world revolves around you but newsflash, Gen, it doesn't."

"It doesn't revolve around you either!" she came back quickly, wiping her wet eyes. "I can't help the fact my Grandmother left us rich. I didn't ask my Dad to die and leave so much to me. But why shouldn't I go out and enjoy the money, it's not a crime! And even if Glen was after me, what makes you think that you could stop him anyway? I've dodged as many bullets as you and it was probably dumb luck that I didn't get killed, nothing to do with your *brilliant* policing at all."

"So you admit at least then that Glen was aiming for you?"

"Yes. No. I don't know!" she cried. "I only know that just because the big brave Mr Pitt is on the case doesn't mean I'll live, after all you couldn't stop Dan from dying, could you?"

The moment the words left her mouth, she regretted them.

"Excuse me, I have to … I just need to…" Cathrynn trembled and left the room.

"Oh God, Cathrynn, I'm so sorry." Genevieve extended a comforting arm but Cathrynn had already gone. "I didn't mean-." She covered her face, sat down on the sofa and cried.

"God damn it, Gen!"

"Oh my God! What on earth is happening?" She asked tearfully. "How did this get so out of hand?"

"Life sucks, that's how," he answered so softly he wasn't sure if he'd imagined it. A moment passed until the tension lessened. He sighed hard, but now his voice was louder and less aggressive. "If I've learned one thing at all in this life, it's never to love anyone, 'cause they're only going to be taken from you anyway."

"Don't say that."

"But it's still true."

"Oh, Casey!"

This was getting complex. He stood quite still, watching her and wondering how she viewed him. He could feel an end to their quest in the air, but he didn't know now if he even wanted to be a part of it any more. He didn't care if he was paid for the job or not, and the likelihood that he wasn't going to felt more likely by the second.

"I caught the news earlier," he told her. "They're still reporting this as an abduction. They found the car an hour ago. They're performing a search for us in the area. Give them a minute to realise we're not there and they'll continue they're original search."

"Really?" she sounded optimistic as thought she was ready and willing to return to the adventure despite tears falling softly down her pink cheeks.

"It's not going to take them long now, Gen, but you know what? I've had it with this," he sighed. Genevieve looked at him. When she entered the room his face was refreshed but now it was worn and tired again. "I guess I'm not as ready as I thought for this kind of action. I'm sorry, I really thought I could do this but I guess I'm beat."

"I don't understand."

"If you want to go to the police, explain your side of it all, there's nothing stopping you. I won't hold you back. Hell, you could even tell them I did kidnap you after all, you know, just to keep in with the media and all. I really don't care anymore."

She gasped, her shock evident. "You're giving up on me? Why? We've come so far."

"Give it a couple of months," he continued, dismissing her question, "and you'll have a bestselling book on the shelves."

"What are you talking about? Sell my story?"

He nodded. "I'm saying, Gen, that I'm not going any further. It won't take them long to figure out I'm here. You go, save yourself the humiliation."

She was dumbfounded. "I don't understand. Humiliation of what?"

"Of being found with me. You're a smart girl, just think if you managed to get away from a suspected kidnapper, imagine how the pubic will react to that. They won't be able to get enough of you. They'd be lapping you up until the end of time."

"But you're not a kidnapper, you've done nothing wrong."

"They won't see it that way, they'll see it exactly how they want to." Casey edged towards the door, his mood level but dropping quickly into hopelessness. "It's just such a mess."

Even from this distance he could hear Cathrynn whimpering in her room

"But what about Glen?" she asked. "What am I supposed to do now, just fall back into my life as though nothing's happened?"

"You'll go back to him and your dream life, I guess."

"But what about you? Us?"

Casey laughed. "Us? What us? There is no 'us', I'm your bodyguard and you were my very first client. That's all. I'm going to be fired one way or another, I might as well just resign and beat them to it."

Genevieve's heart sank. A sudden dry mouth plagued her and the bile in her stomach threatened to travel upwards. She had been awake only a half hour or so and in that time managed to create misery for everyone in the house. Everywhere she went she created that feeling.

"I don't think I can go back to Glen, not now. He's not who I thought he was."

Casey laughed. "You seemed pretty sure a minute ago that he was the best thing you've ever known. With him or without him, you'll be fine but I guess you'll make it on your own pretty well."

"They'll lock you up."

"Yeah," he laughed and shrugged. "Probably."

"If you give yourself in, they'll tear you to pieces," she told him. "It isn't right, none of this. Why are you just giving up on all of this?"

"Like I said, life sucks. I don't exactly know where it all went wrong. I guess between meeting you and losing Danny my life took a nose dive."

"So that's it, is it? You're just ending this whole thing now?"

"Pretty much." He shrugged. "See it from my point of view, Gen. Whose going to believe a guy like me? It took all I had just to convince you."

"I'm so sorry," she sobbed. "I really am. Oh, Casey, I'm so confused. I don't know what to do for the best."

"Take a minute," he said. "Think this through. It's important, a lot depends on your decision, Gen. Let me know what you decide."

Then he left for Cathrynn's room.

Chapter Eighteen

Casey knocked on the bedroom door and his heart sank at the image inside. Cathrynn was lying on her bed in the foetal position. Facing away from him towards the window, she sobbed into the white sheet. He walked up behind her and sat on the edge of the bed, stroking her hair

"I'm here, sweetheart. It's all over now."

She turned her head towards him, her red face and watery eyes broke his heart. There was a look in his eyes, she saw, and it scared her. This wasn't the Casey she'd known all these years. This one was losing it. Again.

"I give up." He said with such simplicity, the words hurt. "I told her to decide. Whatever she comes up with is what'll happen. I don't care anymore."

"What? What are you talking about," she asked. He didn't answer straight away. "What do you think she will do?"

"She's likely to go back to De Salle and play happy families but I don't know for sure. I can never figure her out."

Cathrynn pulled herself up and sat against the pillows.

"What happened to you? What happened to make the bravest man I know give up so easily?"

"You think this is easy?" He smiled weakly. "I don't know, I just can't do it anymore and I hate to disillusion my best girl, but I'm really not that brave at all. This whole thing scares the hell out of me. But I'm stubborn, I guess, arrogant probably, and definitely an idiot, you were right about that," he said. "Part of me died right along with Danny that day and I feel like I'm dead inside all the time. If I carry on like this I'm only kidding myself it's all okay and it's really not. I'm dying inside and it hurts, it really hurts. Too much to pretend it doesn't."

"Of course it hurts, Casey." She stroked his rough jaw, and smiled. "Love does. If it didn't hurt, it wouldn't matter so much. I know she drives you crazy, but you can't give up on her. She doesn't know it but she needs you. You need each other."

"She needs nobody. She'll get by, her kind always does. Money talks and people listen. That's the way it's always been."

"Casey, its more than that. She needs *you*, she needs Casey Pitt the man, not Casey Pitt the bodyguard. You can't let her go back to Glen. He'll kill her, you know he will, if not with a gun, then emotionally. Do you want to read about that in the papers?"

"I won't care what I read, I'll be behind bars."

"What are you talking about?"

"I told her to tell them I really did kidnap her. It makes sense, for her at least. Personally, I don't know what makes sense anymore. She'll come out of it smelling of roses and the press will love her more than they already do. She'll win whatever happens."

"And you'll fade away into the background, a fallen cop and a suspected threat to society? Where the hell did the man I love go?" She asked, her voice a little pointed. Casey looked away but she pulled him back. "Let me tell you a little story," she said. "When I sat in the audience at that medal ceremony, I felt so much pride. I didn't see a cop accepting it, I saw my best friend, a man with inner strength. Enough strength, in fact, to have that medal pinned on his uniform and believe that even for just a moment what he did was the only thing he could have done. My brother died, period. I want him back as much as anybody else but he's not going to. I can't tell you how much I miss him but he's just not coming back. But he knows, Casey, that while we're talking about him, laughing about old times and thinking about him that we are keeping his memory alive and that's all anybody can do to keep their sanity."

"But I miss him so much, Cathrynn." He took her hand and held it against his lips, his eyes filling. "It hurts *so* much." She hugged him, feeling his warm breath against her skin. "I miss him much more than I ever thought I would."

"I do too."

"I'm so sorry."

"Casey, it wasn't your fault, let it go. Let go of the baggage you're carrying around with you, Danny would have. He would have told you to 'focus on the case,' wouldn't he?"

"Yeah," he wiped his eyes and sniffed, "he would."

"You have to find that inner strength again, because without it you won't be able to do what you need to and you know what you have to do. I love you so much and you know I respect you, but I'll be damned if I'm going to let you give up because he died. Danny would hate me if I let you do that." She wiped away her own tears.

"There wasn't a single moment that I thought you could have done more to save him and if I feel that way, you must too. What doesn't kill you makes you stronger, right? Well, get stronger, Casey, because that lady out there needs all the strength you have to save her life."

"If I don't kill her first," he laughed, Cathrynn too. "Or get her killed."

"That won't happen." She reached into her trouser pocket and took out the medal she'd kept from the photo frame. "See this? You know what it says to me?" Casey looked at it in her small palm and shook his head.

"It says that everything I ever loved is right here. Everything. Danny, you and everything."

"It says all that?" he smirked. "But it's just a piece of metal."

"Not to me, it isn't." She held it up between her thumb and forefinger. "To me this represents love. Pure love. And nothing will ever get quite as close."

"You're an amazing woman, Cathrynn." He took her in his arms and kissed her forehead gently. "I'd forgotten how soft you feel. I've missed you, honey, and I love you too. Too much to let you down."

"Then you'll go on with it?"

"If she agrees."

"She does, believe me and she'd be lucky to have you on board. What woman wouldn't want a great looking guy like you around to guard her?" A glint in her eye and an arch of her eyebrow told Casey she was thinking of them in an entirely different light.

"This *is* business, Cathrynn, nothing else."

"Oh come on, do I look like I was born yesterday?"

"What are you suggesting?"

"The fiery comebacks, the constant battle for control? There's so much chemistry there, you two could open a drug store!" she quipped. "I'd have to have been completely stupid not to notice it. She drives you nuts, right?"

"Like you wouldn't believe."

"One moment she's sweetness and light and the next she's a firecracker?"

"Have you been spying on us?"

"You've just spent three days with this girl and you're telling me it's *all* been business?"

"Yeah," he shrugged, "I'm a professional guy. Sure there was the odd moment here and there but she's so wrapped up in De Salle she doesn't even see me, I'm pretty sure of it."

"Do you want her to?" Cathrynn asked, her tears long gone but her matchmaking radar fully operational.

"It's purely professional, I told you."

He couldn't even remember the last woman he dated, though he knew it was before Dan had died.

"I don't believe you! She's an attractive girl and she deserves much better than Glen De Salle. You like her, don't you?"

"Sure I do but there's too much at stake right now without thinking of dating, Cathrynn. Besides, we're from different sides of the tracks. She'd hardly go for a guy like me."

"Don't be too sure of it. She's vulnerable right now and it's the best time to make your move."

"That's pretty insensitive! I can't believe you'd be so blatant about it."

"You can't?" The twinkle in her eye was permanent now, there was no way she'd stop with this subject until he agreed to go for it.

"Well, yeah I can but -."

"So what are you waiting for? Go woo her, Romeo," she nodded smugly.

Casey knew she was right. Getting back into the world of dating was probably the best thing that could happen to him. Dwelling on Dan's death forever and a day was going to do nothing for his future, nor his current circumstances.

"She's confused right now, it'd be totally unprofessional of me to..."

"If you go out there right now, I guarantee she will agree to stay with you until this thing is over. As enticing as Glen is, your role is twice as attractive. I happen to know that women need to feel protected, it's purely animal but then that's human nature for you. Also they love a little action-adventure too." She nodded in confirmation. "You've kept her alive this long, I can't see why she wouldn't fall for you – if she hasn't already – you're a fantastic catch. I fall for you every time we meet."

"Cathrynn, you're bad."

"I know," she grinned. "Thanks. I lived the action thing with you and Danny for a long time, I know how it works and she's practically thriving on it."

"Are you sure?" he questioned, a little dazed. "She seems anything but to me."

"Quite sure. If I find a guy anytime soon, he's going to have to be a something pretty special to better you," she admitted. "Let me ask you, Casey, what do you want?"

"What do you mean?"

"Out of life."

"Right now I just want my life back," he nodded. "Just that."

"You don't hanker for a little romance?"

He laughed. "I don't know that my heart could take it. Let's just focus on the case, huh?"

"Thank you, Danny!" Cathrynn beamed at him then looked up to the heavens. He'd used exactly the same words as Danny would have. "It was hard but I knew he'd come though for us eventually." She pulled him closer for another hug, this time the embrace meant more. "Now, get your butt back in there, Pitt, and see what that girl wants to do. I'll bet you a hundred dollars it's all back on," she said confidently.

Casey moved from the bed. "You sure you can back that up?"

"Hell, yeah. I know how her mind works. I'm a woman too, don't forget."

"And a hell of a woman you are too, Cathrynn."

Genevieve was standing by the window facing the back yard when he walked in, the sun was beginning to set. The voile curtain moved slightly in the evening breeze emphasising her softness and femininity. She looked amazing even if she did look like something the cat dragged in. So much for keeping prim, the girl was stunning without the make up, the plush hair do's and the flash clothes. Right now she looked like an angel, and a *real* woman. Glossy magazines may polish her up creating a shiny sparkling Genevieve Dicing, but this one looked natural and utterly beautiful.

"You okay?" he asked. She turned around, and folded one arm over her chest and held her shoulder.

"Yeah, I'm fine. Is Cathrynn okay? I'm so sorry about what I said. Do you think she will forgive me?"

"She already has."

"I should tell you, Casey, I've made a decision."

He braced himself. "What is it?"

"First of all, I've decided I owe you an apology. I know I can be really hot-headed at times and I just want you to know I am really sorry for all the names I called you. I just don't think before I speak."

"Apology accepted."

"Secondly," she smiled weakly. "I don't hate you, and I never have and I don't think I ever could. Sure you get me riled, but I guess that's mutual. Heck, I do it to everybody, but I was just really confused. Up until a couple of days ago, my life was set in stone. I was going to marry Glen and everything was going to fall into place. I had the dress sorted out, the rings, everything. I guess I was a fool to be that way."

He stepped forwards to comfort her. Extending his arm, his hot hand touched her shoulder and she smiled.

"Not a fool, Gen. Let's just say you were caught up in the moment."

"It was so easy to do," she admitted. "I got a little heady and believed my life was going to be one big fairytale. I'm still a little puzzled as to how I got this far without seeing Glen's other, darker side. If I'd have known what he was capable of, I would never have..." She suddenly gestured towards his arm. "How is that?"

"Newsflash," he raised it with a smile. "It looks like I'm going to live after all."

She grinned. "Good. That's really good. While I'm on a roll, I just want to apologise for the situation too. I got so wrapped up in my life that I just didn't see it coming."

"You know, you really don't have to put this entire rap on your shoulders. Who could've seen this coming? It's not your fault."

"Yeah, it is. I've been an idiot," she confessed. "I've been an egotistical, upper class, conceited, inconsiderate idiot."

"Don't you think you're being a little harsh?"

"Do you?" she asked innocently. He nodded, stepped a little closer and lifted her chin. "Casey, why couldn't I have met you before all this happened?"

"You did."

He closed his eyes and gently kissed her soft lips. As predicted, it was heavenly. Moving his hand slowly up her back and into her hair, Casey left it a moment to savour her taste before breaking away.

"Maybe I shouldn't have done that." He waited to gauge her response before continuing. "I guess I'm the one who should apologise now, huh?" She didn't answer but the happily satisfied look on her face spoke volumes. She was clearly impressed. "You're not going to slap me again are you?"

She smiled, covering her lips with her hand, saving the touch of his kiss to memory. Any kind of embrace Glen had offered paled into insignificance. Casey's kiss was as wonderful as it was unexpected and she didn't know when or if there was going to be another but she craved it all the same. He was definitely something else.

"No."

"That's good to hear. I don't think I could take a beating from you right now. Oddly though, I feel like I could take on the bad guys with my little finger!"

"And that's why I hope that you'll continue with this case."

"You believe me, that I didn't kidnap you?"

"I've known in my heart the whole time. I just needed some confirmation."

"And have you had that?"

"More than just a little." She smiled. "Yes, I have."

Hearing those words calmed him. "What about the press, the things they said about me?"

"I think we've both been carrying some emotional baggage lately. It doesn't matter to me what they say about you, Casey. The man I've been with this past few days has shown me so much about myself I didn't even want to know before. He's taught me how to be a real person. Now it's time to start afresh. The Genevieve Dicing everybody knows is going to be a different woman from now on."

"Are you sure you want to go through with this? It's likely to get pretty ugly."

"It's already been ugly."

"Yes it has," he agreed. "But I'm guessing it's going to get lot worse before it gets better."

"I don't care I just want to know the truth now about Glen. If he wants me dead, then I'd at least like to know why. Nobody takes a shot at a Dicing and gets away with it. My father said it'd take a pretty brave man to take me on, or a pretty stupid one. Well, let's just say I don't think Glen's brave."

She knew the man in front of her had more bravery in his little toe than Glen had in his entire body and that meant the world to her.

"Do you think you still have a future with him?"

"No, but I have some questions I'd like to ask him. One thing I do know though, and that is if it wasn't for you, I wouldn't be here at all so thank you, Casey, for putting your life on the line and being there for me."

"Just doing my job, Ma'am," he winked.

"I know I've been difficult but I really do appreciate everything you've done. I haven't been the best travelling companion either and I'm sorry for that.

"Well, while we are the subject of apologies, I guess I should say sorry for the cheap shot I took earlier. It was out of line."

"It's okay. You were right, if Glen did find me attractive he'd have made his move by now. I guess I'd have more chance with Antonio than Glen," she smiled.

"It did cross my mind, but I didn't want to get slapped again." He pulled her a little closer. "You are so beautiful," he smiled, "believe me."

The moment he said it, she softened even more. Her lips curved and she even blushed.

"You don't have to say that."

"But it's true. Hell, if a guy can't tell a girl she's beautiful then I don't know what's wrong with the world."

Having him hold her without all the problems of the world on her shoulders for five minutes made all the difference.

"Can I ask you something, Casey, something personal?"

"Sure."

"Why did you kiss me before?"

"Promise you won't get violent?" he asked, his eyebrow raised slightly. She nodded. "I kissed you because as much as you irritate the hell out of me when you're mad, you just make me want to make everything alright for you."

Her smile was priceless and a welcome interruption from the seriousness of late.

"So, then we're definitely back on? You'll continue to guard me?"

"I will." He leaned down again and claimed her lips once more

Cathrynn entered with a smile as she edged around the door, coughing slightly to ease the intrusion.

"So what's the plan?" It was quite obvious from the look on her face she'd been eavesdropping. "Of course, you can use my car if you need to and by the way, Casey," she cocked a cheeky eyebrow, "you owe me a hundred dollars and I *will* collect."

He grinned. It was time to re-focus on the job. He didn't know how it was all going to end, but one thing was brought to the forefront of his mind. He reached into his rear waistband and took out his gun.

"What's going on?" Genevieve asked with concern.

He held it in the air in front of her eyes, hit the magazine release catching it in his hand. He put that into his pocket then cocked the gun and deftly caught the round being ejected from the barrel.

"This, honey," he took her hand and placed the weapon squarely inside her palm, "is your new toy."

This was the second time he had given it to her and the second time she felt the solid cold of the metal against her flesh. Her hands dropped in temperature and a deathly sick chill invaded her stomach. Somehow this time felt real, colder and frightening. The look in his eye told her it might very well come to this.

"She gets Teddy bears and I get this?" Genevieve glimpsed Cathrynn's face, which appeared just as curious. A slanted smile touched her lips, unsure what reaction he expected. "What would I need a gun for? *You're* the bodyguard."

"I'm going to teach you how to use it."

"Why?" she asked plainly. "Where are you going?"

"I don't plan on going anywhere, but I'd feel a lot happier knowing you knew."

"Casey, the only reason I can think of that I'd have to use this would be because you couldn't. And I really don't think I want to go any further with that thought."

"Humour me." He gave her a fragile smile. "I'm just thinking if it gets ugly, and I'm down…"

"Why would you be down?" she interrupted, her tone rushed along with her speeding heart beat. "You won't get hurt, you can't, you..."

He touched her arm until the contact calmed he.

"*If*," he emphasised, "If I'm down, Gen, knowing how to use this could save all our lives. If you are at the other end of this gun I'm going to feel a lot happier knowing our chances are that much higher."

"Chances of what? Living? You're going to teach me how to use a gun and hope *I* can save us all? What are you, nuts?" She shook her head pushing the gun back towards him. "I can't do this! I'm not made that way! I don't think I..."

"Genevieve." He held her shoulders with open palms. "Calm down, I need you to listen to me. Okay? It's all going to be alright, I promise, I'm not going to leave you. Just listen to me."

"But you're saying you'll have to rely on me to..." She faltered trying to find the right words. "Casey, don't rely on me. I've never shot one of these things before in my life!"

"I know, that's why I want to show you. You've had security around you from day one, Gen." He reminded her. "You're probably a natural at it already. Besides, it's likely all locked away in your mind waiting for the right time to come out."

She began trembling all over. "I can't!"

"Yes, you can. Anybody can."

"No, I can't," she reinforced. "I really can't. It'd be foolish relying on me, Casey. Worse yet, it would be suicide!"

"No, it won't. I'll show you how."

"No!" she flung her hands up to her head as if to stop his voice from entering her ears. "I can't. You can't do this to me. I need you!"

"And I might need you. Obviously I don't plan to go down but we don't know what to expect. All I'm saying is it'll be better if you knew how to use it. That's all."

She heard his words but they didn't seem to sink in half as quickly as she imagined him getting shot. Seeing him in her minds eye lying on the ground with a bullet wound in his chest tore at her insides. Not Casey, not her bodyguard, her man. She saw it happen for real once before and there was no way she would let her mind take her back there. If he died, there would quite literally be no point in her going on. She breathed deeply, trying to hold back tears of anger and frustration.

"Don't be scared of it, it's just a hunk of metal." He held it up and pushed it forwards for her to grasp. "You remember inside the drain, you understood it was touch and go down there but you listened to my instructions, right?"

She nodded.

"All I'm asking you to do is listen to me again. It probably won't come to this."

"Probably?"

He tilted his head. "Yeah, probably."

"That's not 'definitely'."

"No, it isn't," he agreed. "Just hold it so it feels comfortable in your hand."

He uncurled her fist placing the gun inside her palm. Feeling droplets of perspiration on her upper lip and forehead, she took it in her trembling hand desperately aware of its capabilities. She slid her forefinger into the trigger guard and waited.

Casey looked around at the wall. A family photo hung neatly on it - Danny and Cathrynn as children accompanied by both parents smiled back at him - clearly not a good target option. He glanced at the chimney breast and saw a set of three horse brasses, each below the other. He turned her around to face them and lifted her hand up to take aim.

"You see the middle one?" he asked. "I want you to aim for that and pull the trigger. It's not loaded so you can't hurt anything. I just want you to feel what it's like to take aim and fire at the target. That's all."

"Okay."

"Now close one eye and look down the barrel." He watched her as she followed his instructions. She felt physically sick to the pit of her stomach hoping all the time it wouldn't, *couldn't* come to this. "Once you are happy with the aim," he continued, "I want you to let your trigger finger relax for a moment."

Again she swallowed, her throat was getting dryer by the second. What or at who would she be aiming if it came to this? One of Glen's men, Glen himself? She closed both eyes and exhaled. This was surreal.

"Gen, you're doing great," he said from behind, placing warm arms around her. Slowly, moving his hands down her arms towards the pistol, he steadied her shaking hands. She opened her eyes and breathed him in wanting to think of his skin next to hers instead but knowing she had to concentrate on the gun. "Hold it steady," he told her, adjusting his height and peering down the barrel over her shoulder. "Now I want you to squeeze the trigger gently."

She did, and the gun clicked severing the silence in the room. A small gasp came from her throat. Cathrynn watched quietly from her position.

"Excellent." He stood back a step from her to let her breathe again. "That was great. Now, if that had been loaded, you would have felt a kick as it released the round. But that's the only difference."

Yeah, that and the fact that next time it might be aimed at a real person.

"You okay?" He smiled, hoping to put her at ease.

"Thrilled!" She came back sarcastically, wiping her face.

"It's only for self-defence," he reminded her. "I'm not asking you to become America's best shot."

"Yeah, and with any luck you won't need to do that again anyway." Cathrynn gave a comforting smile. Casey exchanged looks with her then at Genevieve.

"What about her," she gestured to Cathrynn. "Doesn't she need to learn too?"

"I already know," Cathrynn nodded. "Danny taught me."

"And have you ever had to put it into practice?"

"No, thankfully. But if I need to, it's good to know." She smiled and tapped Genevieve's arm. "You never know when you might need it, I've been on some pretty weird dates!"

Lightening the tone was Cathrynn's strong point. Both Genevieve and Casey smiled, thankful for the release. A trickle of perspiration ran down her face and she wiped it instantly, handing the weapon back to Casey.

"You want to take a shower?" Cathrynn asked. "You could freshen up down the hall if you want."

She nodded, grateful for the thought and took Cathrynn's lead for directions to the bathroom.

"I'll call Smith," Casey told them. "See what's going on."

When Cathrynn returned Casey was already on the phone.

"I know it's been a while, things were a little out of control but they're back on track now," he reported. "What's going on there, tell me you have De Salle behind bars."

"I wish I could." Smith told him. "It's all gone belly up here too. The news reports are saying you've kidnapped her, you've got to tell me that isn't true."

The fact that Smith had suggested that got under Casey's skin. He'd put his life on the line for that company and had been given very little in return.

"Jesus! Are you kidding me? Do you honestly think I'd have done something like that? This is all some huge conspiracy, I'm going nuts here! I don't know why the hell any of this is happening."

"Hang in there, Pitt," Smith told him. "You're getting paranoid."

"I don't think so." He sighed. "So what do I do now?"

"Well, the way I see it, you have two options. One is to bring her back to the city and we'll have you both in here for questioning and try to sort this damn thing out once and for all."

"And the other?"

"Carry on as planned and we'll keep in touch."

Casey rolled his eyes to Cathrynn, who stood close by. This was getting him nowhere.

"That doesn't give me much scope. The plan was to keep her away from Glen but if I don't know where he is, how the hell can I do that?"

"You were the cop, Pitt, you figure it out."

Smith's sudden harsh words struck a chord with him. Something didn't smell right, if only he could put his finger on it.

"You guys were supposed to be looking for him but he's always one step ahead of you. He can't be that difficult to find," Casey snarled. "He's always in the papers for Christ sake, find the nearest paparazzi photographer and you've got him!"

"It's not as easy as that."

"Yeah, it is. Is there something you're not telling me? Is something going on there?"

"No, of course not."

Casey put his hand over the mouthpiece and looked up at Cathrynn.

"Something's not right," he mouthed.

"Listen, Pitt, we're on the case, okay? You just carry on with your orders."

"I'm *trying* to, I'm just not getting anywhere! Have you heard from Weston or Baker at all?"

Smith hesitated for a moment then answered. "Yeah, they're…er… doing fine."

"Then can't you speak to them, find out what they know about De Salle?"

"We're doing all we can this end."

"I'm sure you are, but you've got to appreciate this from my angle. This all sounds a little vague."

"Don't forget your orders, Pitt."

That was rule number one, of course he wasn't going to forget them. It angered him that Smith would even suggest it.

"I can't believe this. I took the job with Western to guard a client! I never asked to be put in this position." His voice rose. "My entire career could be over – my life even - and you don't seem to give a damn." He took a breath to calm himself. "Listen, I have no-one, do you understand me? There's nobody I can turn to, you have to help me out here."

"And I said I'm doing all I can from this end."

"What if I find a cop and tell him the truth?" Casey clutched at straws, "Tell them that I'm just a bodyguard with a client and De Salle's trying to cover something up."

"I've got to tell you, it sounds flaky at best."

"This is crazy! I'm not a kidnapper, I'm *not* the bad guy here, De Salle is and I've even got the injuries to prove it!"

Casey listened in the background. He could hear whispers and clicks, there was definitely someone there and unless Smith was right and Casey was getting paranoid, he would swear the noises he could hear were bullets feeding into a gun.

"Okay, relax. Listen, I can get over there inside of thirty minutes and we can work this out for good."

"Over here?" Casey repeated, his distrust rising. He hadn't mentioned his location at all, how could Smith know where his was? "Jesus!" he gasped, "you're tracing me?"

Smith was one of them, he had to be. Were Weston and Baker too? Now he didn't know *who* to trust anymore or what the hell was going on. He slammed down Cathrynn's phone and stared at her.

"Grab whatever you can, we have to leave right now!"

"Me? Why, what's happened?"

"He traced us. Hurry."

"But I can't leave, I've got to go to work in the morning."

"Cathrynn, they're on their way here. You know how this works, we have to get out of here."

"But what about Gen, she's in the shower."

"You grab what you need, I'll get her."

Chapter Nineteen

He flew down the hallway and burst into the bathroom ripping the shower curtain aside with such force the rings popped off one by one into the cubicle. Genevieve screamed covering her body with her hands.
"What the hell -! Don't you *ever* knock?"
Casey grabbed a towel and threw it at her. "No time to explain, we've got to leave, *now*."
"Again? This is becoming a bad habit, Casey!" she yelled back. "Can't I at least shampoo first?"
"Don't start with that again, we've got about five minutes before we're history!"
Her face fell white with shock. "Why? What's going on?"
Without answering he left the room pulling the door behind him hard and leaving her standing naked in the cubicle with a gust of cold air surrounding her.
She ran from the shower naked - all but the towel Casey had launched at her – and wet, and headed for the room she'd slept in at the other end of the hallway. Her unwashed hair spat water droplets onto the floorboards as she ran leaving behind a trail.
She flung the towel over her head to soak up the moisture then grabbed her shorts, shirt and shoes. She was getting quite proficient at dressing with speed and remembered for a split second what it was like to take her time and how heavenly it would be to do it again.
She hadn't a clue what the big rush was but had learned that life was different with Casey Pitt. It was faster for a start and, while much more adventurous than life with Glen, she was starting to revel in it.
Casey and Cathrynn were together in the living room. Casey took out his weapon, replaced the clip he removed and put the last spare magazine from the hold-all into his pocket. Cathrynn stared blankly at him.
"You can't *need* me to come with you," she said. "Take my car by all means but I can't take any more time from work. I have to get back tomorrow. They had a supply teacher to cover for me but I can't let her ..."
He looked up at her. "We don't have time for this! You remember how this works, don't you? They're on their way here, right now. They'll get here, turn the place upside down and anybody who gets in their way. You think for one moment I'm going to leave you here to face that alone?"
She recalled many stories about how he and Danny would have to simply up and leave wherever they were at a moments notice. Sure she remembered that part, but now Danny was gone and Casey was no longer in the force she hadn't needed to consider that way of life anymore.

"But can't I just make a quick call to my boss. I promise it won't take long."

"Cathrynn, in about thirty seconds," he pointed at the door with the barrel of his now loaded gun, "Gen and me, we're going to be out of here and there's no way on earth I'm leaving without you."

"But -."

"But, nothing. You helped me out when I needed it and I'm more than thankful but I should never have put you in this position in the first place. I can't let you be alone right now. If they don't kill you, they'll use you to get to us and I'm not going to let them do that," he told her outright. "Now, go hurry Gen up."

Obediently, she left the room.

"You doing okay?" she asked Genevieve. The red-headed beauty, now dressed, stood with the white towel hanging from her head. As she let it fall, dark red curls spilled out and matted around her shoulders. The look on Genevieve's face said everything. "You could have done with more time in the shower, huh?"

"If I could wash the damn stuff just *one* time I'd be happy!" She rolled her eyes. "Does he drive you nuts as much as he does me? This isn't the first time he's done this you know. He burst through the motel room the other night while I was in the bath. If I didn't know him better I'd have thought he was deliberately making a habit out of it. He was half naked too!"

Cathrynn laughed at the image and covered her mouth. "God, I hope it was the top half!"

Genevieve let out an uncontrollably loud laugh at the image she conjured then quickly covered her mouth as if to retrieve any damage.

"I told you he was a hunk though, didn't I?" Cathrynn admitted, leaning against the door frame. "He's a regular Action Man, that's for sure."

Genevieve picked up the towel from the floor and threw it on the bed sheets.

"Oh yeah, a regular Action Man."

"Don't worry about the gun thing," she said. "It's pretty scary at first but after you get used to holding one, you know you're the only person in control of it. If you don't want it to go off, you don't have to pull that trigger."

"Thanks, but I'd really rather not get used to it at all. The thing scares the hell out of me, turns me icy cold. I don't know how he walks around all day with it in his pants of all places. I'd be terrified to breathe!"

Cathrynn smiled.

"It's good of you to have us here though, that he could rely on you. I really appreciate it and thanks for loaning me your spare room. I needed the water and the rest like you wouldn't believe."

"No problem. Any friend of Casey's is a friend of mine. Dehydration can be a killer."

"Also, I'm sorry about what I said earlier."

Cathrynn hushed her. "All the talk of Danny, it just got to me a little but don't worry. I'm glad you decided to let Casey carry on with this. You've given him a focus and he needs that."

"So, you two were an item?" she asked. "Course, you don't have to tell me if you don't want to."

"No, it's fine, we've never been exactly like that. We almost got it together one time years ago but as much as I love the big lug, he's really too much of a best friend for me to let a relationship get in the way. My brother stopped anything even slightly suggestive from happening which, in hindsight, was probably a good move. Casey's more like a big brother than a lover, you know? I wouldn't want to spoil what I have with him. He's the best though, I love him to pieces and you could never ask for a sweeter guy. You'd definitely want this one on your side." Cathrynn glowed. "But he'll follow orders until it kills him. That's probably his biggest fault – and believe me he has many. But you could do a lot worse than have him around."

Genevieve nodded. "I just didn't expect to meet him again after all this time and under these conditions. It's all been a bit of a shock really. Seeing the two of you together, it's obvious he loves you."

"I rather thought the two of you had some chemistry going on. I think you'd make a terrific couple." The two women stared at each other blankly for a moment.

"It's okay, you know," Cathrynn added sweetly. "He's really a charming guy and I'd love to see him happy."

Another awkward silence filled the room until Genevieve spoke.

"He's amazing at this stuff, isn't he?"

"The best. And please don't feel uncomfortable, Gen, from what I can gather the past few days have been pretty intense for you both. Why not find some comfort together?" She nodded. "Come on, we should get moving before he yells at us again."

"You're coming too?" Genevieve smiled. "Some female company at last! It was turning into 'Testosterone Central' around here."

"When my brother was around, it was all I could do to breathe air!"

"I really like you, Cathrynn," she chuckled. "When all this is over, we should go shopping together."

Their mutual laughter stopped at the sight of Casey.

"You two ready?" He pointed his weapon at the floor and walked towards the front door with the two girls behind him.

"I've just got to get one thing," Cathrynn veered off into her bedroom. "I'll be right there."

"What?" Casey growled. "We've got to go, *now!*"

As fluidly as she went in, she returned carrying her purse. The look on Casey's face was one of astonishment.

"What?" she shrugged. "I might need it."

Casey gasped. "Women!"

The two girls exchanged smiles behind him but followed him out of the apartment and to the car, Casey watching every area for suspicious movements as he went, his weapon out of sight but ready at a moments notice. The three silently walked to the car, Genevieve opened the back door and sat next to Cathrynn as Casey got in the front.

As he pulled out of the driveway and headed away from the city, Casey kept a firm look in his rear view mirror. Nobody appeared to be following them. Maybe Smith was right and his paranoia had gotten to him. Had he moved the girls for nothing? It was difficult to ascertain if anybody were following them since he'd never set eyes on Smith or indeed any of the others. Presumably, Weston and Baker were also in on it – whatever 'it' was.

As the cars flew past, he checked every one for suspicious activity.

"I think we're okay. It was a close call."

"What exactly was all that about back there?" Genevieve asked.

"Casey thinks Smith is in on it too," Cathrynn explained.

"Smith? I thought he was supposed to be a good guy."

"So did I," Casey mumbled. "So it puts a little doubt into my mind about Weston and Baker. You just can't trust anybody around here."

"Hey, I live here," Cathrynn caught his eye in the mirror. "Don't tar us all."

His eyes wrinkled a little which she took as a smile. "I guess some people are just born friendly."

"Amen to that," she nodded.

"Gen, you got that cell phone handy?" he asked, pulling out of one lane and into another. She fumbled for it in her purse without question. A moment later, she held it up in sight of the rear view mirror. "Good."

"And I need it because?"

"I want you to call your mother."

"What?" She stared at Cathrynn, "why?"

"To tell her you're okay of course." He replied. "Why else? I'm sure she would be thrilled to hear from you after all this time. Allay her fears, her baby's fine after all."

"But you said they could trace the call."

"Yeah, but it's a bit late for that now."

"So what do I say to her?"

"Tell her," he paused for thought, "tell her you want to come see her."

"Now?"

"Yeah, say we're on our way. You said she lived in the hills, right?"

"Yeah." She looked at Cathrynn again. "My brother's staying with her. But won't that be a little odd, I mean you've supposed to have kidnapped me and there you are turning up on her like you've hand delivered me?"

Casey nodded and smiled. "Yeah, something like that."

"I don't know what's going on in your mind," Cathrynn said, "but the place is going to be filled with the press. They'll eat us alive."

"Yeah, Casey, she's right," Cathrynn's voice was laced with concern but then she paused. "Unless that's what you're hoping for, to deliver her to safety so you have the entire media there to see you've done her no harm, to prove your innocence."

"It was kind of what I was going for." He nodded. "I don't see another way out of it right now. How does it sound?"

Genevieve swallowed hard. The oddest feeling went right through her. This was the end of their adventure together and if it all went pear-shaped, and the police took Casey away, would they believe his story? She would defend him, of course, and Cathrynn was a character witness too but it frightened her to think this could be the beginning of the end for them both. Maybe she'd never see him again, at least without bars in between.

"Are you sure?" She asked. "What happens if it doesn't go the way you want?"

"Hey, I've got both of you on my side. They have to listen to me."

"Well, you can definitely count on my support, Casey. I want that hundred I won!" Cathrynn grinned. Genevieve looked puzzled until Cathrynn dismissed the comment with a wave of her hand.

"Call her, Gen." Casey told her, "tell her you're fine, and you're on your way."

Before she did, she looked at his eyes in the mirror.

"I have a confession," she said. He remained silent. "You remember the first day when we stopped, Glen showed up and shot you?"

"Yeah, I don't forget things like that easily," he tipped his head.

"I called him. I guess he traced the phone. I'm sorry."
"I know." He nodded. "I worked it out."
"But you didn't say anything?"
He shrugged. "I didn't think we needed another reason to fight. It's okay, Gen," he told her. "Make your call."

She unfolded her phone, tapped down to her mothers number realising Casey's future was all down to the next button she pressed

The pressure built.

"Are you really sure?" her green eyes suddenly watered. Casey swallowed, from the view in the mirror, he seemed to read her thoughts.

"Yeah," he nodded. "Do it."

She pressed the key and instantly heard the phone connecting. Her mother answered but as soon as she heard Judith's voice, she could not help but close it back up cancelling the call immediately.

"What are you doing?" Cathrynn asked, confusion plastered all over her face. "Make the call."

"I can't," she sobbed. "What if it all goes wrong? I don't want him to end up in jail over me!"

"I won't." Casey reassured her, "I promise."

"How can you make that promise, huh?" she asked. "How can you know what's going to happen? I know this has probably been the second worst time of my life, but I..." She stopped.

Dare she admit she had strong feelings for him? She swallowed then wiped her face free of the rogue tear that splashed it. Inhaling deeply, she closed her eyes and put her hands through her damp hair reminding herself of the feelings she had when they kissed. Could she give that up, or the possibility of a relationship – a real one with a real man?

She opened her eyes, unaware another tear had made its way down her cheek.

"If I make this call, Casey, I don't know what's going to happen."

"None of us do. But if you don't make the call..." he told her, his voice was warm, comforting but commanding too. "We can't run forever, Gen."

She looked at the phone and, sniffing back her upset, dialled again, this time with Cathrynn's comforting hand over hers.

Judith picked up.

"Mom, it's me." She sobbed. "No, no it's just because I can hear your voice. I've missed you too. I'm fine, really I am. No, nothing like that. He didn't touch me," she said aloud.

Casey looked in the rear view mirror at them both but caught Cathrynn's expression of sympathy. All he wanted to do was take Genevieve in his arms.

"Mom, it's all a big mistake, we're coming to your place. I know the press are there, we're coming to show them he's innocent. Yes, he is – completely. It's too complicated to go into on the phone. I'll explain when I get there."

She folded the phone again, looked into the mirror at his eyes and wept at what she'd done.

This was going to be some showdown.

Chapter Twenty

Driving towards the city was having a 'déjà vu' effect on him. Even the cars overtaking him looked the same, let alone the people driving them. Every few minutes he checked the rear view mirror to see Genevieve's face and wished he could hold her.

Genevieve sunk into Cathrynn's shoulder, the two looking exhausted as if they had been on an extreme shopping trip all day – minus the bags

"Tell me again, how you and Glen met?" Casey asked, breaking the silence.

"I already told you, it was at a function," she said. "I almost fell over and he caught me. It was fate. That's all, perfectly innocent."

Cathrynn looked up. "Where's this going, Casey?"

"Humour me. Who else was there, at the function that night?"

"Cassandra, my brother, my friends. Just the usual crowd."

"What if it was a set up?"

"What do you mean?" she asked, puzzled. "What are you talking about?"

"You said before that your father left a fortune, right? Who gets yours if you die?"

"Michael. Why?"

"Was that common knowledge?"

"I guess," she shrugged. "I don't know. My close friends probably knew. What are you suggesting, that Michael's behind all of this?" She tried to laugh but fatigue had overtaken. "That's even more ridiculous than saying Glen's responsible. Michael's my brother, sure we fought like cat and dog but he's not going to conspire to kill me for my share of the inheritance. He's loaded."

"Maybe money means more to him that having a kid sister?"

"No, Casey," she shook her head wildly. This was just too ludicrous. "Michael wouldn't do that."

Casey's expression said everything. "You didn't think Glen was capable either but that didn't stop him shooting at us, did it?"

"No, this time you really do have it all wrong. I grew up with Michael, he's my family," she shrugged and posed the question at Cathrynn. "You wouldn't expect Danny to be capable, would you?"

Cathrynn listened but didn't respond.

"This doesn't sound a little convenient to you?" Casey pressed.

"What?"

"Your brother introduced you to Glen. What if they are working together to have you killed and share the money?"

"You need a vacation!" she scoffed. "That kind of thing only happens in movies."

"Think about it. They'd stand to make a hell of a lot of cash if you weren't around."

"No, it's not like that. Michael's a good person, he doesn't have a wicked bone in his body." She stared outside, watching the cars go by thinking about what she was hearing. Could Michael be responsible? The thought ripped at her insides. He was very smart. The suggestion that Glen was responsible was hard enough to take but Michael? This was pure idiocy even to think it. "Anyway, why would he put up a reward if he wanted me dead?"

"It's a cover story," Casey came back quickly. "Perfect defence. He's the loving brother who wants his kid sister back. He puts up a reward, toys with an emotional public and the press lap it up. He played them from the start."

"What? How long have you been thinking like this?"

"A while."

"You've been piecing together my life and you come up with Michael?" Genevieve shook her head again. "No, I really can't see it."

"We'll see soon enough, I guess."

"It does sound plausible," Cathrynn agreed. "I'm sorry but Casey does have a point."

"You two are seriously nuts. My brother isn't capable of anything like this. He's just not made that way. He's smart and studious not a low life sleaze."

Casey turned his head to glance at her wide-eyed expression. "Money turns people into all kinds, Gen."

"Well he's likely at my Mom's house anyway, I guess you can ask him when you see him. Unless he's after Mom's cash as well of course. You might want to check out her teapot in case he's had his hands in there," she giggled. "Wait until you meet him and you'll realise how stupid an idea that really is."

"I will."

After forty five minutes, the rhythmic movement of Cathrynn's car slowed to a halt and Casey turned around to face them both.

"What?" Genevieve asked, looking outside. All she saw was much the same as she'd seen before; sandy soil, cacti, rocks and road. The night was coming in but it was still light out. The odd dwelling here and there pinpointed the journey along the way.

Her mother wanted to live far from the city but still be in contact. Laurel Hills was perfect for her. No interruptions and no unwelcome visitors. Just Judith, her photography and both her children within easy reach either by car or plane. The fact the press were constantly there this past few days must be driving her mad.

Genevieve looked bewildered, as though she'd just awoken from a long deep sleep. She had, of sorts, and after today ended, it would change her life forever.

"Why have we stopped?"

"I'm guessing if we go any further up that road we're going to be surrounded by the press. Before we go I just wanted to make sure you're happy with this. It's going to get pretty frantic."

"I know."

He nodded giving her a comforting smile. "Here we go then."

He faced the front, turned the key and they moved off. Cathrynn fumbled for a magazine behind her head on the back shelf and opened it up.

"You're reading?" Genevieve gave a surprised laugh. "At a time like this?"

"No, this is to cover your face when we get nearer. The press are going to devour you."

She sighed and took it, grasping it in her hands ready to hold it up at the first sign of the press vehicles. Ironically the page she opened showed a small picture of her and Glen at an Awards ceremony the previous year. The caption underneath read: 'Hollywood's Best Dressed Couple'. She turned over the page, not wanting to think about that part of her life any longer.

"Up ahead," Casey announced, spotting the lights on a news crew van. "There's one. Are you ready?"

"As I'll ever be."

"If we're being televised," Genevieve said, suddenly feeling quite nauseous, "Glen will see, won't he?"

"If he's watching."

"Then he could come here too?"

Casey nodded and, despite the first camera crew heading towards them on foot, he continued to drive through them. A woman sporting a beige suite and short blonde hair looked inside as they drove slowly by, her microphone and the camera man behind her both pushing towards the window.

"It's her!" the reporter shouted. "Tell me you're getting this? Genevieve Dicing is in the car! Genevieve Dicing is alive and well!"

"Now might be a good time to cover your face, Gen," Cathrynn smiled supportively.

The first camera crew ran behind the car quickly joining the onslaught of journalists approaching. Camera lights were everywhere in the dusk, so much so, it could have passed for daylight.

"Miss Dicing! Miss Dicing!"

The voices shouted from behind the windows. There was no way on earth she would open any of them. They were going crazy outside, each of them trying to get the one big story, the scoop of the day, and Genevieve sat inside squeezing Cathrynn's hand tightly. She was more than just a little nervous. Under other circumstances she would lap up this kind of behaviour but today she couldn't bare it.

Casey noted her expression in the mirror. "Come on, Gen. It'll be just like old times with the press in your face."

"No, this is different. This is crazy! Don't these people have anything else to report?"

"You're the biggest story out there right now. You're making their day."

"Well, I feel like a caged animal!" She peered over the top of the magazine and looked out the front windshield. In the distance between the reporters she could just make out her mothers house. "Oh, thank God! We're here. Hurry up, Casey, I can't take much more."

"Yes, Ma'am."

Driving the car slowly through the crowd was a craft in itself. He didn't want to hurt anybody but if they were so foolish as to throw themselves in front of it *just* for a photograph, then more fool them. He'd drive right over the top of them if he had to.

"Give us some room!" he growled. "Come on!"

Genevieve took out her cell phone and pressed 'last number redial'.

"Mom, we're right outside. Open the gates, *hurry*!"

Finally a gap emerged and Casey took it. Large wrought iron gates opened as if by magic. He drove straight though and looked behind to see the rabble kept back as they closed just as quickly. He pulled up to the front of the house and stopped the car letting out a long gasp.

"That was fun!" he smirked, letting out the air in his cheeks. "You two okay?"

They nodded.

Judith and Michael ran outside together to greet them. As soon as she set eyes on her daughter, she began crying.

"Oh my God, my darling! Are you alright?" she sobbed. "I've been so worried." She pulled Genevieve out of the car hugging her tightly.

Wearing a pair of white cotton pants and a pale pink blouse, Judith Dicing looked rather less formal than Cathrynn had seen in magazines. She smiled politely before sidling up next to Casey.

"Mom, I'm fine. Really I am. It's so good to see you."

Judith held her in front, at eye level, and inspected her.

"What on earth...?"

Genevieve looked down at the vest she'd been wearing the past few days and the tiny shorts and laughed.

"I'm okay, I'm fine."

Casey checked out the cameras flashing through the gates. If they didn't get inside the house soon, they might as well invite the media in with them.

"May I suggest we get her in the house, Mrs Dicing. They're going crazy out there."

Judith watched as they poked the cameras and microphones through the gates.

"Come on, darling. Let's get you cleaned up. You can tell me all about it inside."

Cathrynn walked after them and Casey after her. Michael stood at the entrance, his expression a mixture of surprise and concern. In blue jeans and a white shirt, he looked every bit the studious brother Genevieve had described though she could see more of his father in his face than his mother.

"Michael," his sister grabbed hold of him and hugged him tightly.

"Hey, Sis. Good to see you back in one piece." He kissed her cheek. "You're making quite a habit of this aren't you?" he winked. "You had us all going there for a while."

Judith pulled her back and took her inside.

Cathrynn smiled up at Michael, their height difference similar to her own brother, but he didn't respond, almost as if he didn't see her.

Cathrynn put out her hand. "I'm Cathrynn Chandler. It's very nice to meet you, Sir. I've read so much about you and your family, it's a pleasure to actually meet you."

Instead of shaking her hand, Michael had his eyes firmly fixed on Casey.

"And this is Casey..."

"I know who that is," he interrupted curtly. "I know *exactly* who he is."

Cathrynn took back her hand and watched as the two men exchange feral stares. She felt like a small child with two grown-ups about to bicker.

An uneasy feeling ran through her stomach and she grabbed Casey's hand pulling him inside behind her.

Michael walked in slowly, watching every move Casey made.

"This is worse than the reporters!" she whispered.

Casey glanced over his shoulder. "I'm not here to collect, man," he said sarcastically. "You know, in case you were thinking about the reward you put up."

"Casey!" Cathrynn tugged his hand throwing him a wild-eyed look.

"What?" he shrugged. "I'm just saying, is all."

Judith linked arms with her daughter, the two walking down the terracotta tiled hallway together leaving the rest of them to catch up. As Casey followed, he saw every picture on the wall was a photograph Judith had taken. By the look of it, she worked mainly in black and white. One picture in particular stood out, it was the very first one he'd even seen of Genevieve, the one Dan and he were given in order to locate her in the storm drain. Such a long time had passed since them, so many things happened.

He tore away his attention and followed them into the back of the house to the lounge. A leather suite took the main area, with a glass coffee table in the middle. To the left was a large brick fireplace where, inside, cubby-holes had been built which displayed candles. It was as sophisticated as Cathrynn had imagined and fitted Judith Dicing's character perfectly.

Casey walked over to a window and looked out. Very little else could be done from a security point of view in his opinion. Cameras had been located in her garden and as he drew up he saw one mounted on her roof but the press still lingered outside for 'the' story of the week. He was thankful for the fifty foot drive in front of the house and the gates.

"Turn that off, will you, Michael?" Judith asked, gesturing to the television screen. Though on mute, Casey could see the reporters outside filming the house right now, anxious for another piece of hot gossip. The band along the bottom of the screen announced in red: *Breaking News...Genevieve Dicing is safe and well.*

Chances were they filmed everything, and Glen could well be on his way. Casey sighed. News sure travelled quickly in this town.

Judith opened the French doors into the garden. The press couldn't be seen from that side of the house so neither could they see her. Hibiscus perfumed the air and the pool looked refreshing and welcoming, illuminated from both above and below.

For Cathrynn this was another world.

"You've got a great place here, Mrs Dicing," she smiled. "I just wanted to say that it's real nice to meet you. I'm Cathrynn Chandler. I'm a close friend of Casey's." She extended her arm which Judith took. "I was at the medal ceremony as well though I was sorry not to meet you."

"Well, it's nice to meet you now, dear, even under such circumstances."

"Thank you. Casey's been taking care of her and I just wanted you to know that I think he's done a fantastic job."

"Do you?" Judith turned to Casey and for a moment he didn't know if she were about to slap him or hug him. He hoped it was the latter. "Trouble seems to follow you around like a stray dog, doesn't it, Mr Pitt?" she noted plainly. "I'm sure you can appreciate the last few days have been horrible for my entire family."

He stood to attention and focus straight ahead. "Yes, Ma'am, I can."

"We've been through it before, of course, but it doesn't get any easier. This time I've had to cope without my husband beside me. Thank God my son was able to fill that gap or I don't know what I would've done." She turned to see Michael watching from the doorway. He'd hardly moved. "But this young lady seems to think you've done nothing but good for my daughter and I'm sure she's not a liar."

"No, Ma'am, she isn't."

She leaned forwards and smiled. He could smell the scent of her floral perfume. It was different to her daughters choice but it suited her.

"Relax, Mr Pitt, I don't breathe fire," she reassured him. "But I wonder though, if you might be able to shed some light on the news reports I was practically forced to watch the past few days. Everybody seems to think you had kidnapped Genevieve and yet, here you are handing her over to me like the national treasure she is. Tell me, is it the reward money you're after? Because if it is, I have it here. It's in the house and it's all yours if you want it"

He wondered if she told him that to gauge his reaction. If anything, he looked offended at the suggestion.

"Absolutely not, Ma'am! The money means nothing to me."

"But surely it would be useful."

"It probably would. But I don't care about it. I never took the job in the first place just for the pay-check, I took it because I believe in protecting lives."

"That's very commendable."

"Maybe."

"Don't sell yourself short, Mr Pitt. I've lived a life in the public eye for a long time. Protection was an essential part of that life. Without it, who knows what would have happened."

He nodded. "Well, all I know is that I took the job and your daughter turned out to be my first assignment."

"You must have been thrilled to see her again after all this time," she said haughtily. "After all, I can only imagine how unbelievably intense your first meeting must have been. There must not have been time to even think."

"It was pretty extreme. But I don't know that 'thrilled' is the right word." He caught Genevieve's eye and the two shared a split second connection of silent flirtation. He smiled and tipped his head, "pain in the butt maybe…"

"Well," Judith ignored his comment. "She told me how incredibly brave you were, how you talked to her, stayed with her and ultimately saved her life. I'll always be thankful to you for that."

"Like I told her, it was just my job. If it were anybody else down there, I'd have done the same thing. No question."

"And now you have another job? I suppose being a bodyguard in LA was a little different to policing the state of Virginia," she smiled. "I've found the people here to be very friendly but an entirely different breed."

"Yeah, you could say that."

"But she seems to fit in very well with the lifestyle." She faced her daughter, still slightly dismayed at her state of dress. "It isn't something I'd enjoy if I'm truthful. Living life in front of the camera has never been my choice but my husband's position called for it."

"Mother, he isn't interested in small talk," Michael interrupted. "Lets just get this over with shall we? Give the man what he came for and get him out of here."

"I told you already. I'm not here for the money," Casey stated clearly, raising his voice slightly.

"Tell me," Judith asked, "what was your response when you realised who you were sent to protect?"

"If I'm truthful, Ma'am, I guess I was a little horrified."

"Horrified?" she repeated, somewhat disappointed. "But she's a very attractive young woman."

"Yes, she is and in my opinion that's what gets her into so much trouble – well," he smirked, "that and her mouth! Anyway, once I'd realised who she was and she remembered me, somewhere between that and the crowd outside right now, I'm really not sure what happened but I do know that Glen De Salle is heavily involved."

"Glen, you say? In what way?"

"Some kind of conspiracy."

"That's quite some allegation. Can you prove it?"

He gestured to his arm. "I have a bullet wound thanks to him."

"Does it need attention?"

"It's fine, thank you."

"I'm sorry you were shot, Mr Pitt, but I'm really not sure a bullet wound proves anything."

"The point I am making is that the bullet that injured my arm could very well have ended up inside your daughter's skull."

Judith nodded, her pose hardly changed despite the colourful description he gave.

"So you've been protecting her from Glen, is that what you're saying?"

"Yes, Ma'am, it is."

"I know you were a Police Officer before all this, Mr Pitt, so I presume you remember that in this country people are innocent until proven guilty."

"Some people are just born guilty," he told her bluntly, staring right into her eyes. "That's just the way it is."

"And you think Glen is guilty or at least in some part? Is that right?"

He stole his glance away and stared ahead. "It is."

"Glen is likely to become my daughter's husband, Mr Pitt. Why would he do something like this? They love each other. Don't you read the papers, they're never out of them." She looked at her daughter and then back at Casey. Clasping her arms calmly behind her back, she went on, her voice laced with cynicism. "Of course, sometimes it's completely unnecessary but she seems to get some kind of bizarre buzz from it." She said rolling her eyes.

"I try to avoid the media in all it's disguises, Ma'am."

"How odd then, when you consider the only times I've ever met you, have been with a host of media attention surrounding you."

"Not surrounding me, Ma'am, they're there for you're daughter."

Cathrynn and Genevieve exchanged smiles. Judith appeared to be trying to give Casey a hard time but he was coping. Not many people scared him.

"Yes," she smiled, "you do have a point." She turned back to the French windows and breathed in the cool evening air. "Michael, would you ask Fiona to bring some tea for our guests, please?"

"Guests? We should be calling the police, not entertaining these people!"

"Why? Mr Pitt says he hasn't done anything wrong." She raised her eyebrows innocently. Keeping her cool only antagonised her son further but it didn't stop her. "Just get tea for us, will you?"

He nodded and left the room. Casey relaxed a little.

"You have to realise, Mr Pitt, that just because you are an ex-police officer, it doesn't automatically mean you are innocent."

"I know that."

"Well, I still don't understand how the news reports one thing and you're saying quite another."

"You said it yourself, you know how the press works. If it sells a story, they love it. Ask your daughter, ask Cathrynn. They'll both tell you the truth. I have nothing to hide, Mrs Dicing. Nothing at all."

Judith scanned both girls who looked every bit as eager to speak as she expected.

"I'd rather get your side of things first if you don't mind. Let me piece things together in my mind and then we'll take tea and *then* maybe we can get to the bottom of this sorry affair. How does that sound?"

"Sounds good."

She gave him a kind smile, confirmation of the genteel woman she was.

"You know when I attended the ceremony and watched you receive that medal it didn't occur to me that our paths would ever cross again. That terrible episode was over, Genevieve was back and everything was fine.

So you can imagine how confused I was when I heard she had gone missing for a second time, and not only had she been abducted but it was by the very same man who had so gallantly rescued her the first time."

"Alleged," he corrected. "Alleged abduction. I was set up."

"You?"

"Yeah."

"By whom and for what purpose?" she took a seat on the edge of Genevieve's arm chair, crossing her legs purposefully.

"I've had a lot of time to think about that, Ma'am." He shuffled slightly on his feet.

"Would you care to take a seat, Mr. Pitt. It appears we may be here for some time."

"No, thank you. I'm fine."

Michael walked back into the room, tucking something into his back pocket.

"I have an idea who might be involved though." Casey went on. "It isn't rocket science."

"And who might that be?"

"I'd rather keep that information to myself for the time being."

"Very well." She went on. "According to the unbelievably constant news reports, you resigned from the police force due to medical circumstances. They said you were 'manic depressive and unpredictable.' Would you say that was a fair assessment of your mental health?"

"No, Ma'am, I would not! And I'd be a lot happier if the media didn't judge me over something so personal. If you want the truth, I left the force because I went through hell trying to come to terms with my partner's death."

Genevieve bowed down her head sympathetically.

"And now you're over it?"

"No, Ma'am, and I don't suppose I ever will."

"Mom, don't give him the third degree, he's been wonderful. If it wasn't for him I'd be dead, I'm sure of it."

"Why are you even asking him anything?" Michael growled. "That's the cop's job."

"Don't interrupt, either of you. Your father isn't here to ask these questions and I have to have it cleared up in my mind before the police arrive."

"He's done nothing wrong." Genevieve said again. "He's completely innocent. I can't stress that enough. He's just wonderful."

"Well, you've obviously impressed my daughter."

"Wasn't my intention to impress anybody, but I think what Gen's trying to say is that I had her best interests at heart the entire time she was with me."

"I'm sure you did," Michael said, "you wanted the damn reward money!"

"I brought her here to clear my name," Casey glared. "I'm innocent."

"Well, let us just suppose for a moment you did come for the money," Judith nodded. "Your request, Michael, was for her safe return. Therefore the money is his."

"Why don't you people listen? I don't want your damn money! I'm not here for that. I just want to clear my name and get on with my life."

At that moment, a young woman brought in a tray.

"Thank you, Fiona. Put it over there please." Obediently, she put down the tray and left the room. "And you thought that by waltzing in here, through the press no less, with my daughter beside you, that it would somehow exonerate you?"

"I hoped so. I told you what happened. I'd like you to believe me and I don't know why you won't."

"Mom, everything he said is true."

"Except the part about his partner," Cathrynn added. "My brother was more than just a partner, they were best friends." She stood politely.

"Mrs Dicing, I don't know if you've ever lost a best friend before but Casey's had a hard time dealing with Danny's death and what you're doing here, if you'll pardon my bluntness, is crap! He's the best there is. I don't care what the press have been saying, someone has set him up. Casey Pitt does not deserve any of this. To treat him this way is not just unnecessary, it's unjust."

"It's so refreshing to see such loyalty," Judith smiled genuinely. "A lot of men would be happy to be in your position."

"Forgive me if I don't enjoy the situation so much as the camaraderie," Casey said.

"And incidentally, Miss Chandler, my late husband was my best friend so I do understand your point. But Mr Pitt," she went on, "there's just something about you I cannot ignore. You come across as the most worthy man I can honestly say I've ever met so I'm puzzled as to why this story has erupted the way it has. I understand news crews take a piece of dirt and let it evolve into an enormous mess, God knows being involved in political affairs there was always some smear campaign going on but you learn to deal with it. You have to. But you," she touched his cheek. "You, I find I *want* to believe."

"*Because* he's telling the truth," Genevieve said, a frustrated edge to her voice.

"For Goodness sake, he's charming you!" Michael spat. "Can't you see that? The man needs to pay for his crime I'm going to call the police."

"No, their likely on their way anyway, if they've been watching the TV at all. No, I want to listen first."

"Mother!"

"Tea, Mr Pitt?" she smiled casually, ignoring her son completely. "Do you take milk?"

Chapter Twenty-One

Walking back to her seat next to Genevieve, Cathrynn stirred her tea carefully. The bone China cups and saucers Fiona brought in gave a very delicate, sophisticated edge to the circumstances.

Now the sun had set and the Hibiscus scent wafted through the room, Cathrynn decided this was a much more refined way of life, one that maybe she could find at some point in her life. She thought, quite flippantly, that there was an element of Genevieve in her too – probably in all women. Finding a rich husband and living the life of Riley definitely had it's plus points. She could imagine herself sitting elegantly by the pool with a tall drink in one hand given to her by some fabulously good-looking, exotic type and, knowing her, a phone in the other ordering pizza.

She was grounded, if nothing else.

Despite seeing just the hallway and lounge, Cathrynn knew their host had the best taste in décor. Judith's personality screamed it with peach drapes and matching cushions furnishing the living room and a beige and tan rug over terracotta tiles. She wouldn't have been surprised to see this room inside an issue of Better Homes and Gardens, the photograph - if the others in the hallways were anything to go by - taken by Judith herself of course.

Casey drank his tea. The Chinaware made him look uncultured and too rough for the delicacies of a cup and saucer. The rosebud painted fluted rim looked ridiculous against his unshaven jaw and manly hands, but the refreshment was more than welcome.

"Casey, please," Judith offered extending her arm to a vacant seat. "It's the least I can do when you've brought my daughter back safely."

"The *least* we could do, Mother, is to turn him in," Michael argued. "He *kidnapped* Genevieve, for Christ's sake! We shouldn't be sitting around here taking tea with him as though this were the social event of the year!"

"Don't be such a snob, Michael! These people are our guests and I'd like you to treat them as such. Honestly, I'm so sorry," she nodded to Casey. "You'd hardly think that we sent him to the best schools, would you? Please sit down."

"I'd rather stand if it's all the same." If the meeting was going to be even slightly confrontational, he'd be better on his feet. He gazed at Michael, who looked more out of his league than Casey was around Genevieve. "Pick up a lot of life skills at school, Michael?"

Michael lifted his chin, unsure where this was going. "I don't know what you are talking about."

"What did you major in? Business? Investment?"

"Casey!" Cathrynn put in quickly, very aware which route this line of questioning was taking.

Judith watched the exchange with interest but said nothing.

"I'm not sure I like your tone, Pitt." Michael went on. "And I'd appreciate it if you changed it."

"I'll bet." Casey put down his cup. The sound of China against China rang through the room. "I was just curious. You can probably appreciate the amount of time I've spent listening to your sister of the past couple of days. She's a big talker," he tipped his head and smirked, "*very* big, in fact, but somewhere inside her she has this idealistic notion that you'll do anything for her."

"Of course, why wouldn't I?"

"I guess you could say I'm more of the idea that you'll do just about anything for her *money* rather than for her."

"Mr Pitt!" Judith sat upright.

He nodded an apology at her. "Believe me, I'm just as appalled but I'm not stupid." He gestured at the Chinaware adding, "the tea was a nice touch but I've pretty much worked out that I'll likely leave here in cuffs…"

"Amen to that," Michael said. "And the sooner the better."

"…so just hear me out. I have nothing much else to lose so I'll lay my cards on the table. I think that Michael is a little more involved with this whole set up than he'd like people to believe."

"Mother!" Michael urged. "You're not going to let him speak to me like this, are you?"

"Michael, they're only words. Let the man have his say. You can have yours afterwards."

"I'm not really a gambling man," Casey went on, "but I'd bet he's so involved that in his back pocket he's got a cell phone and if you tap the last number recall button De Salle's name will pop up. I'm also betting that he's is on his way here as I speak."

"It doesn't take a genius to work that out," Michael said. "If Glen watched the news report, he'll be along with the police and we can all watch when they arrest you."

"I'm kind of hoping he will turn up sooner actually," Casey added. "I'm itching for this whole thing to be over."

"Exactly what is it you think they're involve in?" Judith asked.

"I think I'd prefer to wait until Glen gets here. Rest assured whatever it is, your son wasn't working alone. He plainly doesn't have the guts and I know he doesn't have the spine."

Michael didn't know whether to argue or thank him.

"Michael," Judith stood in front of her son. His height overpowered her but she wasn't going to be intimidated by him. "Do you have anything you want to say, anything you want to get out in the open, share with us all?"

"I have nothing to say, Mother, he's lying and I can't believe you'd even listen to lies like that!"

"Darling," she went on, "if you do have anything to say, I'd rather hear it from you."

"You don't believe me?" his jaw dropped comically. "You'd sooner take the word of a kidnapper than your own son?"

"*Alleged* kidnapper," she corrected. "Mr Pitt hasn't yet been charged with anything."

Both Genevieve and Cathrynn sat on the edge of their seats as if they were watching the climax to a movie. Their heartbeats quickening collectively with the thought that if Casey was completely wrong he would certainly be taken away in cuffs just for the slander alone. The next time they saw him there might be glass between them.

"I hope he knows what he's doing," Genevieve whispered.

"Well, if he doesn't it's too late now."

Suddenly outside the Press roared as another car made it's way towards the gate. Moments later they heard the sound of knuckles wrapping against the door.

"Show time!" Casey smiled. "Hold onto your seats, girls, it's about to get pretty rocky."

Chapter Twenty-Two

Genevieve couldn't bare the suspense. Half of her wanted so badly for him to be right and the other half just couldn't bare the thought of her brother and fiancée collaborating her murder.

Glen charged into the room with vigour wearing a black Versace suit over his well kept body. His dark hair was combed back over his head. He wouldn't have looked out of place in a gangster movie. Faces filled with suspense gazed up from their seats. Glen looked as if he owned the place but instead of pinning his view on his girlfriend, he eyed Judith.

"Perfectly timed," Casey sniggered at the sight. "You might even say it was well rehearsed."

The thrill of seeing him in the flesh sent Cathrynn's heat beating so quickly her hands shook rattling the tea cup against the saucer. Bringing unwanted attention, she placed it onto the side table and stared up at Glen. Seeing a Hollywood heart-throb in real life was exciting enough but the danger he brought with him turned that excitement into fear. It was like watching a movie in 3-D.

"What the hell's going on?" Glen snarled. "Judith, why the hell haven't you called the cops yet? God only knows what this piece of garbage has been doing with your daughter."

Before Judith had a moment to respond to his rudeness, Glen looked her daughter from top to toe then shook his head, clearly unimpressed.

"Glen!" she gasped. Standing to her feet, she ran to him, her long bare legs, resembling those of a pedigree filly. She leaned up to kiss him but he pulled away. She'd never seen him so angry before. The embarrassment of his rejection in front of everyone made her squirm. She reddened. Was he actually angry that she was still alive?

"What's wrong? Aren't you pleased I'm back?" she asked weakly. "I've missed you so much." She tried again to embrace him but received nothing in return. Finally he looked down at her, a sneer planted firmly across his lips.

"You look like a cheap whore dressed like that!" He turned to Michael and shook his head, his nostrils flaring at the disgust of it all. "And you! Can't you do anything right?"

"What?" he shrugged, "it wasn't me who came up with it!"

"With what?" Judith sprung to her feet. "What's going on?"

"Ask him," Casey nodded. "Ask your would-be son-in-law. I'll bet he can tell you everything you want to know."

Glen turned around quickly. "Pitt, you're a dead man!"

"Probably!" he shrugged. "Just tell me one thing. Why me?"

"Why you? You want to know why you?" Glen raked his hair back, his unbuttoned suit displayed the whiteness of his shirt beneath. "Why the hell not you? You are a nothing, you're nobody, you're just a pawn. It was going to be so easy but you're as bad as VP Junior here, you just can't do anything right!"

"Glen, exactly what was going to be *so easy?*" Judith swallowed dryly, holding her daughter protectively, unsure if she even wanted an answer. "What's going on?"

"Shut up!" Glen yelled at her then looked back at Casey. "I won't let you ruin this for me, Pitt. I've worked too hard to let you ruin it all."

"Oh my God," Genevieve gasped. It was all falling into place. "It's true, isn't it? Glen how could you? I loved you! I trusted you!"

"Will somebody please tell me what's going on?" Judith voice rose more than she'd intended and it wasn't becoming.

A final attempt to touch him, Genevieve gave a fragile smile.

"I said get off me!" Glen yanked out his weapon from underneath his jacket and pointed it at Genevieve. "I said...*get off me!*"

"Glen!"

As quickly as De Salle had displayed his weapon, Casey's was pointing his at him.

"Drop it, now, De Salle!"

Genevieve turned cold. Two guns pointed at each other and she stood in the middle of them both. A chill of fear set in her stomach and forced bile up into her throat. This was not how she hoped it would end.

"Oh my God, please don't do this, Glen." She begged. "Please! I'll do anything, *anything*."

"Will you die for me? Huh? Will you do that?" he barked. "This is all very familiar, Pitt. It feels like just minutes ago we were in pretty much the same position. Only this time I won't miss."

He moved his gun from Genevieve and aimed it at Casey.

"You know, it doesn't have to end like this," Casey said coolly. "Drop your weapon and we could probably come to some agreement. It was her money, wasn't it? You were just too greedy, you and the Dicing kid back there. What is it with you people and money? With Gen dead, it all goes to Michael, and, of course, De Salle wanted his share."

"You would kill your own sister for money?" Judith gasped. "Why? Why would you do that? Are you in trouble, did you need if for something? If you'd have asked, I'd have helped you."

"He's not in trouble, he's just greedy!" Casey said. "How about Weston, Baker and Smith, were they in on it too?"

"Actors!" Glen grinned, proud of the fact. "Yeah, they were actors. Hollywood's full of them. Some of them can't get a job but it doesn't stop them being convincing in their craft so I hired them. Pretty good, weren't they? Weston completely fooled you, didn't he?"

"They all did."

"And worth every penny. Deserve Oscars, they all do. I was a little worried at the beginning in the cab. Gen wasn't supposed to call me. I had no idea she'd do that and the whole thing almost ended there and then." He turned to his would-be fiancée. "Sweetheart," his smiled remained, "I *was* aiming at you, you know."

She gasped. "I wouldn't believe Casey, I couldn't. But he was right all along. Didn't you ever love me, Glen?"

"Love you?" he laughed. "You disgust me! I can't bare to even touch you! It was worth hanging around just for the money but, honey, you were never my type."

"But we were about to get engaged."

"You were about to get engaged - *you*! It's pretty hard to stop you when you're going through the motions."

"Tell me," she sobbed, "did my best friend know what was going on?"

"Cassandra?" He laughed and rolled his eyes. "Cassandra and I have been together for quite some time." He saw the look on her face as he twisted the metaphorical knife in a little further. "Had no idea she would be as good in bed as she is! Kinky little fox too!"

Genevieve was silenced. If this foolery didn't stop soon, she was going to throw up right in front of them all. Her boyfriend, her brother and now her best friend. Who else was involved? She let out silent tears and looked at her mother.

"Please tell me you knew nothing about this, I couldn't bare it if you knew."

"Darling, I had no idea. I'm so sorry."

"It's a damn sick game you played, De Salle," Casey said. "And all for money."

"I could never imagine making love to you, Genevieve," Glen added. "The thought of it turned my stomach but your money was pretty attractive so I kept quiet for as long as I could."

"Get out of my house, Glen!" Judith spat. "Now!"

"Gladly. Let me just tell you this. If the first kidnapping hadn't gone bad, I wouldn't have had to go through the whining every time she saw something that caught her eye. I've earned every cent of what I'm after, believe me, every single cent."

"The first kidnapping?" Genevieve wiped her face from the falling tears. "What are you talking about?"

"I hired that guy to take you off the street."

"But - but I didn't even know you back then."

"So, what difference does that make? Mikey knows a guy who knows a guy. I told him to grab the red-head, take her somewhere solitary and kill her but I guess he lost his edge. Instead I find out from the news you got away and a cop had been killed. If that day hadn't gone belly-up we wouldn't have had to go through it all over again."

"I can't believe what I'm hearing," Genevieve said. "You knew about this, Michael?"

Fear kept him silent, but his face said everything.

"That was when I realised I had to hire professionals to do the job right, skilled people. They'd carry it off well and nobody would be the wiser. Needed a job, Pitt, didn't you? Wanted to keep with the action thing, huh?"

Casey shook his head in disbelief.

"Course now Daddy was gone, the money was even better than before," Glen went on. "Kind of made it worthwhile the second time around. I just didn't know that the all amazing Casey Pitt would be the one to do the rescuing the first time but it was kind of a poetic justice that he got to fill the position of kidnapper the second time around. He even came with a motive." He imitated a whiny voice adding, "My best friend was killed, I can't go on!"

Casey's face contorted. "You've got it coming, man. You've got it coming real bad!"

"I thought you'd have found it amusing that one minute you're driving a cab and the next thing the news says you're a kidnapper. Bad news travels so quickly in this town. The press did a real good job. I take my hat off to them. We just showed up as and when and they did all the rest. Just shows you," he turned to Genevieve, "you can't trust anyone."

Cathrynn stood and edged up next to Casey.

"Essentially then, Mr De Salle, if I understand all this correctly, you've just confessed to being involved with the guy who killed my brother?"

"Oh, Jeez! Another one? Who the hell are you, Missy? I don't even know your brother!"

"I'm Cathrynn Chandler," she said quite calmly. She undid her purse, took out a gun and pointed it at him. "And I'm going to make you very sorry."

"Where the hell did that come from?" Casey gasped.

"You don't get to be a cops kid sister without learning a thing or two, Casey."

"Oh, Jeez!" Glen laughed. "Come on lady, like you're gonna use that thing on me! Put it away, Cathrynn Chandler, before you scare yourself. I'm way out of your league, honey."

"No, I can't let Danny's death be in vain. My brother needn't have died that day. You killed him - just for money. You took away my brother and a damned good cop just to line your pockets? You're sick, do you know that. You're a sick bastard!"

Now with three weapons in the room, Judith and Genevieve were frightened beyond belief. Glen took it in turn to aim his weapon first at Genevieve, then to Casey and Cathrynn afterwards.

"Cathrynn," Casey's comforting voice just wasn't enough. " Put that away."

"No, I can't let him get away with it."

"For me, Cathrynn, for me. Put it away for me. I'll end this I promise, just put that away."

"Glen," Cathrynn said, "thousands of people out there admire you, they crave more of you but if only they knew the real you. You're nothing but a fraud, parading around looking fabulous for the cameras and smiling on cue. You've destroyed this girl's life, you've sunk so low you've become a murderer and you did all that just because you wanted more money. You're nothing but a monster, Glen and I'm sorry I was ever excited to meet you."

"Yeah, yeah, whatever!" he dismissed waving his gun hand through the air. "I don't have time for this any longer." Hooking his arm around Genevieve's waist and holding her like a human shield, he moved them both towards the French doors. She had no alternative but to move her feet in the direction he was pushing.

"Your own sister?" Judith sneered at her son. "And you won't even step in now? What kind of man are you, Michael? I hope your father can't see what you've become."

"What's going on, Glen?" Casey asked briskly. "You wouldn't be tryin' to make a smooth getaway now would you? Your infamous press have surrounded this place," Casey went on. "You think they're goin' to just let you walk out of here with her and not even stop you for an interview? Once they see her with you and the piece in your hand they're going to stick all kinds of things in your face. You'll be on TV all over the globe. Your face will be on every news paper first thing in the morning."

"That's nothing unusual, Pitt."

"Well, it won't be for what you're wearing, that's for damn sure! It's over, De Salle, you're finished."

As they struggled through the French doors, he used Genevieve to shield his body from the weapons.

"Stop this De Salle. Let her go!"

"Not gonna happen, Pitt!"

Genevieve pulled at Glen's arm but he wouldn't move. Not now, he had too much insurance like this. She lifted up her hand and scratched his face hard with her chipped nail. Blood erupted immediately, but he didn't release her, instead he grabbed her hair and pulled her outside with him.

"You little bitch!" he shouted. "You -."

Between the French doors and the swimming pool, Glen held her tightly edging away from Casey.

He wiped his face with his suited arm and saw the discolouration immediately. Quickly he smacked her across her face and threw down, discarding her like a piece of garbage. She stood opposite Cathrynn, who edged out adjacent to Casey.

Glen was still caught up with his cheek to notice how close to the pool he was. With God's grace and any luck at all, he'd walk straight back into it and this whole thing would be over.

But God wasn't with them at that moment.

"Watch out!" Michael screamed. Glen turned, saw the pool and grinned at Casey, blood dripping down his face.

"Lets get this over with," Cathrynn said softly.

"Leave it to me, Cathrynn, *please*!" he told her. "I know what I'm doing. Put that thing away."

"Because he's the all-important Casey Pitt!" Glen laughed. "He knows what he's doing, honey, so why don't you just be a good girl and do as you're told. Why don't you put the damn thing away before you shoot yourself in the foot or mess up your hair!"

"Because all the bullets in here have your name on them!" she said through gritted teeth. "That's why, you lousy piece of...!"

"Put it down!" Casey begged, interrupting her.

As she lifted her gun, she could see Casey at the corner of her eye. Half of her knew she should let him do this his way and the other half just had to do something to avenge her brothers death.

"I can't!" she lifted it level with Glen's chest and aimed but before she could pull the trigger, Glen shot her in the calf. Immediately she fell to the ground as if her leg had been shot clean off.

Genevieve screamed, Casey kept his weapon pointed at Glen but his eyes were on Cathrynn.

Judith covered her face in her hands. "No!" she cried, her view shielded by Casey. "Is she dead?"

"I'm fine! I'm fine!" Cathrynn recoiled, her voice shaking. "God, that hurts!" Her gun landed next to Genevieve and she pulled it closer with her foot. Cathrynn watched her, nodding cautiously.

"Put the gun down, De Salle." Casey told him. "I'm not kidding any more. Put it down or this gets very ugly, very quickly."

Judith stepped out to assist Cathrynn but Glen ordered her back.

"Just me and you now, Pitt."

"Yeah and I'm guessing with more witnesses than you could ever hope for." Without another word, and with complete calm, Glen put down his weapon and put his hands up. "Starting to see sense, huh?"

"We'll see."

"Put your hands on your head and turn around." Cautiously Casey moved closer but this seemed all too easy.

"Make me."

"Just do it." He edged further forwards, waiting for Glen to comply. Instead, Genevieve grabbed the gun and aimed it at Glen.

"What the hell...?" Glen looked surprised.

"What's the matter, Glen, scared?" she asked, hoping she could go through with what Casey had taught her. She held the gun just as she'd been shown but it all seemed too real, too cold-blooded. Aiming the gun at Glen was one thing but using it was definitely another.

"You won't shoot me, Sweetheart. You haven't got the guts!" he taunted. "I'm surprised you even picked it up since it's hardly encrusted with diamonds!"

Casey looked at her, tilted his head in a 'it's-your-call' kind of way but wore a sympathetic expression which confused her. Should she shoot Glen or not? She didn't know what to do. She tried hard to recall the way Casey showed her how to use it but in her hesitation, Glen had all the time he needed to swipe it from her hands and push her to the ground.

It was useless. Glen had won the game.

She looked up at Casey. "I'm so sorry."

"Oh, Genevieve, shut up whining!" Glen cut in

Casey took a step nearer but Glen took out a knife from his sleeve and sliced Casey who lunged forward putting his fist into Glen's jaw but as Glen grabbed at him he hurled Casey straight into the water, picked up his gun and shot three rounds into the pool. It happened all so quickly.

"No! Glen, No!" Genevieve screamed. "Oh my God, you'll kill him!"

"That was the point, Sweetheart," he said then shot two more rounds into the water.

She froze.

"Glen," Michael stood at the doorway with a gun in his hand, "I can't let you do this."

Glen turned around to face him. "Oh, Junior has grown a spine after all." He goaded. "Well, come on then, use it. Go on, pull the damn trigger. Let's see exactly how big you are, Michael."

And with that, Michael pulled the trigger. Everybody watched as Glen fell to the floor but nobody was more shocked than Glen himself.

"I didn't think you had the guts," he whimpered.

Cathrynn struggled to her feet but fell on the patio again. "Get Casey out of there!" She yelled. "Help him!" He'll drown!"

Genevieve stood at the side of the pool looking down onto Casey's body sinking. Two red stripes coloured the water above him merging into a mass.

"Oh dear God, he's hit." Genevieve shaking hands covered her mouth. "He's going to die!"

"Then get your skinny butt in there and get him the hell out!" Cathrynn screamed.

"I can't get in a pool. Not since that day in the drain, I just can't do it."

"But he's dying!"

"I can't, Cathrynn, don't ask me! I just can't do it!"

"Gen, you have to get in there now!" she ordered, her words were now plain and clear and calm. "If you don't get in there and save his life like he did for you, I will kill you myself." She lifted up her gun and aimed it at Genevieve. "Don't think for a moment I won't do it. Get him out of there. *Now!*"

Genevieve didn't know whether to throw up or jump in the pool. Her entire body trembled with fear. What if she jumped in and they both drowned? What if she jumped in on top of him and injured him further? He was already shot and stabbed, what more could this poor man go through, she wondered. She kicked off her shoes and watched the water moving below her feet.

"You can do this, Gen. Get in there!" Cathrynn yelled, her voice now hoarse.

I'm going to drown! I can't move – help! Don't let me die!

"Do it, Gen!" Cathrynn pulled back the trigger on her gun and winced at the impending sound. Genevieve pinched her nose tightly, inhaled deeply and jumped in just as Cathrynn fired her gun

Judith fell onto her knees inside the house. "Not my daughter! No!"

"I didn't get her," Cathrynn reassured her quickly. "She's fine, I wasn't aiming for her anyhow," she added then looked back at the pool and whispered, "Please get him out, Gen, please."

Under the water, Genevieve opened her eyes, saw Casey floating and grabbed hold of his shirt. Bubbles vacated his mouth, floated above and through his fair hair which wriggled in the water like seaweed. She pulled him to the surface and swam to the side of the pool. Cathrynn dragged herself to the side so she, Michael and Judith could pull him to safety.

Genevieve left the pool and pushed her hair back. "Is he alright?"

"Michael," Judith gasped, panic filling her voice, "call an ambulance quickly!"

He ran back into the house, jumped over Glen's unconscious body and made the call.

Cathrynn lifted back Casey's head, pinched his nose and covered his mouth with hers blowing life back into his body. The three watched his chest rose and fell.

"One, two, three," Cathrynn's hands pushed against his chest. "One, two, three." She sobbed and went down to his mouth again. "One, two three." She pushed his chest and waited.

Suddenly, he coughed, choked up the water and spat it out.

It was only at that moment, Genevieve looked to see where he had been shot. A bullet had hit his left thigh and another through his right bicep. Two more for the collection, plus a blade mark across his stomach. But he was alive! Thank God he was alive!

He opened his eyes and smiled up to see Cathrynn and Genevieve. Judith inhaled sharply and shook her head trying in her mind to work out what had just taken place.

"My God, Casey Pitt, you don't know how close you came just then. An ambulance is on it's way. You're going to be just fine." Judith reassured him.

He smiled back, looked at each of the women in turn until his gaze remained with Genevieve, whose entire body and hair was dripping on the ground between them.

"You're wet, Gen," he said huskily. "I didn't think you liked swimming."

Chapter Twenty-Three

The green of the grass twinned with the blue sky above her shiny brown hair, made the scene look idyllic around Cathrynn. The colours in the park shone out as if somebody had just finished painting them. If Casey didn't die that day, he would swear he had died now and gone to heaven.

"Hey good-looking," he limped closer, his arm resting in its sling. He handed over the hundred dollars he owed her and grinned. "You look great."

"I wish I could say the same about you," Cathrynn stood up from the park bench to kiss him, wincing slightly as she put pressure on her leg. "A bet's a bet," she winked. "Thanks. You look awful, rugged and damned sexy as usual, but awful. But you look like you're recovering well enough. Are you?"

"Yeah, it's been almost a month. Can you believe it? I don't understand where the time goes." He shook his head. "How's your leg?"

"Fine. Still hurts like hell." She folded her newspaper and put it beside her. "I got off pretty lightly all things considered."

"Yeah and you'd have suffered less too if you had listened to me."

"You still on about that? Come on, Casey, when are you ever going to learn that women don't listen?" she laughed. "Anyway, you read the news?" She gestured to her paper.

"Yeah, they'll put the slime away," he nodded. "Once he's made a full recovery, he's going down. Michael's on probation, the family pulled out all the stops when it came to him. I guess blood is thicker than water, huh?"

"I'd have happily watched him go down for his part too," she admitted, "but then I guess it's not up to me. He did have the guts to stand up to Glen in the end."

"Well, you know how these rich kids are. They're all alike," he winked, trying to find some humour in it. "Beats me how Michael stayed out of trouble this long. They'll watch him like a hawk now though, if he even steps out of line once they'll be on top of him."

"I'm just pleased Glen got what was coming to him. I don't think I could have lived with myself if he'd gotten away with it." She let out a deep sigh. "I'm just sorry I wasn't the one who got to shoot him!"

"Cathrynn!" Casey scolded. "A dear sweet girl like you, and you want to go putting bullets into people. Shame on you."

She smiled, tipped her head to one side and laughed. "I'm just pleased the whole thing is over and I can get back to regular life."